BEAT BLUES

BEAT BLUES

San Francisco, 1955

A novel
JONAH RASKIN

coolgrove press

Coolgrove Press, an imprint of
Cool Grove Publishing, Inc. New York.
512 Argyle Road, Brooklyn, NY 11218
All rights reserved under the International and
Pan-American Copyright Conventions.
www. coolgrove. com
For permissions and other inquiries write to
info@coolgrove. com

ISBN: 978-1-887276-96-2
Library of Congress Control Number: 2021942600

Front cover photograph of City Lights Bookstore
courtsey of Jeanne M. Hansen

Jazz Cellar photo by C. R. Snyder, courtesy of the Beat Museum,
San Francisco.

Sketch of Natalie Jackson by Robert LaVigne, courtesy of the estate of Robert
LaVigne by D.L. Gremmels and W. F. Bloxom.

Book cover and interior design by Coolgrovearts

Coolgrove Press is a member and past award recipient of
Community of Literary Magazines and Presses [CLMP].

This book is manufactured and wholesaled to the trade by Ingram Spark

Media alchemy by Kiku

Coolgrove Press

This book is dedicated to the Swanhuyser tribe.

"A well-woven novel set in the seething and influential Beat Generation milieu of San Francisco, 1955. Raskin has done his research. He's good at depicting the moiling lives of Beat era figures, such as the tragic Natalie Jackson, featured in Kerouac's *Dharma Bums*. When Kerouac, Ginsberg, Bob Kaufman, Lawrence Ferlinghetti, Shig Murao and Gregory Corso speak, the results are in the ballpark of reality. The novel skillfully blends important activities of the burgeoning Civil Rights movement with the liberation-loving Beat era."

—Ed Sanders, co-founder, the Fugs,
author of *The Family,* historian, poet, artist.

"Good fiction can be the truest telling of a time and a place. Raskin's novel *Beat Blues*, San Francisco, 1955, tells a story that excites and teaches. It brings to life well known representatives of the Beat Generation such as Kerouac, Cassady, Ginsberg and others as well as Ferlinghetti's famed City Lights Bookstore. It's a time of upheaval when young people wish to stretch beyond the borders of the lives they've been handed. Norman, the character through whom we view the scene, must face his white skin privilege as racial killings occur and another civil rights movement responds to the horrors of injustice. Accessible, beautiful, telling and more, this novel is a must read."

—Beverly Gologorsky,
acclaimed writer, and the author
of the new novel, *Can You See the Wind*

Jazz Cellar photo by C. R. Snyder, courtesy of the Beat Museum, San Francisco.

"In *Beat Blues*, legendary Beat historian and biographer, Jonah Raskin, spins an historically accurate tale that reads like a true alternative reality. Fictional protagonist, Norman de Haan, takes us deep into the underground of the Beat counterculture a year before it burst into the public consciousness in an orgiastic wave of infamy and glory, obscenity trials and national bestsellers. Jammed with an all-star cast of real life Beat figures living and loving, right where they're supposed to be, Raskin creates a wild Cassady-esque ride where fact and fantasy overlap, swirling together like a pea soup fog over the streets of North Beach and beyond. If you've ever fantasized about being a fly on the wall at an underground poetry reading or after-hours jazz session in the 1940s and 1950s, you're sure to love *Beat Blues*."

—Jerry Cimino,

Beat Blues: San Francisco, 1955

You came to me with the blues in your body and now
you want to jazz me into your holy bed, rock me to sleep
my baby while the atomic nightmare wraps us in her arms.

—Anonymous

1

When all was said and done, he was at heart a fugitive from his own past and an exile in his own country, a man haunted by his ancestors and a spook of sorts—albeit a white spook—in a world blighted by whiteness. This book about him begins in the middle of a brutal January, with the streets of New York blanketed with snow and the wind cutting him to the bone. Norman de Haan received a telegram, that ancient means of communication, that offered him a job at a new bookstore called City Lights. It was just what he wanted: a virtual passport to another country and a guaranteed income. He read the telegram for the first time in his apartment and danced a kind of jig by himself as he stood in his bathrobe, his brown hair uncombed, and a toothbrush sticking from his mouth. Celebrate, baby, he told himself.

Norman dressed warmly in a camel hair coat, boots, a scarf, and a tweed cap. He took a flower from the vase in the living room, stuck it behind his right ear and whistled a few bars from Hank Ballard's "Work with Me, Annie," though he changed the name Annie to Natalie, the woman with whom he was hopelessly in love. On Sixth Avenue, the wind roared, but inside Norman was on fire. He aimed for the Nirvana, which was founded by a longtime wanderer who settled in Manhattan, and who wanted a café for the neighborhood and for world travelers like himself who found themselves beached on unfamiliar shores, and wanted release from their earthly sufferings.

Norman gazed at the black-and-white photos on a blue wall that depicted the waterfronts in Marseille, Tangier, Liverpool and places he did not recognize. He nodded to the regulars who sat at the small round tables and smoked, drank coffee and whispered to one another, which lent the place a kind of conspiratorial air. Norman sat down at the counter and cast his eyes on Gwendolyn, better known as Gwen, who ran the café in the absence of the owner, and gave it soul. Hipsters came just to play the tunes on the jukebox and they were made to feel welcome. Gwen placed a cup in front of Norman and filled it with hot coffee.

"Are you hungry this morning?"

Norman looked at Gwen as though she was crazy.

"A short stack, an egg over easy and a side of bacon. I'm celebrating, Gwen."

Gwen never wrote anything down, but kept all orders in her head. She turned and shouted to Sasha, the short order cook, who had jumped ship in New York at the end of the war and who had recreated himself as a kind of American Adam: an innocent in a place he thought of as paradise.

Norman nodded to Sasha and waved the telegram above his head.

"I'm splitting the Big Apple and going to California."

Sasha smiled and revealed his gold teeth.

"Your breakfast is coming right up."

Gwen shook her head. She didn't look happy.

"We're gonna miss you, Norman. You better watch out for the nuts and fruits. I hear California is crawlin' with 'em."

Norman waved the telegram in front of Gwen's big round smiling face.

"Yeah! I got a job."

Gwen refilled Norman's cup.

"Hallelujah."

From the front of the diner came a cry that echoed in the café.

"Hallelujah."

Norman didn't recognize the voice and couldn't identify the accent that sounded like a mélange that was part cosmopolitan, part unsophisticated, and part something else that he couldn't place.

Born with a good ear, Norman had learned to recognize and identify the voices he heard on and around battlefields where he had waged war, from North Africa to Italy and Germany. Now he was puzzled about the voice and person who uttered the single word, "Hallelujah."

Norman turned away from the counter and made eye contact with a man who had short curly hair and who might have been a light-skinned Black man or a dark-skinned white man. The man held hands with a white woman, who had shoulder length hair, beautiful white teeth and who wore large hoop earrings in both ears. All the tables were occupied, and there were no side-by-side seats at the counter. The City Lights telegram had put Norman in a gracious mood. He leapt to his feet.

"I can move."

The man shook his head.

"Unnecessary and unneeded, but *merci beaucoup mon ami* for offering. Me and my woman can sit either side of you. That way we get to share."

Norman returned to his seat and looked down at the platter that Gwen had placed in front of him with the short stack, the egg over easy and the bacon. The woman took the stool to Norman's left and the man took the stool to his right.

"I'm Bob and this here is Lucy."

Norman shook hands with Bob and with Lucy. With a knife and fork he cut his pancakes into small pieces, began to eat, and spoke in between bites.

"I'm leaving New York before the end of the month and headed for San Francisco. I've got a job at a new bookstore."

Bob stroked his goatee.

"Hallelujah." He paused a moment before he went on.

"You'll love San Francisco. I did when I was there. But you gotta find the hip places and the hip people."

Lucy sipped the coffee that Gwen had automatically poured for her.

Bob glanced at the specials that were written on a chalkboard above the counter and ordered the vegetarian hash and explained to Gwen that he and Lucy would share. Norman listened to Bob while he finished his breakfast. Bob added milk to his coffee and stirred with a spoon.

"North Beach is the district where it's at. I hunkered down in '52, but I was moving so fast I didn't leave a thumbprint or footprint. I knew Pete Martin, who helped to open City Lights, but Pete's long gone. Now it's Ferlinghetti's. You'll dig him when you get to know him, and you'll dig Shig, too, a cool Japanese cat who sits at the front counter, Buddha-like. He'll connect you to all the hipsters."

Bob reached inside the pocket of his jacket, produced a sheaf of papers, selected a single page and offered it to Norman, who read the title, "Abomunist Manifesto," along with the name of the author, "Bomkauf," obviously an alias.

"Keep it. It's a gift."

Norman read the opening line: "Abomunists join nothing but their hand or legs, or other same." B. Kaufman joined in and recited from memory: "Abomunists spit anti-poetry for poetic reasons and frink."

The room fell suddenly silent and so did the kitchen.

Gwen stood behind the counter with her hands on her hips. Sasha, who held a spatula in his right hand, peered out from his little window to the world to see what was happening. When Bob finished the recital of his manifesto, Sasha whistled his appreciation. Gwen gazed at the regulars who had all stopped whatever they were doing to listen and to watch Bob who threw his whole body into his performance. Gwen put her big brown hands together and clapped.

"Come on folks, show some appreciation for the poet."

The applause, while not exactly deafening, was definitely enthusiastic.

Norman stood and clapped.

"I like it, especially the part about the abomunists not writing for dollars, but writing the dollars themselves and also the part about crackling anti-poetry."

Norman handed Bob the single sheet of paper with his handwritten poem.

"Sounds like you've been around the block a few times. Sounds, too, like you've been burned, once or twice, and come out of the fire reborn."

Bob lifted his fork in his right hand and held it above the plate with the vegetarian hash.

"A baptism of fire."

He began to eat, a little at a time, and pushed the plate toward Lucy who looked ravenously hungry. Norman watched them share breakfast. He liked what he saw and decided to gamble. Why not? He was a new man, or at least, on the way to becoming a new man on the other side of the continent, where men and women, he had been told, recreated themselves. He removed his wallet, tossed two singles on the counter, held his tweed cap in his hands and twirled it around clockwise and then counterclockwise.

"Say, if you need a place, you can have my pad while I'm gone."

Kaufman smiled, Lucy smiled and Norman also smiled.

"I'm going to my pad now. You can come with and see."

Bob wanted to pay for breakfast. He placed his money on the counter, but Gwen lifted it and gave it back.

"You paid already Mr. Poet, with your words."

She looked at Bob and at Lucy and at Norman.

"I can see that you all have a long road ahead of you. I'll pray for you to get where you are going, safely."

Bob and Gwen followed Norman out the door and along the sidewalk that ran parallel to Sixth Avenue, which was clogged with cars, busses and trucks, drivers honking madly. A roly-poly cop threw up his hands as though to say he could do nothing and don't blame him. Norman took a left on Cornelia and looked back to make sure Bob and Gwen hadn't gotten lost in the crowd.

"It's always noisy and there's always traffic, but Washington Square Park is nearby and you're not far from the Hudson River. I think you'll like the neighborhood. Folks are pretty respectful, and the old bohemians are always good for a laugh and a glass of wine."

Outside his building, which was old, but well-preserved and clean, Norman removed the keys from his pocket and unlocked the lock to the door at the front entrance. He led Bob and Lucy up five flights, pausing at the landing to catch his breath. Inside his apartment, he turned on the lights and wandered from room to room, all of them small, but with plenty of natural light from the large windows that looked out at Cornelia Street.

"This here is the kitchen, and this is the dining room and over there is the bedroom, which is the coldest room in the pad, but you can cuddle and keep warm." He paused a moment. "Have a seat."

Bob looked at the stove in the kichen. Lucy eyed the books on the shelves.

"Look, Bob, he's got Rimbaud!"

She handed a thin paperback to her man who read the quotations on the backcover, opened the book to the contents and then turned to "The Drunken Boat" and read, "As I was going down impassive Rivers/ I no longer felt myself guided by haulers."

Then he closed the volume and placed it on the table.

"First person is where it's at." He sat down and from memory recited, "I went to a masquerade/ disguised as myself/ Not one of my friends/ Recognized me."

Norman brewed a pot of mint tea, let it steep, and after a few moments poured three cups. Bob sipped and savored.

"I've sailed the seven seas and seen strange sights. I've never been inside a pad that feels so heavenly. I could write poetry here and be happy, not for eternity but for a while."

Norman stretched out his legs and rested then on the ottoman, the only piece of furniture he really cares about.

"In Paris after the war, I met up with the surrealists who hipped me to Andre Breton and his manifesto. I'd like to follow in their footsteps, if that's possible."

Kaufman gazed at the unframed print that was fixed to the wall with thumb tacks.

"Joan Miró would knock my socks off, if I wore socks."

Norman gazed at Kaufman's feet and noticed that they were, indeed, sockless, though that didn't seem to matter to the poet or to Lucy. It certainly didn't matter to Norman.

Bob stared at the Miró print and read the title, which was in small letters and difficult to read.

"'The Birth of the World' is one of my favorites, I suppose because the world is always giving birth to itself."

Norman refilled the cups with mint tea and wiped the steam from his glasses.

"I know the crazy bastard senator from Wisconsin was censored, by his colleague, but I'm not so dumb as to think there won't ever be another Red Scare."

Bob removed his shoes and wigged his feet.

"I'll tell you, Norman. I went to San Francisco to organize on the waterfront and had the shit beat out of me by cops who tossed me in jail, told the judge I was a criminal anarchist. Ha ha ha. I'm an anarchist, communist, abolitionist, humanist, and I'm as Black as the Earth and as Blue as New Orleans, my birthplace and home town."

Kaufman leaned forward, removed a wallet from his back

pocket and produced a faded newspaper clipping, which he offered to Norman who put on his glasses and read from *The Pilot*, the Maritime Union newspaper, which had published a letter signed by "Bob Kaufman" denouncing "the present hysterical campaign against the Communist Party by the House Committee on Un-American Activities." Norman nodded his head.

"What bugs me about this country is that intellectuals want to keep writing and politics separate.

The French don't do that nor the Italians, or the Russians. What is it with the U.S.?" Bob allowed himself to take a long, slow look at the living room and all its nooks and crannies. He liked what he saw. "Yeah, yeah. I know what you mean. It sometimes feels like poets aren't welcome in the U.S.A. They are in San Francisco, more than any other place I know of, and the sound…well…it's different. You'll see and hear for youself."

Norman tore a blank sheet of lined paper from a yellow pad and wrote, on the top of the page, "January 1955, rental agreement between Norman de Haan and Bob Kaufman, for apt. 5C at 89 Cornelia Street, N.Y. N.Y. $25 a month to be paid in cash or check to Toni de Haan, 11 Fifth Avenue." He leaned back in his chair and admired the instant document he had created.

"I hope abomunists are willing to sign informal contracts. $25 a month sounds like a sweet deal to me. Toni is my sister. We don't need a notary and you don't have to pay a deposit. Either of us can terminate this agreement whenever." Lucy read the document, opened her purse and handed Bob a pen. He signed with a flourish and then Norman signed, also with a flourish. Lucy opened her purse removed two tens and a five and handed them to Norman, who pocketed them.

They all shook hands. Norman gave Bob a set of keys and walked him and Lucy through the apartment once again and provided them with all the salient information he thought they might need. "The switch for the overhead light in the living room is broken, the sofa folds out into a bed, you can set traps if you don't like mice, and I'd appreciate it greatly if you said to anyone who asked, including the landlord, that you're my overnight guests. Collect my mail, please, and forward anything that looks important to me at City Lights. Oh, and if a woman named Natalie Jackson happens to show up, tell her I split the scene."

Norman escorted Bob and Lucy to the corner of Sixth Avenue where the traffic was moving again, and where the same cop they had seen an hour earlier stood in the sun, ate a hot dog and looked very pleased with himself, indeed. "*Au revoir*, pal."

"*Au revoir, mon ami*." Lucy embraced Norman and kissed him on both cheeks.

"Thanks, for putting your trust in us."

2

Norman de Haan looked at his reflection in the mirror in the bathroom and wondered where the dark cloud had gone that had hung over his head. Where was the grim expression that he wore like a mask and why didn't he look like the brooding soul that he knew? He blinked his eyes, stared again and looked for signs of the moody fellow who had big mood swings and who could be iffy about nearly everything. His capital letter "A," unlike Hester Prynne's in Hawthorne's *The Scarlet Letter,* he told himself, had stood for "Ambivalence," not for Adultery, though he had also been a most curious fellow who surrounded himself with big ideas and odd ball friends who challenged both his orthodox and his heretical beliefs.

Like many of his peers, Norman de Haan relied on pop sociology and pop psychology. The books and magazines that he devoured, informed him that he and his peers belonged to something called "The Silent Generation." The phrase seemed to fit and yet it did not fit one bit.

Norman took little or nothing for granted. When he examined his life, he saw that he was often lonely, even when he was in the company of others. Unlike many of his friends in the Village, he didn't carry signs in the streets, shout slogans from the Right or the Left, or make lots of noise, though he had done plenty of that in uniform. So had the members of his platoon. Their guns resounded all across Europe, followed by a kind of eerie silence that instilled in Norman an inner sense of quietude. He would never go to war again, he told himself.

If anyone had asked him what his philosophy was, he would have said, "I'm an existentialist." He read Jean-Paul Sartre in French and thought deeply about the existentialists who seemed to speak for him (and for the Silent Generation) by placing emphasis on choice, not on chance. From now on, Norman would aim to choose his own fate.

Short and wiry, with soft eyes and a gentle smile, he usually wore a serious expression. What he wanted most of all, he told himself, was to feel loved and to love another person. He had tried very hard to love Natalie Jackson, who was tall and thin, with curly red hair and prominent cheek bones. She belonged to the same generation as Norman, though she was a bit younger than him. Norman's sister, Toni, who fancied herself a matchmaker, connected them.

"I think the two of you will hit it off. You'll have fun together."

Fun! Now there was a novel idea. He hadn't had fun since Paris in the Spring of '45. Toni provided Norman with Natalie's phone number, but it took him about ten days to phone her. He had a tendency to be spacey, and he was also shy, especially around women his own age. That was the narrative that he repeated to himself. A rationalization, he realized. When he finally rang her, she had nearly forgotten his name and that he was supposed to call.

"Your sister told me about you. When you didn't get in touch, I thought you weren't interested in me."

Norman looked out the window in his bedroom and listened to the rain that fell steadily on rooftops and on the pavement below.

"No, no, that's not it. I'm interested. In fact, I'm very interested. I want you to go to the movies with me."

There was a long pause before Natalie spoke again.

"Okay." She sounded tentative. "What movie did you have in mind?"

Norman paced back and forth in the hallway.

"I'm not sure. I can look at the paper, see what's playing and get back to you."

Later that morning, he picked out *Dial M for Murder*, called Natalie and arranged to meet her in front of the box office. Norman arrived late; Natalie seemed frazzled. They missed the first few minutes of the flic, and then sat together silently. Later, they compared notes at a café on the upper east side. Norman loved Hitchcock. Natalie admired Grace Kelly in the role of the socialite, but she didn't care for the men in Kelly's life, one of them played by Ray Milland and another played by Robert Cummings. That first date was a bust, a fiasco and a debacle. But maybe he was exaggerating, as he was wont to do.

The second date got off on a better foot. Norman met

Natalie outside the MOMA. Inside they checked coats and hats and wandered about, gazing at painting after painting, and discovered that they both liked the work of Salvador Dali. Natalie bought a postcard of one of Dali's works.

"I'm gonna put this on my refrigerator."

Norman browsed in the museum's shop and bought a post card that depicted Hieronymus Bosch's "The Garden of Delights."

"I think he's more surreal than Dali. Maybe that's because, like me, he's Dutch."

On a stroll in Central Park later that day, with the trees bare and a cold wind whipping the branches, they held hands and kissed. Norman assumed that Natalie liked him; she didn't back away when he kissed her, nor did she object to holding hands. On a bench in the park, Norman tried his best to share intimacies, though his disclosures might have sounded more appropriate for a slide show of his family than for a romantic encounter.

"My mother was and still is a socialite who works with charities. My father operated a bookstore and sold rare prints. He passed a while ago. My mother's a widow. I studied English at Yale and I hope to write one day."

Natalie watched a ground squirrel stop and look both ways before crossing the path and disappearing in the underbrush.

"It's different for girls. At least it has been for me. I was told to not speak up, first by the nuns and then when I went to work in a shop on Lexington Avenue selling rouge, lipstick and perfume."

Norman listened and tried to understand, though he quickly realized that he and Natalie came from very different worlds. He wondered why his sister thought he and Natalie would hit it off.

"I guess we're from opposite sides of the tracks. Star-crossed lovers."

"I wasn't aware that we were lovers."

On their third date, Norman downed too many martinis and said things he didn't know he was going to say until he said them.

"Natalie, you are very beautiful."

She sighed.

"Thank you, Norman, but I'm not sure why you'd say that."

After that comment he went silent. He walked Natalie to the subway, gave her a peck on her cheek and watched her descend the stairs for the PATH train to New Jersey. In a kind of daze, he walked home and wondered what he had done wrong, what he could have said, what he should have talked about.

When he conferred with his sister, Toni, she listened patiently and chose her words carefully so as not to hurt Norman's feelings.

"Guys have been telling Natalie she's beautiful since forever. Everywhere she goes and everywhere she turns, it's the same broken record. Guys who want to get into her pants tell her she's beautiful. I thought you'd be different."

Norman surprised himself by breaking it off with Natalie, though he was miserable afterward. His problem, he told himself, was that he didn't have the precise words to describe his feelings.

He decided that he was intellectually overdeveloped and emotionally underdeveloped.

After he and Natalie stopped "seeing one another," as he put it, there was nothing to hold him in New York, certainly not his mother, or even his sister Toni, whom he adored. Natalie mailed him a matchbook photo of herself, signed with her name and the word, "fondly," but he didn't change his mind. He still vowed to leave the city. Distance was what he needed now. He heard from his sister that Natalie was already dating his wartime buddy, Charlie Wilson.

Please, someone rescue me from the doldrums, he told himself. Who gives a fig for fondly?

Salvation came in the form of the telegram from Lawrence Ferlinghetti in San Francisco. Mr. Ferlinghetti had known Norman's father, who sold rare volumes of poetry (and under the counter, pornography, which would have landed him in prison if the cops had raided).

Books, books, books, he told himself as he walked north on Sixth Avenue, booted and bundled from head to toe. There were no escaping books. He stopped and window shopped, and at the Western Union office on Sixth Avenue and 14th Street he drafted a telegram to Ferlinghetti: "Offer accepted. Stop. Wrapping things up New York. Stop. Ready for adventure of my life. Stop. Norman de Haan. Stop."

He headed north again, walking faster, with snowflakes falling and melting on his overcoat. He remembered that he had met the San Francisco bookstore owner and bibliophile his senior year when he played football at Chaminade, the high school for boys in Mineola on Long Island. The priests had taught him to pray, and told him and his classmates they were the fittest of the fit: superboys.

Aside from Ferlinghetti, Norman knew no one else on the West coast, no family, friends, and no war buddies, either. Traveling to California would mean going to another country. He was eager to leave, and yet he didn't get up and go. So he felt like one of the characters in a Samuel Beckett play.

"New York has its claws in me," he wrote in his journal. "I'll have to pull them out one by one." At Herald Square, where he stopped to buy a pack of Lucky Strike, he noticed the cover of a magazine with a photo of his favorite actor, Richard Widmark, who often played the part of the villain, though sometimes he was a likable villain. He shared top billing in *No Way Out* with Sidney Poitier, a movie about a Black doctor who has to treat a white supremacist, and that prompted Norman to think about race and about his own future.

He went back to his pad on Cornelia Street, gathered his father's books, boxed them and carted them to The Strand, where he sold them for cash. Then he went to the bank, and withdrew his money, a whopping $345.67. Back at Corneila again, he packed his service revolver from World War II (a 45 caliber Colt), which he wrapped in a pillowcase and tied with a string and squeezed into the bottom of a bulging duffle bag.

He added a sweater, then picked up and held in both hands the only book his grandfather had given him on his 16th birthday: *Narrative of a Five Year's Expedition against the Revolted Negroes of Surinam in Guiana, from the year 1772 to 1777 by Captain J.G. Stedman*. Norman read the date of publication, December 2, 1793, then turned the pages, stopped and studied an engraving by William Blake entitled "A Negro Hung Alive by the Ribs to a Gallows." He wrapped the volume in newspaper, tied it with a string, and added it to the duffle, which soon contained his whole world and came to symbolize his eclectic life.

The phone rang. He let it ring, thinking the caller would give up, but after it stopped ringing, it started again. He answered begrudgingly.

"De Haan here."

"Oh, Norman, Dr. Lindenhoff. I've been concerned about you."

"You needn't be!"

"No more nightmares?"

"Correct."

"No more obsessive thinking?"

"I'm good!" He laughed.

"I wish you'd come to my office."

"No can do. Leaving town. Won't be back for a while."

"Please, just for a checkup and you'll be on your way. I owe you one."

Nearly everyone he knew in the Village saw a shrink. Norman had joined the crowd whose members wrote down their dreams and interpreted them.

In Dr. Lindenhoff's office, he tossed his duffle bag in the corner, lay down on the couch, gazed at the ceiling, and smelled the smoke from Lindenhoff's pipe. Dr. Lindenhoff wore a tweed suit, a white shirt with cufflinks and a tie with a tie clasp. His hair was parted down the middle of his head. Norman knew the ways of the doctor who was partial to Sigmund Freud.

"I suppose I'm suffering from what you'd call survivor guilt. I had buddies who never made it home. It's all a tangled knot. I think I should take a sword and cut through it, not try to disentangle it."

Dr. Lindenhoff stood up and looked down at the patient to whom he had grown attached, beyond a professional relationship.

"It might help if you could remember what happened to you during the war. Then perhaps you wouldn't feel haunted by the past."

Norman folded his hands, rested them on his belly and smiled at Lindenhoff.

"Who said anything about haunted? I told you I killed a Kraut or two. Okay! It was them or me."

He wet his lips.

"If you want to know, I don't remember being shot and being wounded and being transported to the field hospital where

14

they stitched me up and gave me morphine. Got it doc!"

Dr. Lindenoff puffed on his pipe.

"Perhaps it's better you've forgotten. Otherwise, you might not have been able to live with yourself."

Norman got to his feet, grabbed his duffle bag, tossed it over his shoulder and beat what he called a hasty retreat.

3

I n the thick of the crowded Port Authority Bus Terminal, which he thought of as "the big bug house," Norman paid in cash for a one-way ticket to San Francisco and stuffed it in the pocket of his bombardier jacket. Then he found a pay phone and called his sister.

"Forget about me, Toni, at least for a while. I'm off to the Coast. Just sublet my place to a cool cat and his girl. He's a poet. We dig each other. He'll send you the rent. Check him out. He won't bite. Hug mom and remind her I love her."

Toni shed a tear or two and quickly put on a smiling face.

"I'm here for you when you need me."

Norman was the last passenger to board the bus, the last passenger to find his assigned seat, and the next-to-the-last passenger to stash his luggage in the space overhead. From the back of the bus he heard a voice that sang, "California, here I come." Norman checked his jacket pocket, removed his one and only pack of cigarettes, opened it, and saw he only had three Lucky Strikes left.

You'll make them last, he told himself.

He sat down, stretched his legs as far as they would go, which wasn't very far, and reread the quirky poem, "Abomunist Manifesto," by "Bomkauf" that Bob Kaufman had gifted him. Indeed, Kaufman, or at least his words, were among Norman's cross continental companions. Was this guy for real? Was he a communist, an anarchist or something else, for which a word hadn't yet been coined?

Above and beyond any meaning the poem might have had, it prompted Norman to take his notebook and pen and to sit still, not knowing what to write, hoping he might be inspired.

A young woman with brown skin and long black hair, who sat across the aisle, leaned toward him.

"Bum a cigarette, friend?"

He felt sorry for her; she seemed worn out. Surely that was why she wore the plaintive expression on her face. He was a sucker.

"Help yourself."

He extended his arm across the aisle and watched the woman reach her long, thin fingers into the pack.

"Much obliged."

He pulled out his matches, lit her cigarette, and turned to face the large woman who sat next to him and looked like she lived on biscuits and gravy. Her face was as white as freshly fallen snow in Central Park and she was nearly twice his size—Norman was a spindly 5' 9" and 145 pounds—but she had somehow managed to squeeze into her seat.

She wrapped a horsehair blanket around her shoulders, opened her Bible, and turned to Luke. From the corner of his eye, Norman noticed the passage she had selected for study. She read silently, though her lips moved.

She paused, prayed and fumbled with her rosary.

"You reap what you sow."

"Yes, ma'am and Praise the Lord."

He didn't have to think. The words had been drilled into him and came automatically.

He leaned back, looked down at his notebook, and wrote the word "Chronology" on the top of the page, followed by "First memory, the color of the Mediterranean and the faces of the women. Second memory, fish soup with bread. Third memory, the barn where Charlie studied the maps. Fourth memory (though not exactly a memory), the sensation that I had been shot and that someone— it must have been Charlie—saved me. Bullet missed my heart by inches."

The Greyhound flew across New Jersey, slowed down in the wide open spaces of Pennsylvania, and made half-a-dozen stops in Ohio to let passengers off and take other passengers on. Having logged thousands of miles by tank and truck, often with other soldiers packed tightly around him, he was not new to long distance travel in close quarters. But the Greyhound got on his nerves. He felt claustrophobic and yes, even alienated—that was the word, he told himself— from the other passengers, all of them strangers. Feeling oddly weightless and as though floating in space, he might as well have been going to the moon.

Ennui, but not *nausée*. He laughed and gazed out the window at the surreal landscape. Enough room out there to get lost several times.

He fell asleep thinking about empty space, white space, and blank space without streets, houses or people. He woke suddenly when the bus stopped outside the Lincoln County, Nebraska courthouse. The Bible woman lifted herself slowly from her seat. Norman lugged her suitcase down the aisle and handed it to the driver who carried it out to the street and offered it to a boy sporting a crew cut, wearing a white T-shirt and black pegged trousers. Norman watched him wrestle the suitcase and vanish with the Bible woman in the night.

4

A Black woman, who wore a brightly colored scarf over her head and rings on the fingers of her left hand, stood on tiptoes and lodged a leather valise in the overhead rack. Her hip accidentally brushed against Norman's right shoulder.

"Excuse me, sir."

"Excused ma'am."

Norman stood up to make room for her. The woman must have been twice the age of the young brown-skinned woman with the long fingers who sat across the aisle. The Black woman arranged her body, opened her purse, and removed a pocketbook sized map of the U.S. with each state brightly colored. She put her thumb down near the heart of Nebraska, where she had climbed on board.

"Many, many miles to go. Might as well enjoy 'em."

"I'm trying." He paused. "Going home?"

"Yes, and you?"

"I have a job waiting for me, but I don't know anyone anywhere on the coast."

The older Black woman nodded as though to say she understood his plight.

The younger Black woman with the long black hair wanted another cigarette. Norman offered her the next-to-last Lucky Strike, and took the very last one for himself. They smoked together in silence until he asked, "Mind if I sketch you? I'm not a great artist, but I want to very much."

"Suit yourself."

She turned slightly so that Norman had a good look at her profile.

"Thanks, perfect."

When he finished the sketch, which he admired, he showed it to the woman seated next to him who smiled and nodded.

"You got her likeness."

Norman signed his name and asked the young brown-skinned

woman for hers.

"It's Beulah Hannah."

At the top of the page, Norman wrote, "For Beulah Hannah." He gave her the paper.

"It's a gift."

She rolled it up and placed it inside her suitcase, which she retrieved from the overhead rack with Norman's help. She thanked him and offered a timid smile.

The white man who sat at the window next to the young Black woman cleared his throat and coughed. He was big and brawny, with tattoos on his left forearm, one of which depicted an anchor, another of a mermaid. The brawny fellow wore a white T-shirt that showcased his muscular body. He couldn't or wouldn't stop wiggling in his seat and puffing out his chest.

Just watching him made Norman jittery.

"You got a problem, man?"

"I don't see why they have to sit up here."

Norman exhaled forcefully and gulped for air.

"Be nice, please, sir, we gotta get along on this frickin' bus."

The muscle-bound man gave Norman the finger and spread his knees as far as they would go, which prompted Beulah Hannah to shrink in her seat.

Norman glared.

"Listen, guy, don't hog the space."

When the bus stopped at the next station, Norman stood up, waited for the passengers ahead of him to move forward, and then ran for the concession stand. He bought two packs of Camels, a coffee, a ham and cheese sandwich on white bread, and a package of Oreos, which he placed in the pocket of his jacket.

He boarded the bus and handed the young Black woman the pack of cigarettes that he had purchased explicitly for her.

"I didn't want you to be without."

"That's very decent of you."

He devoured the sandwich while he sipped the coffee, and then leaned back in his seat. The Black woman who sat next to him clearly had something burning inside that she wanted to share. Norman knew by the way she turned her body toward him and the expression on her face.

"What is it ma'am?"

"You heard 'bout Sarah Keys? My son told me 'bout her and I read about her in the newspaper, too. She wouldn't give up her seat to a white boy on a Greyhound. They arrested her and brought her to jail, but she took her case to court. We're waiting for the ruling, but I just know she can't lose."

Norman listened and nodded thoughtfully.

"I know what you mean, ma'am. I've read about the case in Topeka, Kansas and the judges saying separate is unequal. It's about time."

The Black woman nodded her head and looked around furtively.

"You better take care what you say, you hear?"

She sounded like she cared and didn't just mean to be polite.

She began to hum. Her humming put Norman to sleep, though not for long. The bus took too many of the bumps on the Interstate and rattled his bones. When he woke, he stretched his arms and legs.

"Thank you 'ma'am, that helped."

"I wasn't humming to you. But I'm happy you got your zzz's. My name's Zora. How 'bout you?"

"Norman. Norman de Haan. Nice to meet you."

Crossing the Mississippi elevated his mood. The Continental Divide made him feel he'd accomplished something major, and the Rockies raised him up higher than he'd ever been before. He borrowed the Black woman's tiny map of the U.S., studied it, gazed out the window and saw a bright white desert with tall cactus.

The landscape reminded him of the Dali painting with the melting watches he'd seen at the MOMA with tall, thin, red-headed Natalie. Too bad it hadn't worked out between them, but as his sister said, "There are plenty of fish in the sea."

Only, he had noticed that he couldn't find anyone else as appealing or attractive. New York without Natalie felt small, and now they were separated by half of the continent. She was behind him in her little world, while he had a big wide world ahead of him to explore, to map and to make his own.

He shifted his weight in the seat, changed the hands of his watch so he was on Pacific Time, and leaned toward the woman next to him. She noticed his squirming and didn't seem to mind. Norman sensed that there was already a bond between them, tenuous indeed, but still something to build on.

"I served in Germany. They needed translators and I was fluent. The de Haans, my ancestors, did awful things before they arrived in New York, where they tried to clean up their act."

There it was. His story wrapped up, all tidy and in only three sentences.

Zora hummed again, only softer this time.

"The sins of the fathers."

Her voice cocooned Norman and seemed to have a calming effect on her own mood, which rose and fell as the bus raced and sputtered, stopped and started. He wanted more humming, but thought it would be improper to ask.

Norman turned the pages of Zora's book and gazed at the map of California.

"My dad passed a while ago. Everything went to my mother. Now it's going to my sister, Toni, who thinks she's going to be a Hollywood star."

"Got to keep your eyes on the prize."

Zora reached into her traveling kit and removed a small pie-apple from the look and the smell of it—which she cut in half with a pocketknife she produced from somewhere on her person. She shared the pie with Norman, who held it in his right hand and ate it slowly, one bite at a time.

"Thank you 'ma'am. That's kind of you."

She didn't talk while she ate, and he didn't either, not after his initial "thank you." He finished his share of the pie and licked his fingers clean.

"For a time after I broke up with my girl, I lost my appetite."

"You did fine with the apple pie."

"They gave me an honorable discharge and a Purple Heart. When I came home, I moved in with my mom, killed a year doing nothing, and spent nights at Minton's, where I heard Billie and Lester."

"We have jazz in San Francisco, too, which, if you don't know already, is a big town with two halves: one for whites and the other for colored."

She opened the thermos, poured coffee, and offered Norman the cup.

"Go ahead, you first."

"No, you."

"Please."

"Okay."

He sipped slowly. It was strong coffee, still warm, and it felt good going down his throat.

She dabbed her lips with a white handkerchief.

"My son, Ezra, is meetin' the bus at the end of the line. He was in the service, too. 92nd Infantry."

Norman bounced up and down in his seat.

"The Buffalo soldiers! I knew them well! They mopped up the last of the fascists."

5

When they arrived at the Greyhound terminal, Norman turned to Zora and paused. He wanted to say something meaningful.

"Pleasure meeting you, ma'am. I won't soon forget your kindness."

He stood up and grabbed her suitcase, along with his talismanic duffle, both of which he placed on the seat he'd vacated. With his head down low, he walked along the aisle and nodded to the driver who seemed relieved to have made it to San Francisco. He'd delivered his passengers safely.

"Watch your step."

Norman stood on the sidewalk, held his duffle bag with both hands and probed the darkness. Across the street he saw a building that said, "Post Office." Nearby, a neon sign flashed "Blackhawk."

So, that's the Blackhawk that Bob Kaufman mentioned. It was late, but Norman heard a sweet, sweet sax. The Black Hawk sounded like a jazz club where the likes of Bob might revive and thrive.

The cars on the street moved like sharks in the sea. The bus driver closed the door and honked his horn twice, as a kind of farewell. The engine groaned and roared and the bus disappeared around the corner. Norman craned his neck and searched for a star overhead, the fog obscured the sky and he saw nothing in the blue black space that looked endless.

A young man with brown eyes and a sweet smile, dressed in dark slacks and a blue shirt open at the neck, approached Norman.

"Momma says you're a vet and a standup guy. If you need a place for tonight, you can bunk with us."

He extended his hand.

"My name's Ezra."

"I'm Norman. And yes, I was in the war, though I usually don't advertise my military record."

"92nd Infantry."

"Yeah, man, Buffalo Soldiers. Your mother told me. You guys are famous."

"Infamous and segregated."

The two words echoed in Norman head.

His platoon had been one-hundred percent white. All his life, his contact with "colored people," as he called them, had been limited. A Black woman from Tupelo, Mississippi came once a week to his mother's house and did the laundry, washing, drying and ironing. A colored kid on scholarship played on the football team at Chaminade. Norman had tried to befriend him. He thought it was the Christian thing to do, but the kid didn't seem to trust Norman's offer to train together, run laps, do pushups and situps.

In New York, he would surely have shied away from an invitation to stay with a colored family. Now, in San Francisco, he was alone and nowhere to go. Ferlinghetti had not offered him a room, nor had he even recommended a hotel where he could sleep for a night or two.

"Thanks, Ezra. That's very kind of you. It's very much appreciated. I'll take you up on the offer."

Norman's initial impression of Ezra was that he was physically fit in a body builder kind of way. His second impression was that he was "queer," as he called it. He had certain gestures and facial expressions that Norman had learned to recognize when he was in the service. There were more queers in uniform than anyone realized.

Ezra lifted his mother's suitcase.

"My sedan is around the corner. Our house sits at the outer edge of the Fillmore. A bunch of G.I.s live on the same street. One of 'em has a TV. We haven't gotten that far, not yet, and maybe never will."

He paused a moment, and placed Zora's suitcase in the trunk of the sedan, along with Norman's duffle bag.

"My mother tells stories, some 'bout our folks down South, plays the drum and sings at times, visits with our neighbor, Mrs. Cornbrake."

Ezra slammed shut the trunk of the car; the rear bumper bounced up and down.

"My father died of a heart attack down at the shipyard."

Norman found his place in the back seat. Zora sat next to her son, who gripped the steering wheel with both hands and navigated the tangled streets of the city.

Ezra cruised first through a neighborhood where white folks had made their mark; there were white folk's cars, white folk's houses and white folk's picket fences, like in the movies. Next came the neighborhood where Black folks congregated.

It was late and chilly, but men and women sat on their front steps, watched kids play in the street, nodded their heads, lifted brown paper bags, and brought bottles to their lips. They sipped and savored and followed Ezra's blue four-door sedan as it stopped along the curb and the doors opened.

A strange-looking white man emerged from the back seat, lugged a duffle bag, and followed Zora into her two-story house painted orange, red, and blue, with green shutters and a front porch made for sitting and watching the river of humanity.

Inside, the house smelled of spices: cinnamon and nutmeg, along with butter and flour, which brought back a memory of Norman's grandmother and her big kitchen in the big house in Oyster Bay on Long Island where he spent boyhood summers, happy as Huck Finn without Tom Sawyer, who was a pain.

Zora smiled as she removed her coat and scarf. She sat down and played a big, old drum which seemed to mimic the beat of Norman's heart. Or maybe, he decided, his heart mimicked the drum. He knew drums and drummers, like Gene Krupa, but nothing like this drum and this drummer. They seemed to be a single entity. Ezra danced, or rather the dance danced him. Norman leaned against the wall, took out his notebook, and sketched a few simple lines that depicted Zora and the drum.

Ezra learned against the wall and watched.

"It's a hountar from Haiti. Must have been brought from West

Africa by folks who were kidnapped and shipped across the Atlantic."

Norman nodded his head, then plunged ahead on his own and disappeared into the darkness of the dining room. As the sound of the drum grew fainter and fainter, he suddenly realized how sleepy he felt, surely because of all that time on the bus as it hurtled across the U. S. of A.

He opened the refrigerator and helped himself to the bottle of milk on the top shelf. He shook it so that the heavy cream blended with the rest of the liquid, poured himself a glass, removed the Oreo from his pocket, and nibbled until it was gone.

He looked out the window at the neighbors across the street.

Nobody and nothing ever goes in a straight line, he thought, certainly not a bus which takes every twist and turn in the road. Us humans follow a downward spiral that ends in darkness. That's the war talking, he heard himself say, the war that brought you to black tar and brown sugar that you cooked and that nodded you out. New York noir, Harlem noir. Yes, indeed, junk had taken away his pain, until a buddy from the platoon overdosed and Norman went cold turkey. He rinsed his hands at the kitchen sink and dried them on a towel.

"I helped myself to milk."

"There's more where that comes from. The milkman delivers."

"Your bedroom is at the top of the flight of stairs. First door on your left."

"Goodnight and thank you."

"Bless you."

He climbed the stairs, stowed his bag, and bounced on the bed. In the bathroom, he located a thumb tack and fixed his sketch of Zora and her hountar to the white wall above the toilet.

Sleep came to him easily, mercifully and he woke feeling refreshed and new and whole.

The first night at Zora's led to a second night—Zora insisted—and the first week led to the start of a second week.

Why do I go on staying here? Why do I not move out and find my own place? Well, I like the company and I am flattered that Zora and Ezra seem to like me. They're not colored people in a movie. They're real; as real as any colored folk I'm liable to meet, ever. So as long as it works for me and for them, I'm settled here in the Fillmore.

After ten days, he raised the topic of money.

"What about thirty-dollars a month?"

"Seems like a lot."

"I have a job. I can handle it."

"Can we agree about twenty-five?"

Once he began to pay for the room, he felt even more settled and more at home. The money had made a difference for the better.

∾∾

6

By the end of the third week, Norman learned to recognize the daily rhythms of Zora's life: reading the newspaper, *The Defender*, which came in the mail, playing the drum, cooking mustard greens in fatback, making apple pies, praying, laughing, washing, ironing, gossiping with her neighbor, Mrs. Cornbreak, and listening to Bessie Smith records. He soon came to the realization that the Fillmore didn't look, sound, or smell like Harlem, though it was inhabited by Black families, some recently arrived from the South, others longtime residents who had come during the war to work in the shipyards.

Nor did the San Francisco peninsula, surrounded by water on three sides, feel like Manhattan Island. Union Square in S.F. didn't feel like Union Square in NYC. The City by the Bay felt unlike any other city in which he had ever lived, including Left Bank Paris, where he bivouacked after he reconnoitered with the Russians along the Elbe, drank vodka with them and fraternized more than he should have. But what the hell, weren't the Russians allies?

Later, in Paris, and no longer in uniform, he gorged on foie gras and French fries with mayonnaise and guzzled huge quantities of Burgandy. Bravely, he knocked on the door of the apartment for Richard Wright and his white, Jewish wife, Ellen, whom he had met once when he worked in his father's bookstore, Pegasus. Wright told him: "I couldn't stomach the racism." Ellen added, "The French aren't perfect, but no one here treats us like second-class citizens."

For a month, Norman skated around the edges of the ex-pat colony. He, Chester Himes and James Baldwin talked and argued and shared their dreams and their nightmares, about a world that seemed to hover between disaster and some kind of new and wonderful configuration.

Norman would have liked to join their circle, and, while he and Baldwin sauntered along the Seine and admired the gargoyles and the churches, he felt like an outsider among outsiders. Perhaps if he had been a published writer, or a tyro, he might have been accepted, but he had no work to show or to share.

In a bookstore in the Sixth Arrondissement, Baldwin leafed through a copy of Jean Genet's *Our Lady of the Flowers*, bought it and gave it to Norman as a going away present.

"You have to go back, man. Believe me. I know. Just as I also know my place is here."

Later, at the Café de Flor, Norman, Baldwin and Chester Himes smoked, drank and enjoyed rambling conversations. Norman noticed Baldwin's long thin fingers, expressive lips, firm chin and furrowed brow. Most of all, he admired Baldwin's ability to dig deep down inside and express his innermost feelings which seemed to illuminate national dilemmas.

"Paris is a good place for you to write, isn't it, James?"

Baldwin laughed, lit a cigarette and watched the smoke curl up toward the ceiling of the Flor. He smiled and went on smiling.

"Hotels are less expensive here than in Manhattan, and the Parisians don't bug me about the color of my skin and my sexuality. Nobody tells me 'get over it,' meaning slavery. I will never get over Jim Crow, lynching and goddamned discrimination in the very heart of New York, where I was born and grew up. I was outside. You were inside. You're still inside. Hell, you're a de Haan. I'm a descendant of slaves."

Norman liked to think that he carried some of Baldwin's wisdom back with him to the States, and all the way to the West coast. When his collection of essays, *Notes of a Native Son*, was published, Norman took the initiative and ordered two-dozen copies of the book for City Lights. All of them sold instantly. He ordered more and curled up with his own copy. Baldwin's essay, "The Harlem Ghetto" walked him through a place he had only known from a distance, and with detachment mixed with fear he didn't like to own.

Norman de Haan, the descendant of Dutch Calvinists, didn't fall in love with City Lights at first sight, but rather by the end of his first week when it dawned on him that the bookstore had a certain French charm that was contagious. It was also thoroughly American with a global twist. When he took the time to look, he found García Lorca's *Blood Wedding* and *Poet in New York*, plus Vladimir Mayakovsky's plays, *The Bedbug* and *The Bathhouse*, which he revered even before he learned that the Soviet government and the Moscow literary establishment both wanted to shit on dear dear "Vlady," as he came to think of him.

Ferlinghetti also grew on him by leaps and bounds. At the end of his second week at City Lights, it came to Norman that Lawrence Ferlinghetti, his kindly boss, was a Francophile. Not a bad thing to be in whitebread America in 1955, when Swanson's TV dinners had become all the rage. In the quiet hours of the morning, Norman and Lawrence spoke French together, and again in the evening when shadows lengthened and the noises of the city were muffled by the ubiquitous San Francisco fog, which was unlike any other fog he had ever known. A few years older than Norman and a war veteran, Ferlinghetti boasted the odd distinction of having served in both Europe and in Asia in World War II. He was reserved, and rarely initiated a conversation with Norman, but occasionally he shared a thought or an idea.

"This place, this city and me are tied by an invisible umbilical cord to the Left Bank of Paris, the good bank, the bohemian bank, not to the bourgeoisie banks."

Norman chuckled.

"I shouted '*Non* to the banks' in '45 near Shakespeare and Company, where I smoked Gauloises with George Whitman."

Now, a decade later, and with Paris a bright shining memory, Norman recognized that Lawrence's fledging, anarchist bookstore on Columbus Avenue was closer to Charlie Chaplin and to silent films like *City Lights*—with its tramp, millionaire and blind girl—than it was to George Whitman's Paris shop. George had been born in New Jersey and raised in Salem, Massachusetts in the shadow of the witch trials and had to escape from the Puritan blight, which Norman knew all too well.

Or maybe, Norman thought, Lawrence was a mongrel who melded Chaplin with Walt Whitman, and who mixed the waters of San Francisco Bay with those of the Seine.

"What are you reading now? You're not in Kansas anymore, kid."

Norman shrugged his shoulders.

"I'm reading nothing now, I'm sorry to say, sir."

"This is a bookstore, man, you'd better start reading something fast."

"What do you recommend?"

"*Dago Red* by John Fante. He was all the rage, once. Now he's all but forgotten. That's America. Famous one day, unknown the next."

Maybe so, Norman told himself, but Lawrence seemed all too quick to dismiss the whole North American continent, from coast-to-coast and to embrace Europe. Didn't Lawrence know the Huck-Finn-and-Jim-Mississippi River, the Salvador Dali cactus in the Nevada desert, and the Rockies in winter that nearly destroyed Meriwether Lewis and William Clark had it not been for Sacagawea, the sixteen-year-old native who saved their lives? Where was Lawrence's love of his native land? It had to be lurking somewhere. Indeed, it was there, though not in red, white and blue. One simply had to look for it where one least expected it, under the surface, in the margins and among the subterraneans.

Norman found a used copy of Fante's novel, *Dago Red*, in Lawrence's office and read a few pages at a time while he sat at the front counter. He fell in love with Fante's characters and realized he'd never be able to let go of books. They'd never let go of him. They were as much a part of him as his de Haan ancestors.

He saw, too, that City Lights was a nifty niche for Lawrence, a scholar who had studied at the Sorbonne and who aimed to be a poet who straddled centuries and oceans. His visage reminded Norman of the sketches he'd admired of the French poet, Apollinaire. He saw Apollinaire in Ferlinghetti when the dying light on the horizon hit him at just the right angle.

An anarchist proprietor: a strange combination, Norman told himself. Where else was that possible? In Paris, for sure, and maybe in London, but not in Moscow or Tokyo, and not even in New Orleans with its Creoles and Bourbon Street blues.

The Golden Gate was as American as the Normandy beaches were French. Norman observed the Italian men playing bocce and watched his boss *cherchez les femmes* in North Beach which boasted beautiful women who spoke English, Spanish, Italian and more. When Norman ached for a taste of New York, Lawrence advised him to give up hunting for a real bagel, a real bialy, an authentic doughnut, or a veritable Manhattan crueller, and go instead for sourdough bread.

He also said to forget about *petite madeleine*, a not so obscure reference that Norman got and which brought a smile to his face. The breezes from the Pacific seemed to erode his Manhattan profile little by little. He softened. He relaxed. He let his guard down and let people into his life, even while he maintained his own space.

Norman's spartan room on the second floor of Zora's house had a bare floor and no curtains on the windows that leaked cold air on windy days and nights. The bathroom down the hall looked like a relic of Gold Rush days. He would not have been surprised to find a miner from Chile or China sitting on the ancient can, reading Oscar Wilde and smoking a handrolled cigarette.

Norman slept late most mornings, dressed, walked to the bus stop on the corner, and climbed aboard the number 22. After a week or so, he knew every twist and turn of the route. He would descend at Columbus, trudge uphill and open the front door to the store.

"Hello, Shig."

"Hello, Norman."

At the start they rarely said more than half-a-dozen words to one another. Then, Shig issued a warning and an adviso.

"Don't call the boss, Larry. He'll be mad as hell if you do. You might remember that he was raised first by an aunt and later by foster parents. Lawrence never knew his own father. I think of him as an orphan. Book by book, City Lights has been his way of creating a family."

Shig lent Norman his copy of Oswald Spengler's *The Decline of the West* and unpacked his notions about the West and the East, the fall of western civilization, and the cyclical nature of history.

"We are doomed. We are the last of our kind and had better make use of our time here wisely."

Next he shared D. T. Suzuki's *An Introduction to Zen Buddhism* and encouraged Norman to sit, face the wall, meditate and try to empty his mind of all the clutter, which proved to be more difficult than it seemed.

"Ah, so, you have monkey mind like the rest of us."
Norman nodded.
"How do I stop it?"
Shig laughed.
"You can't."
"Then what's the point of sitting and meditating?"
"Maybe there is no point."

Shig guided Norman around the city on foot and by cable car, and showed him where to eat a bowl of sukiyaki—pronounced "ski ah ki"—for $1, along with cold beer and hot sake. He also led Norman around the bookstore, which wasn't much more than the proverbial hole in the wall, but it boasted nooks and crannies on the ground floor, and secret spaces upstairs, where Lawrence wrote poetry.

The bookstore was conveniently located next door to a friendly florist who sold fragrant white and red roses and bouquets which Norman bought and brought home to Zora, who put them in a vase and added to the dining room table.

"Thank you for the flowers."
"Thank you for your southern hospitality."
She laughed.

Afternoons at the store, Norman rolled up his shirt sleeves, hunkered down in the basement, unpacked boxes of books from publishers in New York, and catalogued every single one, all of them paperbacks and not a hardback anywhere in sight.

If he missed anything about New York, it was the jazz scene. He had fallen in love with Billie Holiday and had secretly longed to be like Lester Young. The saxophone belonged to Norman's soul. Or maybe he belonged to it. Bebop and the blues got under his skin. They jazzed him, sexed him and rebirthed him. Norman heard Young in his head, as real as if they were in the same space together. His sax sounded real and not imaginary.

Norman's "sax narrative," as he called it, triggered laughter from Lawrence, who seemed to be permanently lost in thought, or maybe eternally entangled in words, both French and English. He told Norman that what he experienced had to be an "auditory hallucination" and that he ought to get tested at the Christopher Columbus Ear, Nose, and Throat Clinic.

"Better to know than not to know, at least in this instance."

Lawrence climbed the stairs to his office. Norman picked up, and held in both hands, a hefty paperback of James Farrell's *The Young Manhood of Studs Lonigan.* He had finished the Fante. The cover of the Farrell novel was meant to look sexy, but wasn't. It was garish.

He opened the book and read the first line; by the end of the first page, he merged with Studs. I've done this before, he heard himself say. There were so many unholy ghosts in his head from Zorro and Julien Sorel, to Odette and Nick Carraway. Norman closed the book, lifted his eyes, and watched Lawrence descend the stairs that had been worn away by thousands of human footsteps: someone always going up, someone else always coming down.

Norman remembered that when he was five or so, his father had said, "You can't step into the same river twice," a remark Mr. de Haan attributed to a Greek named Heraclitus. Norman's father also told him, "Let not the sun go down upon your anger," which made no sense to him at 13.

Mr. de Haan lectured his son about morality, mortality and about their ancestors.

"Your schoolmates aren't fit to associate with any of the de Haans, least of all with you, Norman."

Mr. de Haan had robbed him of his boyhood, all through his real youth and adolescence. He robbed his son again when he died of a heart attack when Norman was 14, just beginning to understand the workings of his own body and who imagined that he would live forever.

A kind uncle tried to disabuse him of his illusions.

"Pegasus, your father's bookstore, served as a front."

Norman knit his brow.

"Front for what?"

"Laundering money, stupid."

7

Norman had worked at Pegasus on weekends. Strange men in sharkskin suits entered the store carrying brown paper bags, which his father received and stashed. Norman couldn't stop himself from entering the back office and poking around when his father was out. There was more money than he had ever seen, or would ever see again. He helped himself to a handful of bills, which he thought of as his share as a junior member in the de Haan tribe. Norman confessed to his priest, who admonished him and gave him more Hail Marys to say than he had ever said before.

Now he was working in a bookstore again, although he had sworn "never again." Lawrence's emotional remoteness reminded Norman of his own father. Still, Lawrence meant well, especially when Norman talked about the saxophone he heard, or thought he heard in his head.

"I know what it's like to hear things. All kinds of voices go into my poetry."

Norman smiled. Lawrence had opened up to him, if only a tiny bit. Still, he was thankful.

"I'd like to channel my sex drive and become a writer."

He read one novel after another, wrote page after page in his notebook, and still he heard the sax, only louder now than in New York.

On the house phone—not Lawrence's private line— which lived on the ledge beneath the front desk Norman made an appointment to see a hearing specialist at the Christopher Columbus Clinic. In the office of the clinic, he told Doctor Ivan Ivanovich about the saxophone he heard. The next day he arrived with high hopes that his problem would be solved, but the doctor struck him as a con artist.

"I know how you feel. I have had the same experience. You've come to the right place."

Ivanovich instructed him to sit in a chair in a box. Then he fired bizarre and not so bizarre questions at him, none of which Norman took seriously, though he provided some serious answers.

"Where and when were you born?"

"Long Island, 1922." (That was true).

"Do you ever play a musical instrument?"

"No, sir!" (That wasn't true. He once played boogie woogie piano).

"Are you constipated?"

"Fuck no! " (Sometimes he was).

"Did your parents speak English at home?"

"Esperanto." (A lie).

Doctor Ivanovich brought out the wise guy in Norman, albeit not for long. He got on Norman's nerves. The doctor was setting him up for something.

"Served in the military?"

"European theater."

"How long?"

"'42 to '45."

"Any hearing problems during the war?"

"Only when I couldn't hear."

"Why was that?"

"Bombs exploding."

"Where and when do you hear this mysterious saxophone?"

"Could be anytime, anywhere, mostly in New York but it has followed me out here."

"Recognize any of the tunes?"

"D.B. Blues."

"What about the musician?'

"Lester Young."

"Not Charlie Parker?"

"Correct. Not The Bird, not his syncopation."

Ivanovich put earphones over Norman's head, exited the box-like space, and closed the door so Norman could not see him, though the doctor could see Norman.

I know how Dorothy must have felt in the land of Oz with the wizard behind the curtain, he told himself.

The doctor created sounds that sounded random; they grew louder and louder and then fainter and fainter.

Norman followed Ivanovitch's instructions: he listened to the sounds, and with his index finger, pressed a button that turned on a red light. He felt less and less like Dorothy and more and more like a rat in a lab, his brain waves fried.

You will turn into a zombie, he told himself. But he kept pressing the button and watching the red light come on.

After an agonizingly long period of time, Doctor Ivanovich released him, sat him down, and told him he passed the test, but just barely. He suggested that Norman keep a record of the times he heard the saxophone, plus the duration of the sound.

Norman stood and walked toward the exit. This guy just wants my money, he told himself.

"Thanks. I'll do that."

Ivanovich opened the top drawer of his desk and removed a hearing aid.

"Wait a second."

He demonstrated how the device worked. Too complicated, Norman thought. He held it in his hands.

"I'll think about it."

The doctor frowned.

"It's on sale. Take it home and try it. Buy it in the next 48 hours, and you save an additional ten percent. Or purchase on the installment plan."

Norman took a big step toward the door.

"I'll think about it."

He did for a split second or two. Once he hit the street, he didn't give the hearing aid another thought, though he continued to hear the sax.

"The sax is my Holy Ghost," he told Shig.

They had ghosts in common, though Shig's were mostly Japanese.

"They talk to me, remind me of things I've forgotten and point me in the right direction when I get turned around and don't know which way to go."

Shig and Norman didn't have a work schedule with days and hours marked off for each one on a calendar. They improvised and covered for one another when need be, though Norman was the real troublemaker of the two and needed a front. When Shig went out for a smoke and miso soup, Norman gave away copies of Lawrence's *Pictures of the Gone World,* simply because he liked the smile on a woman's face, or appreciated the paperbacks she wanted to buy.

One afternoon, after a morning of shelving new books, Lawrence invited Norman upstairs.

"Someone is pilfering copies of my book. I want you to be on the lookout."

Norman's free book policy came to an end and copies of *Pictures of the Gone World* piled up.

In the basement and at the cash register, Norman had time to think long and hard about Zora's son, Ezra. He wondered where he made the money he threw around for gas, booze, and snazzy shirts. He also wondered if Zora truly cared for him, as she claimed, or if she was setting him up for a fall. That was his paranoia talking.

On a Monday before the book store opened, he walked to the Rincon Annex Post office, rented a box, bought stamped envelopes, and wrote two notes. In the one to his mother, Bea, he explained, "Have landed safely, rented a small room in a large house, am well fed, sleeping good, won't be home for Easter, Love, Norman."

In the note to his sister, Toni, which was more personal, he wrote: "Living with a mother (a widow) and her queer son in the Fillmore. You'd call them both Negroes, though they don't use that word. From the very Deep South, not totally citified. The widow plays a cool old drum from Haiti. Her son goes to school on the GI Bill. Me, I'm my same old, same old. Don't worry. Let me know when you hit the big time in L.A. I'll come down and treat you like a starlet."

He posted the letters and admired the colorful murals on the walls of the post office, which were titled "The History of California," and painted by an artist named Anton Refregier. Norman especially liked the portrait of Sir Francis Drake, holding a sword in his right hand, with his left hand resting on a replica of the globe. Drake looked very dapper, indeed, and not like the pirate who pilfered for the Queen.

He tried the key for his box, found it worked, and watched an elderly man shuffle along and stuff his mail into the pocket of his jacket. The man took Norman by the elbow and swirled him around so he was facing the mural that depicted crowds in the street and cops with billy clubs.

"They tried to remove them."

"They?"

"You're a smart guy. You know who I mean."

"I'll come back and study 'em."

Back at the store, he asked Shig about the murals.

"What I know is that crackpots complained that Anton Refregier's art didn't show how happy we all are in California."

Norman nodded.

"Nothing depresses me more than the Pollyannas of the world."

Shig snorted.

"They believe what they read in the newspapers and blame teenagers for the blackboard jungle they see everywhere."

A letter for Norman de Haan arrived c/o City Lights with his old address on Cornelia Street in New York. He knew it had to be from Bob Kaufman and he worried that something bad had happened. Norman tended to imagine disaster. He need not have worried. The letter, which was, indeed, from Bob, contained only good news. It was one long, unbroken sentence without punctuation. "Dear Norman you can't imagine or maybe you can since you're an imaginative human what a joy it is to be in your apartment and to have a fixed address something I have not had for some time since I have been shipping out from various ports beginning in '42 when I departed from Galveston, TX. was discharged in N.Y. in '44 when I went all the way to Calcutta India which is probably one of the wildest and most wonderful cities in the world and too bad the British fucked it up but India is now its own independent nation and then soon after that voyage I became a pastry chef on the *Hood Victory* and my final voyage was in '46 on the *Mormacport* since then been writing pretty steadily had some time the other day to do some digging on the de Haans maybe some of your ancestors might have put some of my ancestors in chains and carried them across the Atlantic not to freedom but to bondage and now look at us me in your pad and you at City Lights in solidarity and love Robert Kaufman."

Norman wrote back and used short simple sentences, Hemingway style.

"Learning to sit and meditate. Might turn into a Zen Buddhist. Monkey mind is killing me. I walk a lot. This place is all hills. It's segregated, too. Colored folks are in one place. Whites in another. I go back and forth between the two. An old colored lady calls me a white spook. I trust I'm not spooking here. Your pal, Norman."

8

Early one morning, he stood on the landing at the top of the flight of stairs in the creaky Fillmore house, and overheard Zora in conversation with Mrs. Cornbrake, whom he thought of as the neighborhood snoop.

"How long that freeloader gonna go on livin' in your house, Zora?"

"Oh, I don't know. I don't think 'bout time the way you do, Mrs. Cornbrake. Maybe he be here for another day, maybe 'til Juneteenth. I don't rightly know."

Mrs. Cornbrake chewed on a wad of tobacco.

"I thought you didn't care a fig for white folks, claimed they was the ruination of Black folks."

Zora chuckled and turned her whole body until she stood in the middle of the doorway, soaking up the rays of the sun.

"I mostly don't truck with white folks, but this here white boy, he's decent. I saw that on the bus coming' across the country. Somebody got to care for him, 'cause if I don't, he'd fall in with the wrong people. That would be the end of him, and I'd have to buy a casket and arrange for a funeral. Then where would I be, Mrs. Cornbrake? You see what I mean?"

Zora chucked again and peered into Mrs. Cornbrake's eyes which seemed to see everywhere.

"Someday before long I'll be buried in the ground with Black folks. Meanwhile, Norman saves me from thinking too much about myself. I guess I'm trying to prove something. Maybe that I don't have hate stored up inside me. Hate will kill you."

Mrs. Cornbrake huffed and puffed.

"He's a white spook, make me nervous."

Zora stood resolute and unbowed.

"That boy makes me feel calm, not nervous."

Zora looked up, noticed Norman looking down, and smiled.
"Maybe he'll spook you into being more Christian."

The back and forth between Zora and Mrs. Cornbrake,
which took place in the shadows of the doorway, answered some
of Norman's questions about Zora, but he wanted still more blank
spaces filled in.

He liked Mrs. Cornbrake's phrase, "white spook," and began
to think of himself as the reverse of an Oreo. He was white on the
outside and black on the inside. He wasn't surprised when he signed
a letter to Toni, "the White Spook." Norman began to feel like he
belonged in the Fillmore.

"Morning, Mrs. Cornbrake."

It was early and chilly and Norman wanted to find a café for
coffee and someone to talk to.

Mrs. Cornbrake watered the red roses in her front yard.

"You talkin' to me?"

"I said 'Morning, Mrs. Cornbrake.'"

"How you know my name?"

"You grow beautiful flowers."

"Thank ya."

"If you need something ask."

"I worked in the shipyards. I can take care of me fine."

"I'm sure you can. Anyway, it's a beautiful morning."

Mrs. Cornbrake went back to her red roses and Norman
prowled the neighborhood hoping to unearth a café, but found
nothing that suited him. He returned to Zora's and made himself
coffee. He sat in the kitchen, reading a story in *The Defender* which
came in the mail, along with letters, flyers, and post cards for Mr.
Norman de Haan from his sister.

Zora loved *The Defender* and swore by it as though it was her
Bible. A newspaper story, which came with a Johannesburg dateline,
bore a headline that read, "Non-whites Evicted." Norman watched
Zora read it once, and then again a second time as though she didn't
want to believe the news it conveyed from South Africa, the land of
apartheid.

"Non-whites. I guess I'm one of them."

Norman sat down next to her.

"If you don't mind, Zora, I was wondering what or how you feel, and even if you do feel anything at all, about this thing they're calling integration in our own country?"

Zora folded the paper and rested her hands across her belly. "I don't *feel* nothing 'bout what they call integration, segregation. White folks do what they mean to do, same as in the slavery time, only with more lies and more bullets. I'd believe in the Lord and not in the Man and I believe in *The Defender*, which tells it like it is."

She reached out, touched Norman's chin and brushed away a stray crumb.

"It's best if colored folk don't pay white folks no mind and just do what they got to do by themselves."

She got up slowly and went into the kitchen. Norman followed her and watched her gather bowls and utensils for cooking. Zora opened the door to the pantry in the hall, removed jars and brown paper bags, reached into the icebox, and came out with her hands full.

Then she began to make something—he didn't know what—with flour, eggs, milk, cream, and peaches in syrup from a can, humming to herself. She baked her concoction in an ancient oven that looked like it might have been used on a plantation in the Deep South. That evening Zora served peach cobbler for dessert.

Norman learned that Zora revealed herself in bits and pieces that made him think of the patches in the quilt that lived in the spare bedroom beyond the landing. The patches didn't seem to fit together in any kind of pattern that he recognized, and yet, he sensed that they fit together in an awkward but beautiful way.

Norman grew to admire Zora. At the same time, he found himself wishing that Ezra would show who he really was. Why isn't he more like his mother? Norman asked himself.

"Enigmatic Ezra," he called him, though not to his face. Norman's uncertainties about Zora's son built up week after week. One evening in the dead of winter, he heard from Ezra about a teenager in Montgomery, Alabama who caused a ruckus on a bus.

"This news goin' around the world."

Ezra waved a copy of *The Defender* in the air, his eyes bulging, his face on fire.

"This girl, she refused to move to the 'colored only' section. Cops carried her off in handcuffs, feet first, trying to do her harm."

Ezra folded the paper, gathered his books for school, put on a blue V-neck sweater and gave Norman a pat on the back.

"Carry on spook, carry on."

9

The morning after Ezra's rant about the brave young woman in Montgomery, Alabama, Zora gave Norman a letter and three pennies. She asked him to please buy a stamp at the post office, place it on the envelope, and hand it over the counter to the mail clerk on duty at the window.

He returned the pennies.

"Not to worry. I got you covered."

He glanced at the writing on the envelope that was addressed to "Miss Cadillac Colvin, Money, Mississippi," and in the upper left-hand corner, "Mrs. Zora Colvin, San Francisco, Calif."

"You omitted the name of your own street and the one for Miss Colvin."

Zora squeezed the three pennies in the palm of her hand. "That's right. Dollars to doughnuts, the letter reaches my niece just fine."

"Yes, ma'am. I'm sure that's true."

He didn't want to pick a fight with Zora about the letter to someone in Mississippi, which he associated with William Faulkner's *Light in August,* the novel his father had given him as a Christmas present, and *Sanctuary,* the potboiler which he read in boot camp. Norman hoped he never met anyone like Popeye and Temple Drake, both of them, in his view, sicko.

On his way to the post office, Zora's letter to Mississippi burned hotter and hotter in his hand. Walking up Columbus, he resolved to make the contents known to himself.

"Morning, Shig. Got to go to the post office soon."

"Morning, Norman."

On the second floor, in the bookstore's makeshift kitchen, Norman added water from the tap to a kettle, lit a safety match, turned on the gas and lowered the heat. When steam came through the spout, he separated the sticky from the dry side of the flap. The adhesive gave way and the envelope opened without tearing.

At a small desk in the basement, where he would have privacy, he sat down and removed the letter from the envelope. He placed the letter on the table and read silently: "Dear Cadillac, Word of your Doings in Alabama reached me here on the Coast. I do Believe that you must be a Brave Girl. Once when I was your age, I was Braver than I am now.

"It is my deepest Hope and fondest Belief that you won't allow your Self to be used by nobody, no matter what the color of their skin. I do not expect you to reply. I am an old Colored Lady with no more expectations in Life. I keep you in my prayers, send you my Blessings and ask you to remember our Lord, Jesus Christ. Sincerely, Aunt Zora."

"Well, well, well."

Norman sputtered.

Why didn't she pick up the phone and call or wire a telegram?

Inside the letter he found a five-dollar bill which he snapped. Not surprisingly, he soon began to feel guilty. To assuage his conscience, he opened his wallet, removed a five-dollar bill, and inserted it in the envelope. He resealed it and placed it under a stack of books to help remove the creases, and to enable the remaining stickiness to regain some of his former strength. Then he placed the letter inside a paperback copy of *Fahrenheit 451*—which he had not read but wanted to.

Norman glanced at his watch, figured he had time to write to Kaufman. Hurriedly, he put his thoughts down on paper:

Kaufman, Sir

You are a modern day, proletarian Ishmael who has lived to tell his amazing seafaring tales. No doubt you will go on telling more of them. I appreciate your writing style. I know about automatic writing, stream of consciousness and James Joyce. So far I haven't gotten the hang of it. I blame the English Dept. at Yale. Yeah, I'm a card-carrying Yalie. I need to break free. Fortunately, I've fallen in with a bunch of guys who aim to write without stopping and sometimes even without thinking, but being in touch with their unconscious and their dreams which at first sounded easy to me but it's harder than it appears to be because it takes discipline and practice. Sweet Jesus, I see that I've just written what my English prof would call a run-on sentence. So be it. I'm a run-on kinda guy. Gotta go now. See you in Frisco.

He signed the letter, "Norman de H," inserted it in an envelope, added his old address on Cornelia Street, climbed the stairs to the ground floor and waved to Shig.

"Going out. Won't be long."

He hoofed it to Washington Square. There, he admired the statue of Benjamin Franklin and the lovely poplar trees. He entered the post office, bought two first-class stamps for six cents, fixed them to the envelopes and handed them over the counter.

"Will these go out today?"

The clerk gave him a puzzled expression.

"Daddy-O, you can bank on it."

He wandered into Saints Peter and Paul Church, knelt down in a pew at the back, looked at Christ on the cross, and tried to pray the way he'd prayed as a boy, but couldn't. He stood up, brushed the lint from his trousers and made for the exit, hoping to avoid a tall, thin priest who came right at him like a bullet fired from a gun.

"Afternoon, father."

Norman offered a courteous smile.

The priest pressed his hands together and squeezed.

"You don't have to be a lapsed Catholic forever, my son."

"Nothing is forever, father."

Outside the church he shuddered for a moment or two. Escaped again. Close call. Encounters with priests pushed Norman's buttons and stirred up memories of confessions he wanted to forget.

On the walk back to City Lights, he imagined Zora's letter traveling from North to South, crossing the Mason Dixon line, making its way from spaces for white people to spaces for black people, all the way to Money, Mississippi. He saw Cadillac, whom he imagined as a girl in bare feet and pigtails, open the letter and read it, hold the two bills in her hands and show her mother and father.

Upstairs in Lawrence's office he found an atlas for the U.S., located Mississippi, but couldn't pinpoint the town of Money.

That evening he turned to Ezra for information.

"Do you know of a place called Money, Mississippi?"

Ezra nodded his head, and, when Norman asked, "Is Cadillac a strange name for a girl?" Ezra shook his head. Nothing seemed to rattle him, not even an encounter with two bulky officers with the San Francisco Police Department, which took place on Van Ness Avenue. He and Norman were on their way to the Blackhawk on Hyde for an evening of jazz. Ezra seemed euphoric and more talkative than usual.

"My dad took me to the Blackhawk when I was a kid. It was special. I heard Johnny Mathis and Cal Tjader, who played the vibraphone, turned me on to Latin jazz and mambo, man. Mambo's where it's at."

While he walked, Norman eyed the brightly painted little houses with their tidy front porches and the miniature well-kept gardens that bordered the street.

"I heard about the Blackhawk from a colored fellow with a German-Jewish last name, Kaufman, just before I quit New York. Kaufman is a poet and a frickin' original. I have one of his poems, 'An Abomunist Manifesto.' I'll have to show you, 'cause you'll dig it."

Ezra and Norman shared a menthol cigarette, a Kool, which they passed back and forth until nothing was left except a tiny bit, too small to hold. Norman flicked it into the gutter, where it sputtered and died.

"I never did like the word *fag*."

He hoped that Ezra would take the bait and was disappointed when he didn't.

His companion looked spiffy in his army uniform, which he had exhumed from the hall closet and dusted. Ezra had polished the buttons, then revived his military bearing and doused himself with cologne. Norman wore his civvies and wished he had brought his uniform across the country and could dress up as a soldier and play the part of the liberator. That was a role he enjoyed. In France in '45 everyone loved a liberator.

Straight ahead and fast approaching them were the two bulky cops loaded for bear. Ezra saw them before Norman did. He reached into the right pocket of his jacket, removed a small brown paper bag, stuffed it swiftly in the left pocket of Norman's bombardier jacket and whispered, "Get lost."

He did precisely what Ezra told him to do, asked no questions—
there wasn't time for that—and walked back slowly the way they
had come. Norman gazed over his shoulder once, for a second or
two, before he turned sharply at the intersection. He stopped long
enough to see that the two officers flanked Ezra, one on either side of
him, hands on their revolvers, faces drawn as though they were in no
mood for funny business. Ezra suddenly went limp. His whole body
seemed to say, "You have nothing to fear from me."

Norman froze for a moment.

Should I go back and stand with my buddy? He wondered.
No way. Ezra told me "Get lost." Norman was almost certain what
was inside the bag, but he dared not look, not on the street and in
plain view. Nor would it do to go back to Zora's, open the bag, and
make sure of the contents. Zora would wonder why he had come
back without Ezra, and wonder, too, whether something bad had
happened to her son.

Norman walked for a block, keeping an eye out for trouble.
He spied a yellow cab, hailed it, jumped into the backseat, slammed
the door, shouted, "Blackhawk," and then, since he'd watched zillions
of detective flicks at the Thalia in Manhattan, added, "Step on it."

It was a fun ride, uphill and downhill, weaving around cable
cars and running red lights. Norman got his money's worth and then
some. He gave the cabby— a young woman with short dark hair and
no lipstick or eyeliner—a tip that put a smile on her oval face.

"Call me anytime. I'm your girl."

She handed Norman her card which had her name, Abbie
Stein, and her phone number.

Halfway out of the cab, he turned and faced her.

"Later."

She pursed her lips.

"Don't be shy."

He stood on the sidewalk under the neon sign.

Now you know where Ezra gets his money, he told himself.
He's a reefer man.

☞☜

Jonah Raskin

10

The Blackhawk felt funky, as in rough around the edges, and funny, as in strange, not ha-ha funny. Except for a few couples who might have been described as "interracial," white folks and black folks sat at separate tables, with only jazz to bring them together. The place wasn't segregated, but it wasn't really integrated, either. A few young kids accompanied adults and sipped through straws from bottles of Coca Cola.

A couple of guys who struck Norman as queer leaned against the bar and a couple of women he thought of as lesbians stood near the back wall. This place is gonna be raided, Norman thought. I don't want to be here when that happens. His paranoia was acting up again.

He remembered that he had first heard bebop in Harlem six months after he came home from the war. At first, he resisted it and wanted to go back to the days of swing and the big bands when he danced in a clumsy, albeit graceful sort of way. He missed the dancing, missed Gene Krupa on drums and Dizzy on his horn, but bebop wore down his resistance, swept him up and carried him away.

Dancing, he decided, was for squares. He had been a weekend hipster. Now he was a fulltime hep cat. The sax became his deity; he worshipped at its shrine. No wonder he heard it at odd hours and in odd places.

Ezra arrived at the Blackhawk after the first set came to a close, and found Norman seated at a small round table, where he sipped a cocktail. Norman reached discretely for the brown paper bag in his jacket and surrendered it before Ezra asked for it. His pal held it in the palm of his hand, scampered across the floor and ducked behind the curtain on the stage.

A few minutes later, Lester appeared with his sax for the start of the second set and began to play slowly and sweetly. He transported Norman to a place that felt blissful. A photographer took Lester's picture with the band members, and pictures of the audience, too.

Ezra returned to the table, sat down, folded his arms across his chest, and let the music wash over him. It helped that he was stoned. There was no doubt about it, the reefer had worked its magic. Norman could smell it.

But it wasn't just on Ezra; it was all over the Blackhawk, mixed in with, but not dominated by the smell of tobacco, beer, perfume and perspiration. Norman's own bittersweet longings welled up from inside and made him feel hornier than he had felt for a long, long time. Perhaps he had a contact high.

Ezra clapped Norman on his back and roused him from his reverie.

"You did right bro! The cops didn't find nothin' on me. Let me go once I showed my driver's license and papers from the army. I carry 'em to keep me outta trouble. The uniform didn't hurt, neither."

Norman surveyed the room.

"Great show! Fantastic audience. I could stay here forever."

He noticed parents with their children in tow.

"What gives with the kids?"

"They gotta get with jazz same as adults."

"What about the guy with the camera?"

"That's Fred Lyon. He nails 'Frisco, from the Golden Gate to Coit Tower and Nob Hill; he's famous all over town. If you pay him he'll take your photo."

Norman watched Lyon move around the room like a dancer, snapping shots of the audience, as well as shots of Lester Young, who wore a pork pie hat. Norman fixed his eyes on Ezra, who didn't look or sound like the man he had seen on the sidewalk, hemmed in by the cops. Ezra snapped his fingers. His head bobbed up and down.

"Man, oh man, Prez is hot tonight. Did you hear that riff?"

"I did! It's better to hear him in person than to hallucinate his harmonies."

When Lester played "D.B. Blues" Ezra looked like he was lodged in jazz heaven.

"Fuckin' outrageous that he was busted with booze and reefer, locked up, kicked out of the military and court-martialed."

"Dishonorably discharged! Disgraceful!"

Ezra's lithe black body moved to Lester's elastic blues.

Seemingly taller and more robust now than he had been on the street surrounded by the cops, Ezra leapt to his feet, sashayed across the room, pulled up a chair and sat down at a table opposite a woman who wore a purple evening gown that revealed her back. In his spiffy uniform with his hair slicked back, Ezra looked, Norman decided, like a confidence man who might talk a man or a woman into or out of most anything. He was cheeky.

Norman could not see the woman's face, though he twisted this way and that way and tried to find a clear line of sight. There were too many people sitting and standing between them. Her face was turned away from him, though for a few moments he had a good look at her slender neck and shoulder blades.

He thought he remembered them, especially now with the sax swirling around and around. Lester, the funky bebop king and the woman with the beautiful shoulder blades, a white queen reigning effortlessly over the crazy scene at the Blackhawk. Norman didn't want to be her vassal, or express his fealty, and he resented the intimacy she seemed to share with Ezra, her black prince.

The Blackhawk was a kind of pressure cooker that heated everyone. It intensified Norman's red hot rage and his cool green jealousy, and something he didn't want to know and acknowledge, the noir at the heart of noir: the blackness of his own whiteness.

His ancestors were talking to him, though he didn't want to hear them. He calmed himself down by sheer willpower and crossed the room at a diagonal, the music growing louder and louder. He glanced over his shoulder and found Natalie's flinty eyes—yes, yes, Natalie's eyes—as hers found his, their eyes locking until he blinked, his head pounding.

Lester was fucking his sax, the music rising and falling until it climaxed and the room thundered. Then came a moment of silence and clarity. Natalie had the same hard eyes and soft mouth that he remembered.

Who am I? He asked himself. Who is Norman de Haan, who traces his ancestors from Holland to Suriname on the coast of the Atlantic Ocean? He didn't like to admit it, but he thought that the white queen was threatened by the Black prince, who was supposedly his buddy and obviously as queer as the queers who stood at the bar.

Race trumped everything every time. It whipped friendship, sex and class, too.

Where was his Oreo self now? Nowhere. He was white on the outside and white on the inside.

"Mind if I join you?"

Norman didn't wait for an answer. He grabbed a nearby chair, sat down and drilled Natalie with his eyes.

"Long time no see."

He was instantly embarrassed by the cliché that told him he was at a loss for words. It was cliché time at the Blackhawk. The clichés piled up and crashed down to the floor along with the notes that spilled from Lester's sax.

There they were, the three of them: the two army veterans and the woman between them. New York Norman and San Francisco Ezra, east entangling with west, white coexisting and colliding with Black, and the noir queen at the crossroads. There would be no balancing act. Something or someone had to give. It wasn't going to be Norman. He would stand his ground, even if there was no ground to stand on.

Ezra piled another cliché on the pyramid of clichés.

"I might as well break the ice."

To Natalie he said, "This is my buddy, Norman," and to Norman, "Meet Natalie, a Jersey girl, just blew into Frisco." At least he didn't say "my girl." Norman was thankful for that. Maybe Ezra went both ways. Maybe he bedded women as well as men.

Norman vowed not to seem too curious and vowed, too, not to toss out another cliché. He didn't want to utter another fake phrase, or make a face that would reveal his invisible connections and disconnections to Miss Natalie Jackson, formerly of New Jersey.

She was more beautiful than he remembered her, more womanly and less girly, more sophisticated and less rough around the edges. He knew he was still dangerously in love with her.

"Pleased to meet you."

He tried to hide the embarrassed expression he was sure had to be on his face. He wanted to slap himself.

Natalie wore a bemused smile that seemed to belie her anxiety.

"Pleased to meet you, too, Norman. Do you come here often?"

Norman shook his head.

"No, this is my first time." Once he started to talk, he couldn't stop talking. Words concealed his own nervousness.

"Ezra brought me here and I'm glad he did. Lester is amazing and the Blackhawk is the coolest club I've ever been to, including Birdland, though Bird was phenomenal until he started shooting up. Truth to tell, I love Shearing's lullaby to the place. It's a classic."

He heard himself speak and thought he sounded like his glib prof in Jazz 101.

Natalie lifted her cocktail glass.

"Bebop is ancient history. You should hear 'Shake Rattle & Roll.' It's the newest thing. I have a stack of 45 RPMs. You know, don't you, the DJs call it 'rock 'n' roll' and say it has already blown bebop out of the water. Elvis is bound to hit 'Frisco ASAP.'"

Norman wanted to be cantankerous.

"I would not like bebop to go the same way as the novel, which is dead or at least dying, according to my friends who read *Partisan Review*."

He turned toward Ezra.

"What about you, pal. What do you think?"

Ezra took a deep breath.

"I'm partial to Muddy Waters and Ray Charles and turn a deaf ear to the Crew Cuts, and as for Patti Page, that doggie in the window she sings about ought to pee all over her lily white shoes."

Natalie laughed until her whole body shook. She turned from Norman to Ezra and then back to Norman, and wore a smug expression on her face that said she wanted to pick a fight.

"You sound like you've got a stick up your royal Dutch ass."

"No reason to jump at every new fad."

Norman growled.

Natalie growled back.

"It's not a fad."

"What is it if not a fad?"

"You wouldn't understand."

Ezra listened to the verbal volley with amusement and seemed disinclined to add his own feelings to the mix. But then he broke his stony silence.

"If you pay attention to rock and roll, you'll hear rhythm and blues. He didn't say "rock 'n' roll or rhythm 'n' blues, He used the word "and" which lent a certain formality to the terms.

Natalie glared.

"If you listen, you'll hear country and western in rock."

Ezra huffed.

"A lot of white boys tryin' to sound like they come from Tupelo."

Natalie practically jumped out of her seat.

"Some of them are from Mississippi."

When it came to rock 'n' roll, she obviously knew what she was talking about. The table went suddenly silent until Ezra leaned forward and roared over the din in the room.

"How 'bout we hit my mama's place and dig her race records."

Natalie glanced at her wristwatch.

"I don't know. I'm a workin' girl."

Norman's ears perked up.

"You workin'?" He sounded incredulous. "You don't seem the type."

"Yeah, I'm a little shop girl. You heard of us? Nine to five Monday to Saturday. Pays the bills."

On the street outside the Blackhawk, with the neon sign glowing in the dark, Ezra stood on the sidewalk and tried to hail a yellow cab. First one driver and then another switched off the light on the roof and accelerated when Ezra came into view, a dark shadow outlined by the streetlight.

"Off duty my ass. Fucking cracker oughta go back to Johannesburg."

Ah, finally, Norman thought, he's expressing his true feelings.

⊙⊙

11

Natalie shivered, adjusted the slim shoulder strap on her evening gown and stepped into the street as though she owned it. She inserted the tip of her thumb and the tip of her middle finger in her mouth, curled her tongue back and squeezed the corners of her mouth. When she spied a yellow cab barreling along, she whistled loudly. The driver slammed on his brakes; the vehicle skidded to a stop.

Natalie turned to Ezra.

"What's the address, baby?"

The bald taxicab driver rolled down the window nearest the curb. He leaned across the front seat, eyed Natalie up and down, and winced when he noticed Ezra standing in the shadows.

"I don't carry no spades."

Norman lunged forward.

"Fuck you."

He yanked the rear door open and hurled his body into the back seat.

"You'll go where we tell you to go."

He was surprised by his own rage. Don't carry no spades! That was unacceptable. Natalie leapt into the front seat. Norman held the door ajar on his side of the taxi. Ezra jumped inside and smiled a big smile that revealed his white teeth.

"Corner of Fulton and Scott."

Norman moved his body forward so that his face touched Natalie's face.

"Where you workin' miss?"

It was no idle question. He was genuinely curious.

Natalie lifted her dress above her knees and showed off her long legs.

"Union Square. I. Magnin. They call me a floater 'cause I move from cosmetics to jewelry and do some modeling, too. I ain't getting rich if that's what you think."

They tumbled out of the cab at the corner of Scott and Fulton, along Alamo Square. Norman craned his neck and saw that the windows in the house that he now called home were dark. Zora had obviously gone to bed; that was a relief. She wouldn't blow a whistle, read the riot act and curtail their mini party.

Ezra climbed the front steps, removed his keychain from his pocket, unlocked the locks on the front door, and held it open for Natalie and Norman. He closed it behind them, tip-toed from the foyer to the hallway, flicked on a light in the back parlor and removed the plastic that covered the chairs and the sofa.

"Get comfy."

He moved the knob on the turntable to "On," sorted through a stack of 78s, selected a record, and played a recording of Bessie Smith singing "Cemetery Blues."

"I'm going down to the cemetery,/ 'Cause the world is all wrong!/ Down there with the spooks to hear 'em sing my sorrow song/ Got a date to see a ghost."

The song sent chills up and down Norman's spine. After all, de Haan spooks and de Haan ghosts were his companions. His eyes climbed up the walls towards the carved angels in the four corners of the ceiling. Bessie Smith's voice took him somewhere higher up, someplace far away.

Ezra rolled a humonguous joint, fired it up, puffed and puffed and passed it to the white spook who inhaled, held the holy smoke in his lungs, and offered it to Natalie, who put her lips together, sucked on it, and placed it on the windowsill. Then she removed the straps on her evening gown. She kicked it into the air with her right foot, watched it land on the sofa, and shimmied and shook until the song came to an end.

Norman heard the needle in the groove. Natalie began to perform her striptease again when Ezra played Bessie singing, "A Good Man is Hard to Find." Like Norman, Natalie seemed to be in heaven, though hers didn't have room for him.

"Fuckin' A. A goddamned half-decent man is impossible to find in 'Frisco. I know. I've looked from the bay to the breakers, all 49 square miles. This town is crawling with queers who don't know how to treat a lady, present company excluded, of course."

She stared at Ezra apologetically.

"You could teach your brethren manners."

Bessie sang, "My heart is sad and I'm all alone/My man's treating me mean."

Natalie removed her lace bra and slipped out of her white silk panties while Bessie poured out her heart.

"Just when you think that he's your pal/ You look and find him foolin' 'round some old gal."

Natalie's pubic hair was as red and curly as the hair on the top of her head. She folded her elastic body, stretched out on the floor, placed her hands across her breasts and closed her eyes.

As Norman knew, men regarded Natalie as a body and nothing but a body ever since her adolescence. Now, in San Francisco, her body accorded her a certain power that she enjoyed.

Neither she, nor Ezra and Norman (who were both in a bluesy mood), heard Zora descend the stairs. Nor were they aware that Zora stood at the entrance to the parlor and watched Natalie's performance with a look of sadness on her face. Her unhappiness seemed to derive as much from Bessie's voice and the words to the song, as from the spectacle of a white woman lying on her back, on display on the floor.

Natalie sensed Zora's presence before Ezra or Norman, who was stoned and exhausted, too, after a long day at the store and after listening to Lester wail at the Blackhawk.

Zora sat down on the sofa and wrapped her arms around her purple robe. Natalie opened her eyes and blinked. When the recording ended, she picked up her bra and her undies and put them on. She slipped into her evening gown and bowed ceremoniously to the lady of the house, who sniffed the air, caught the lingering aroma of reefer and smiled knowingly.

"I see you have good taste in music, if not in manners. But don't let me wreck your party. It wasn't that long ago I spent nights at the juke joint by the Delta, a stone's throw from my mama's home. Help yourself to my wine and pour a glass for me."

Norman expected Zora to kick him and Natalie out of the house, and maybe her own son, too. He was surprised when she accepted the glass of red wine that Ezra handed her, and surprised, too, when she raised her glass and sipped.

"To my favorite, Mississippi John Hurt."

"Here's to juke joints and Muddy Waters." That was Ezra.

"Lester and Bird, too." That was Norman.

"Bill Haley and the Comets." That was Natalie's rejoinder.

She finished the red wine and placed her glass on the round table with the carved legs.

Ezra retrieved the corkscrew and would have opened a second bottle, except Zora laid down the law.

"Closing time, children."

Natalie nodded her head and grabbed her purse.

"Time for me to hit the road." She turned to Zora. "Thanks for the dance floor." Her comment brought a wry smile to Zora's sleepy face. Ezra followed Natalie toward the front door, unlocked it and opened it. Norman heard them descend the steps and begin a conversation, though he couldn't make out any of the words that passed between them.

Zora turned off the Victrola, removed the 78, slipped the record into its sleeve, and returned the album to the shelf on the wall, underneath a sepia-tinged photo from far away and long ago. Norman recognized the Spanish moss dripping from an old oak tree in a landscape that Mr. Faulkner might have peopled with the likes of Popeye and Temple Drake.

He squinted his eyes and stared at Zora, who glanced in the direction of the front door and toward the sounds of the conversation between Ezra and Natalie. Zora turned and faced Norman.

"Child, I'd watch my step 'round that gal. She be poison for the likes of you."

Norman did not hear her words, or see her round, black, sleepy face. The wine and the weed had dispatched him to dreamland where he entered a house and climbed the cobwebbed staircase that led up and up and up, until he reached the attic and saw manacles and Black bodies. His ancestors haunting him again.

❦

12

He opened his eyes slowly, afraid of what he might see and stretched his arms and legs. Someone had covered him with Zora's patchwork quilt and placed a pillow under his head. Someone had cared. He wasn't alone or lonely, though he was groggy. His bones ached and his stomach growled. In the kitchen, he made coffee and toast, which he slathered with butter and jam. He sat at the table and listened to the creaking of the floorboards above his head. Someone else was up, moving about and making sounds.

He wasn't ready to receive another human being in the space he created for himself. He tried to remember everything that had happened the previous night: Ezra's encounter with the police, Natalie's evening gown that revealed the shape of her body, Bessie Smith's voice, and Zora's unexpected appearance at their party. Something inside him had shifted. He could feel it, but he couldn't put words to it.

On the other side of town, halfway up Russian Hill in a tidy apartment that looked down at North Beach, Natalie Jackson rose soon after dawn, turned on the lamp next to her bed and inserted her feet into her slippers, one at a time. In the bathroom, she showered, shampooed, and shaved the hair in her armpits and on her legs. She stood in front of the mirror, turned her face into a mask and barely recognized herself.

"Who are you, Natalie? What do you want from life, from men and from yourself?"

She shook her head, finished the maquillage, courtesy of I. Magnin, puckered her lips, and stared at her reflection.

"No one will know. No one will suspect."

Living a double life appealed to her sense of adventure and love of mystery and the mysterious. At night, the little shop girl turned herself into a raging hipster who dug rock 'n' roll, smoked weed and drove men like Norman crazy.

Natalie wrapped a paisley scarf over her head, walked down the stairs to the street and hoofed it to Union Square. At the Doggie Diner on the corner, she bought a coffee (black, no sugar) and a jelly doughnut. After one small bite of the doughnut, she tossed the uneaten portion in the trash, along with the paper napkin she used to wipe her fingers clean.

She arrived early for work and punched her timecard, which put a smile on the face of the dour supervisor.

"Ten percent discount when a customer buys twenty-five dollars or more worth of merchandize. Only today. Offer ends at 4 p.m."

"Wonderful!" Natalie sounded elated. "I might take you up on the offer."

The supervisor frowned.

"It doesn't apply to employees."

In a huff, Natalie dashed past the leather gloves, the handbags and the accessories.

Behind the counter, she made sure her glass display case—it was hers and no one else's—had no smudges, no fingerprints and no cigarette ash, and that her hands were immaculately clean and her lipstick perfectly straight. For the first half hour, she was alone and lost in her own thoughts.

Also, for the next half hour or so, she enjoyed the company of a young woman, perhaps her own age, who wore a sparkling diamond on her ring finger that was so big and showy, it was obscene. The young woman, Bette Green, purchased a makeup kit and listened to Natalie describe how she managed to keep her face wrinkle-free and looking like it belonged to a 23-year-old. Not a difficult task; she was 23.

"You have to love your face."

Natalie admired Bette, a bleach blonde shopper with a diamond ring, a push-up bra and cleavage who was obviously trying to look like Marilyn Monroe. The movie star's face was plastered all over town to promote the release of *The Seven Year Itch*.

Natalie smiled her I. Magnin smile at the Monroe wannabe.

"Love *your* face; put your *whole self* into it. Try our other super skincare products. Buy twenty-five dollars' worth and you get a ten percent discount. Trust me: it's a great deal and it won't last forever."

Natalie sounded as though she believed every word she spoke.

From around the corner, Norman watched and listened. He was impressed. With her contagious smile and seductive voice, Natalie could sell anything, no matter how ridiculous the claims for the product. He saw that selling stuff at I. Magnin provided her with an opportunity to be more than just a body. At the counter, and in her own space, she had a memorable face and an unmistakable voice. She told a story and captivated her audience.

Norman watched the object of his desire. Yes, he had turned her into an object. He wanted to consume her. No, he wasn't spying on her, he told himself, but rather looking out for her welfare and gathering valuable information about marketing and sales which he could bring to City Lights.

For starters, he decided, Shig would have to smile when he sat at the front desk, and act like an Ivy Leaguer. It would be better if customers regarded Shig as a bookish fellow who knew what was on the bestseller list and what *ought* to have been there.

(Indeed, Shig had compiled a list of the books that practically ran out of City Lights on two legs. He posted his list—"Shig's Selections"—on the wall behind the cash register.)

Norman stood on the edge of the women's department and considered the pros and cons of following Natalie home, wherever that might be. He might lurk at a safe distance until she entered the house, wait until the time was right, knock on the door, wear a salesman's smile, and then listen to her footsteps and her, "Who is it?"

After deliberating for a few moments, he shot down the idea. When he was back home, he approached Ezra before he went off to his class on electrical engineering at City College.

"Listen, pal, how 'bout you drop Natalie's address on me? I'd sure appreciate it."

Ezra raised his eyebrows.

"Why you think *I* got it?"

"I know *you* got it. You got the hots for her despite your natural inclinations."

"How little you know! You got to forget about the sick bitch, or she'll run circles around you, again!"

"Whatcha mean?" Norman sounded innocent, but he didn't fool Ezra, who scowled.

"You know what I mean, motherfucker. She'll run circles around you once and she'll run circles around you twice. But go ahead, torture yourself, you masochistic white boy. Natalie hangs out most days at 1144 Gough, a big old Victorian painted yellow. The color might make you puke."

"You've been?"

Norman didn't really want to hear the answer to his question. A lie might have satisfied him better than the truth.

"Yeah. Does that make you happy, my man?"

Norman swallowed hard.

"Good to know. Thanks. You won't regret it."

He paused a moment.

"Did you just call me a white boy?"

Ezra laughed.

"Last time I looked you had white skin and I had black skin. I'm just saying. Don't take it personally, pal."

Upstairs, Norman washed his armpits and his private parts with soap, hot water and a washcloth, and dried himself with a big white towel. Next, he put on jockey briefs, tight jeans, a black turtleneck sweater and pointy black shoes that were not his own, but that he found on the floor of the closet in his room, and that once belonged to another boarder, another ghost, perhaps another spook.

He admired himself in the full-length mirror where Zora always checked her appearance before leaving the house and venturing into the world. Before he knew it, his thoughts had turned to Money, Mississippi.

Was Zora's niece, Cadillac, a good Christian? He wondered, and what about the young woman who refused to move to the back of the bus in Montgomery? Was she also good? Obviously not by the standards of the White Citizens' Councils that had taken shape, so *The Defender* claimed, in the wake of *Brown vs. Board of Education*, which Norman had read about in the pages of *PM* when he was still in New York.

Regular folks and ordinary people were making history, though he wasn't one of them. Envy took possession of him, though he didn't know how he might insert himself into the stream of time and bury his ghosts.

Norman liked his new sexy look, which he had borrowed

and stitched together with refinements from the ads he scrutinized in *Playboy* magazine. He was too embarrassed to buy it, but he perused it at the newsstand near the Greyhound terminal. He liked the interviews, the fiction and the centerfolds, but he was too timid to suggest that City Lights carry *Playboy,* along with serious magazines like *Minority of One, The Reporter,* and *The Saturday Review* (SR, as he called it), which he read cover-to-cover.

He especially loved the pieces on jazz by Wilder Hobson, who managed to have something intelligent to say about Dixieland, the Big Bands, and Benny Goodman, though bebop was beyond his reach.

Maybe one day, Norman told himself, he would follow in Hobson's footsteps and write about Lester and Billie. He would drop himself into the pages of history and make a name for himself.

13

Norman learned every zig and every zag of the journey by bus from Zora's house to Lawrence's bookstore. He paid attention to the route for the first week or so, but he soon lost interest, faded in and faded out of consciousness, snoozed and woke and snoozed again.

Was his mother having a meltdown in Manhattan? He wondered and had his sister, Toni, ended up on the casting couch in Hollywood? Had she actually landed a part as a floozy in a western or as a femme fatale in a mystery? That flic he would like to see.

The bus waited at a red light. A motorcyclist revved his engine. An elderly woman crossed the street with a cane. Norman made a mental note to send his mother a telegram.

He pulled the cord to alert the driver that he wanted to get off the bus at the next stop, walked to the rear exit, waited until the door opened and descended the steps. On the sidewalk, he tamed his hair with a pocket comb that had broken teeth. He also polished the tips of his shoes by rubbing them along the back of his trousers. The wind blew from the Pacific and white clouds galloped from west to east.

On the corner of Gough and Market, Norman noticed a Western Union office and kept walking.

Then a minute or so later, he stopped, went back, and drafted a telegram.

"Mom. Stop. Job is great. Stop. Living situation dream come true. Stop. Out of my comfort zone but happy. Stop. Reachable City Lights, 261 Columbus Ave. Stop. And at house in the Fillmore, too. Stop. Love, Norman. Stop."

He summoned the clerk.

"Send it now, please."

He paid $9.94 with a ten spot and collected the change.

On the street, Norman stopped for a smoke, summoned

his courage and arranged to meet Natalie at her own apartment on Russian Hill, not at the Gough Street addresss that Ezra gave him.

She opened the door, stood in her bathrobe and invited Norman inside.

"I don't know how much longer I can hack it."

Norman looked at the boxes of cereal on the kitchen counter.

"If you need, I can help financially."

Nothing more was said or done on that subject on that day, but the following Friday Natalie persuaded Norman to phone her supervisor and recite the lines she'd written for him.

"This is a friend of Miss Jackson in cosmetics. She's running a fever and is confined to bed. Doctor's orders. I'll keep you posted."

Natalie had lost weight, but seemed healthy and energetic. They played hooky together—he from City Lights and she from I. Magnin—and had fun hiking around the Sutro Baths, and at the Mermaid at Fisherman's Warf shared Manhattan clam chowder with oyster crackers. But the fun didn't last long. Before Natalie finished one cigarette she lit another. That was worrisome.

What really got to Norman were the Milltowns she swallowed for her nerves and her anxiety; they had side effects, she explained, including headaches and nausea. When he visited Natalie at her apartment again, he found her in bed watching TV in the afternoon. He tidied the living room, the bathroom, and the kitchen, but the place grew messier and messier by the day and he gave up.

"You are beautiful even when you are down and depressed."

"Thank you, Norman. That's sweet of you."

Maybe, Norman told himself, she will put on a fresh face, and go back to I. Magnin. He went on hoping and trusting that all would be well.

14

San Francisco was an island, he decided, and also a part of the mainland, a backwater town and not really a city. The distance from New York made a huge difference. Cut off from parents and teachers, the hipsters began to throw off hoary traditions and the idea of tradition itself.

Fuck tradition, Norman heard himself say as he pushed the iron gate at 1144 Gough, sauntered up the stairs and knocked on the front door which was painted a brighter yellow than the rest of the house.

A colorful mural on an outer wall depicted an extra-large ripe banana with the skin peeled back about halfway, along with an image of two ruby-red lips, a mouth wide open and the initials "RL" in purple letters in the righthand corner. Someone, "RL" no doubt, had taken credit for the work, which was pretty good in a comic book kind of way.

What the hell was "RL" selling, Norman wondered? He had to be selling something, though Norman wasn't certain what it was. Probably not bananas. Peddling, trafficking, vending, and flogging were the names of the game in Frisco as much as they were in Brooklyn, the Bronx, and Manhattan. Ivanovitch wasn't really a doctor, but a salesman for hearing aids. Ferlinghetti wasn't just selling books, but also popularizing and democratizing a whole way of life outside American norms and conventions.

Why were all the San Franciscan hipsters not natives but exiles and fugitives from elsewhere? Would the town have any culture to speak of if it weren't for folks like Ferlinghetti, who was born in nowheresville Yonkers, and Shig who sprang from Seattle?

Standing outside the yellow Victorian, he felt like he was on the very edge of the edge.

The City by the Bay, he realized, had its own version of

commercialism. The Dow Jones Average quietly kicked ass from the financial district, to the Cow Palace and the Zoo. Every day, Norman met hucksters eager to bilk, fleece and defraud their fellow citizens all over the 49 square miles of the peninsula, where members of the Ohlone tribe once danced on what they called "the edge of the world." California *was* the edge, and its inhabitants were edgy.

From day one, or close to it, Lawrence had taken Norman under his wing and told him about the Ohlone, who harvested oysters, heaped up huge mounds of shells called midden, and hunted deer until they themselves were hunted down and slaughtered. The members of the tribe were pushed over the edge and into near oblivion by the civilization of the white man with his rifle, and the civilizing ways of the white woman with her Bible, and yet some Ohlone survived.

The pioneers and settlers, Lawrence explained, unsettled the continent and gave birth to children who grew up and raised their children who went to the university at Berkeley and became doctors, teachers, lawyers, hipsters and bohemians. Lawrence explained all this and more to Norman, not only at the store, but also over espresso at the Trieste, which felt like the coffee houses in Greenwich Village.

Norman wasn't unprepared for the new and the strange when he showed up at 1144 Gough. Lawrence reminded him that William Blake had said: "You never know what is enough until you know what is more than enough." Ah, yes, the wise, visonary William Blake who wrote *Proverbs of Hell*. The same Blake who illustrated Captain Stedman's account of the repression of the revolt by the Negroes.

Norman was ready for Blakean excess and ready to rock his own boat. Revolutions, he told himself, were not for the faint of heart. Follow Blake and be brave!

When no one answered Norman's knock, knock, knock, he tried the knob, found the door unlocked, let himself in, closed it behind him and stood quietly in the foyer.

"Hello, it's me, Norman de Haan from City Lights, come to look see."

He paused a moment.

"Anyone home?"

If someone was at home, it seemed unlikely he or she would

have heard him. Organ music composed by Johann Sebastian, or one of the other Bach boys (Norman had taken a music appreciation course at the New School on the GI Bill), but he wasn't sure which Bach. An organ blared from the loudspeakers which were placed strategically around an octagonal-shaped room that occupied the heart of the house.

Choked with books, magazines and manuscripts, it also contained sketches of ripe bananas, puckered red ruby lips and color paintings of penises and vaginas, too, bigger than life and neither appetizing nor aesthetic, except in a grotesque kind of way. They didn't turn Norman on. This place is a mix of hipster frat house and sex palace, he told himself. Maybe it was also a haven for drugs where the wildest kinds of beasts not seen since the days of William Blake and Samuel Taylor Coleridge (of "Kublai Khan" fame) stalked the imagination. Here, no doubt, the hipsters and the cool cats foretold the end of the world and the birth of a new age where mothers and fathers would love their sons and daughters and the sons and daughters would love their mothers and fathers. Was that too much to ask for? Would he ever make his peace with his own mother?

Two typewriters, a Royal and an Underwood, sat opposite one another on a table thrown together with two sawhorses and a sheet of thick plywood. Norman saw a Kodak, a tape recorder, a ream of paper and what looked like a manuscript. Too polite to proceed without a formal invitation, he leaned forward, twisted his neck and took in the bare floor and the big windows that let in streams of sunlight and sent dust bunnies flying. On three walls he saw framed paintings of oversized penises and vaginas. The paintings had price tags, as Norman could see, even from a distance.

He gave up the waiting game, followed the trail of the music, and skirted the bicycle with the two fat tires that leaned against the wall in the hallway. He stopped in his tracks outside the open doorway to his right and peered into a rectangular-shaped room with a small bed. Three individuals propped up by big, fluffy pillows passed a cigarette back and forth, each one taking turns inhaling and blowing smoke into the air. The smoke didn't smell like unadulterated tobacco, but rather tobacco mixed with something that had to be illicit.

Instantly, Norman recognized the woman wedged between the two men, one of them short, stocky and bearded, the other tall, thin and clean-shaven. His heart sank down, down, down to his ankles. The scene triggered a memory of his war buddy, Charlie Wilson, in bed with his girl. Bad things happen to me twice, he told himself. I'm cursed. He was still thinking like his New York self. The metamorphosis wasn't done yet.

The room with the bed, the smoke, and the bodies took shape in Norman's mind as a combat zone with land mines just beneath the surface. A rock-like lump formed in his throat and made it hard for him to swallow. He couldn't have imagined a more devastating scene than the one that unfolded before his eyes. I will have to navigate carefully, he told himself, and watch for explosives that might go off and rip apart my heart. He sighed, he murmured, and he coughed. Courage. Don't chicken out now. Go into the darkness and discover what's there. The lovers—no one else but lovers or fuck buddies would be so intimately entwined—were sprawled on top of a blue and white comforter. Neither the woman nor the two men wore clothes, though oddly enough, the clean-shaven fellow wore a pair of scuffed-up cowboy boots which went well with his muscular build and angular face. He looked, Norman concluded, like a wrangler.

Natalie—that's who the woman was—crossed and uncrossed her slender ankles, wrapped one arm around the neck of the bearded fellow and wrapped the other around the neck of the clean-shaven cowboy. She shot daggers at Norman who tried to glide and slide away.

"Come on in, baby, and join the party."

Norman wanted to do just that, and, at the same time, he didn't want to do it. Confusion caught him in its crosshairs. For a few moments he wore a vacant expression on his face, and shoved his hands in his pockets. He was sure he looked stupid, and, while he didn't consciously choose to enter the bedroom, he didn't choose not to enter it, either.

This was real life, not an abstract existential dilemma. A million thoughts bombarded his brain and his feelings threatened to overwhelm him. He took a baby step forward and then another and crossed the threshold, aware that he was outside the realm of any environmental niche he had ever explored, much less inhabited. Intrigued by the spectacle in front of him, he told himself that he could remain an observer, take mental notes, write up what he witnessed, and publish a firsthand account entitled, "A Report on the Sexual Practices in Bohemian San Francisco." It would be anthropological, he told himself, in the manner of Margaret Mead.

He was dizzy, but he managed to tell himself that the scene in Greenwich Village in the Twenties must have been similar. After all, Mabel Luhan Dodge caroused with John Reed and Margaret Sanger. Or more than half-a-century earlier in Paris, with the *grisettes* and the bohemians, Paul Verlaine and Arthur Rimbaud, whose poetry he discovered while browsing in the library. Surrounded by the four walls of the bedroom, which seemed to throb, Norman glanced around and noticed in the far corner a man with a neatly combed head of hair. He perched on a stool and held a large pad of paper in one hand and a piece of charcoal in the other. The artist was putting the finishing touches to a sketch of the three lovers. Natalie's toenails, Norman noticed, were pink. The booted fellow boasted an uncircumcised and uncommonly large, erect penis that seemed to have a mind of its own. Indeed, it rose and fell, and moved from side to side, though the head always ended up pointing in Natalie's direction. It knew what it wanted. These folks are out of their minds, Norman told himself. They don't care a fig or even a fig leaf what anyone thinks or says about them. They are barrier breakers. I had better leap into the fray now and risk losing everything, rather than stay in my own safe little world.

This is precisely what you need, de Haan: an antidote to your goddamned, hell and brimstone Dutch Calvinism that has kept you under lock and key nearly all you fuckin' life. This is your last chance, my boy, before you wither and die on the vine. Seize it and squeeze it, mother fucker.

Obscenities tumbled from his dark, dark mind like they had never tumbled before, not even when he stormed into Berlin in '45, fucked a fräulein in a bombed out building and knew that the fascists had been crushed.

The artist stared, first at Norman, who looked like he'd seen a ghost, and then at Natalie who looked like she really was one. Natalie waved her hand.

"This is Allen Ginsberg."

She turned her head to the side and indicated the bearded

fellow with a paunch and glasses who gave Norman the "V" for victory sign.

"He answers to Ginzy. He's a wannabe poet, a symbolist no less."

Norman thought she sounded like the poet's publicity agent. Natalie turned her head and faced the clean-shaven fellow with the spectacular erection and the alabaster body without an ounce of fat.

"This is Neal Cassady, the king of the road and the crown prince of all the pimps in Frisco. He and Ginzy are con artists. Hold on to your wallet and your ego, too, or they'll steal them both from under your nose."

Neal scowled, gave Norman the finger and smiled.

"Sit on it."

Natalie turned modest, covered her breasts with her hands, raised her chin, and aimed it at the man in the corner.

"That's Robert LaVigne. He's an Artist with a capital "A." Money in the bank doesn't matter to him, or so he says, though his paintings have price tags."

The artist spelled his own name, letter by letter, murmured "LaVigne," and added," capital V for vice, which is nice when you can get it, so don't knock it."

Neal guffawed.

"Yeah, but incest is best."

With her elbow, Natalie poked him in the ribs.

"LaVigne owns this dump and rents rooms, but if you let him suck your cock, he'll allow you to stay for free until he tells you you're boring him to death. Robert hates boredom. So do I. That's why I hang with con artists. They're never boring and they put their lives on the line."

Ginzy, the hirsute fellow on the far side of the bed, adjusted his glasses, stared at Norman, and said, "Don't be uptight, man. We won't bite your head off."

Neal laughed like a mad man.

"Drop your trousers so we can see your dick, daddy-o." Natalie looked like a provocateur.

"Take it from me, his dick isn't much to look at."

Obviously, she could trade barbs with the guys when the spirit moved her.

"Norman wasn't a Bridge and Tunnel guy back in New York. He's old, old money, New Yorker going back to the fuckin' Dutch, who gave Indians beads in exchange for the keys to the kingdom. He feels bad about it."

"Waa." Ginzy wailed.

Neal teased.

"Poor baby."

Norman shrugged his shoulders as though to say that Natalie's disclosures didn't irk him, though he realized that she couldn't be trusted to keep secrets. He sniffed the air, smelled stale sex and profaned perfume, hiked up his trousers, tightened his belt and stood behind the artist with the sketch pad and the charcoal.

"I like it."

If he thought that the artist would protect him, he was mistaken. He should have known that an artist might wield a sword as well as a paint brush. LaVigne folded his easel.

"Others will want to destroy Natalie's beauty. My art will preserve it."

Ginzy bounded from the bed, bowed from the waist, crossed both hands in front of his circumcised penis and wore a sly grin.

"I'll show you mine, if you show me yours."

He was a playful devil. Norman folded his arms across his chest.

"Are you guys still in junior high school?"

Indeed, they were liberated adolsecents.

Ginzy issued a raspberry. Neal slapped his own bare ass.

"Kiss it, kid."

Natalie sashayed toward Norman, wrapped her arms around his body and purred.

"Come on, honey, don't be a party pooper. Get with the program."

She held Norman in an embrace that made him feel uncomfortable, but he was loathe to break away from the warmth of her body. It reminded him of their days together in New York, "old New York," as he now thought of it.

"Well, I would get with the program, if I knew what the program was. I can't be expected to follow something if you haven't explained it."

Neal crept behind Norman, threw his arms around him and pressed his body against his.

"You gotta relax and be way more spontaneous, man."

Neal moved his pelvis back and forth.

"You're in Dick City, capital D, capital C."

15

The image of the peeled banana on the front door now made a lot more sense to him than when he first saw it. The inhabitants of 1144 were selling the almighty phallus, and something that one of his New School profs would have called "the polymorphous perverse."

But was it perverse? And what did it mean to be perverse, if no one was a victim and the participants were adults who had clearly given their consent? Natalie seemed to be enjoying the three-ring circus. Norman held back his moral yardstick.

Ginzy slipped into a pair of baggy pants, pulled them up as high as they would go, and tied the drawstring.

"We're a boy gang and Natalie's the den mother."

He winked.

"She cracks the whip and keeps us in line. You know, a little S&M never did anyone any harm. Ha ha ha."

Ginzy pried Norman loose from Natalie and Neal, who had sandwiched him. He propelled the interloper down the hall and thrust him into the large octagonal-shaped room. A man with thick black hair, wearing jeans, moccasins, and a green and red wool shirt fit for a lumberjack, sat and pounded the keys of the Underwood. He looked troubled.

"This friggin' machine is too slow. The space bar sticks."

He turned his head and glanced over his shoulder.

"Neal, I need you, man."

He sounded like he was calling for help for an older brother or an uncle.

Neal burst into the room, still naked, except for his cowboy boots, walked bowlegged toward the typist, removed the sheet of paper from the roller, and read the unfinished sentence at the top of the page.

"The beautiful, sad, lonely railroad earth in Frisco…"

Neal placed the single sheet of paper on top of a stack of books that included a paperback of William Saroyan's *The Daring Young Man on the Flying Trapeze*. He turned the typewriter upside down, examined its guts and poked around with his index finger.

"Jack, my main man, the spring's loose. Somebody, gimme a Phillips head."

Natalie scrounged around and delivered the screw driver. Neal loosened a baby screw, fixed a tiny spring, and tightened the works.

"Now you can beat the shit outta your Underwood. You got no more excuses, Jacky boy. Finish the fucker before it finishes you."

He turned to Norman.

"Mr. Jacky Kerouacky has been writing the same fuckin' book over and over again ever since I met him in New York in '49 and tried to fix him up with my ex, LuAnne. The priests and the nuns really did a number on him. He wouldn't fuck her and now he can't make progress with his work in progress. Can't keep a hard-on for more than a New York minute."

He laughed at his own feeble joke.

"Jacky is in his head way too much and not enough in his body. I'm tryin' to get him to improvise. The way he's going 'bout this road novel of his, you'd think he was that faggot Frenchie, Marcel Proust."

Ginzy moseyed up to Neal and offered what sounded like an official pronouncement.

"Jack is Marcel redux. He's the greatest Franco-American writer of his generation, bar none."

Jack shook his head.

"No, no, no, I'm just a dumb Canuck who can barely speak and write a word of English. I don't want no prizes. I just want to be left alone to write."

Norman leaned forward, glanced at the typewritten words on the page that Neal had read aloud, and then read the next line.

"Dean had just been released from the reformatory for boys after serving a sentence for carjacking in Denver when …"

Neal placed his hands on Jack's shoulders and massaged his neck.

"Fact is, I didn't do no time for that caper. It wasn't carjacking.

I borrowed a jalopy from the owner. He didn't make any trouble for me. Smart fella. No one bets against Dean Moriarty. I mean Neal Cassady."

Jack banged away at the typewriter.

"It's a novel, Neal. I'm fucking with the facts and making up shit. Poetic license, you dig, so don't expect to find a true to life portrait of yourself or anyone else, including Ginzy."

With his hands on his hips, Neal screeched.

"Don't mess with my life, motherfucker."

He wobbled across the room in his boots, aimed for the stack of records in the far corner, scratched his balls, selected an LP with Al Cohen on sax, placed it on the turntable, and moved the switch to the "On" position. The sounds of the first track blared from the speakers. Neal danced by himself, his big head bobbing up and down rhythmically.

"Sweet, sweet. I could listen to Al blow all day and all night." When the track ended, he sat down opposite Jack.

"What have you decided, my brother?"

That's the way it was in the big yellow Victorian. The guys were brothers, though they weren't always brotherly in the most positive sense of the word. They could tease, prod and poke, as brothers are wont to do. The fact that Ginzy had been raised Jewish and Jack raised Catholic meant that they were divided by family histories and family habits.

Jack lifted his hands and held them above the keyboard.

"I'm stayin' put. You make for the Big Easy by your lonesome. It will do you good. Send me a postcard and make sure you bring back weed from New Orleans."

Neal leaned back and roared.

"If you ain't goin', I ain't goin'." He glanced from Jack to Norman and back to Jack. "This here stranger, Mr. Norm, I can see he needs a shot of spontaneity. Anyone got a needle?"

"It's Norman."

He sounded like he was ready to defend his name, his honor, and his very manhood. Neal waived his right hand in the air as though it was a magic wand that might make Norman vanish before his eyes.

"Puff."

Norman turned his right hand into a gun.

"Bang, bang."

Jacky drummed on the table with his fingertips, wet his lips, opened his mouth wide, and read from his manuscript.

"I saw the deadbeat dads abandon their lonesome wives, forget about their itty bitty children, hit the road with Dean Moriarty and fall off the map."

Ginzy lit a cigarette and placed it in a long cigarette holder.

"See. It's easy to improvise. Now you go, Norm."

"It's not Norm, Ginzy. It's Norman, like Norman Rockwell. You've heard of him, haven't you?'

Norman glanced at a sketch of Natalie that hung on the wall as though he hoped her image might provide instant inspiration. He paused a few moments and heard a sax in his head.

"August is the cruelest month… mixing memory and desire…" Before he could go on, Ginzy interrupted him, shook his finger and groaned.

"That's not improvisation, that's a parody of Thomas Stearns Eliot."

Norman put up a spirited defense.

"I know it's T. S. Eliot, but I'm not reading. I'm reciting from memory and I'm giving the words a twist. Doesn't that count as spontaneity?"

Jack rose from his chair, bounded across the room and looked accusingly at Norman.

"You're going to have to do much better than that if you're gonna hang with us, my dear, sweet brother."

Puff! Just like that, he might belong to the brotherhood, if only he learned to improvise!

Norman glared at Natalie, who seemed bemused by the comedy that unfolded in the eight-sided room. There was no sand, but the boys in the gang seemed to have reverted to an earlier stage of development when they were not yet mature. If given the chance, they would rebel against themselves and their own bodily functions. Natalie sat down, closed her eyes, and wiped away her tears. Neal feigned sympathy.

"Ah, she's crying, poor baby. I musta said something that hurt her feelings."

Natalie dried her eyes.

"Nothing to worry about. I get choked up sometimes."

Norman had seen her like this before: smiling one second and weeping the next, and for no apparent reason. When she was in that space, he wanted to shield her and let her lick her own wounds.

He cleared the frog in his throat and rocked back and forth on the balls of his feet.

"What about this… give a listen…The four soulful hipsters walked the Negro streets of Frisco searching for Heaven, for somebody cool to love and to be loved in return."

Ginzy clapped him on the back.

"That's the idea, Norm. Keep at it."

At the table in the middle of the room, Ginzy helped himself to the Kodak and began to take pictures of everyone, including Norman, who looked from Ginzy to another man, a bruiser who had just entered the house through the backdoor and began to circle the room.

The bruiser touched everything and peered under nearly every surface, as though trolling for something to make his own. The typewriters looked awfully tempting.

Jack clapped him on the back,

"Yo, *Monsieur* Gregory, *bonjour.*"

"Ditto." Neal whimpered.

Ginzy raised his voice.

"What happenin' cap'n?" He snapped Gregory's picture.

"This'll make a nifty mug shot. Perfect for an ex-con like you."

Norman moved his eyes furtively about the room.

"You're all trying very hard to be a new Lost Generation like the artists after World War I. That's what it seems like to me. You're obsessed with yourselves and can't see beyond your shadows."

Ginzy removed his glasses and, with Norman's shirttails, cleaned the lenses.

"No, no, no. All wrong. We have a New Vision, capital N and capital V. We're beyond modernism and surrealism. We are the future bards of humankind and we're in tune with our ancestors who lived in caves, chanted, danced and fucked."

Jack rubbed his chin.

"We're not a second Lost Generation, we're the Second Coming."

Norman laughed. "You're humble, too, and a veritable work in progress."

Gregory Corso, the bruiser with the curly hair and fat lips, circled the room and dispensed reddish-orange pills. Jack instantly popped his into his mouth and swallowed.

"Here's to walking on water. You know, it wasn't made in Heaven, but here on earth and not by saints, but by sinners."

Like Lawrence, Jack uttered one-liners, or two-liners at most, and thought he was brilliant.

Ginzy placed a pill on his tongue, sipped orange juice from the bottle, and swallowed.

"Down the hatch."

Gregory stopped in front of Norman and turned toward Ginzy.

"Is this dude cool or what?"

Ginzy laughed.

"He's the most uncool cat I know. But you can trust him. He won't rat you out."

The bruiser handed Norman a pill.

"Abandon your ego, fella. This is the end."

Norman stared suspiciously at the pill.

"The end of what?"

At that precise moment, Ginzy riveted his eyes on Norman. With his wild hair and wilder eyes, he looked like a prophet who had walked off the pages of the Old Testament.

"You know, the end of the road, the end of time, the end of western civilization and the end of your innocence, sweetie-pie."

"Oh. Thanks." Norman inserted the pill in the small pocket of his jeans. "For later."

Neal squawked.

"I want another one. Since Jacky boy won't go to Louisiana with me, Nat and me's drivin' to L.A. to check out the new Walt Disney place, meet Mickey and Minnie. We're not stoppin' 'cept for gas so we need something to keep us awake, tide us over, right Nat?"

Natalie curled up catlike in a corner of the sofa.

"Yeah, that's right, honey, so Mr. Gregory, man, please, lay a few more of your magic pills on me. It's Disneyland or bust."

Gregory sat down next to Natalie, put his arm around her and puckered his lips.

"Kiss me four times, one for each upper."

"Deal." Neal roared. Natalie scowled, but she gave Gregory four chaste kisses. Gregory tried to stick his tongue down her throat, but she kicked his shins.

"Eat shit, mother fucker." She could be ornery when the spirit moved her.

Oddly enough, her rebelliousness made Gregory smile. He got to his feet, crossed himself, and like an unholy priest at communion offered Neal four little pills.

Neal juggled one on the tip of his tongue and turned to Natalie.

"Open your sexy mouth and stick out your crazy tongue, baby doll."

Neal transferred the pill from his mouth to hers. She swallowed it and rolled her eyes.

Gregory placed a pill next to Jack's Underwood, added a sheet of paper to the roller, tested the space bar, sat town, began to type madly, and immediately read aloud what he had written. "In the name of the Father, the Son and the Holy Ghost, I bless you in this era of the atomic nightmare."

Jack clapped.

"Very good. You gotta start somewhere."

Norman chuckled to himself.

"Say, Jack, how old are you?"

Jack fired back. "And how old are you, sonny boy?"

"Thirty-Three."

"Same as me! Ginzy is 29 and over the hill. Neal is 29, too, but he hasn't peaked yet. Come back in ten years and you'll be amazed… Say, maybe you can be in our movie, *Pull My Daisy*, Norman. It's still in the planning stages. You could play the uptight New York academic."

☯

16

Neal circled Norman—a kind of island detached from everyone else—as though to see if he had strings attached. When he found none, he stopped inches in front of his face.

"You oughta come with Nat and me to Disney. We need ballast. Yeah, man, meet us at the movie house on Market tonight. There's a triple feature: *Tarzan the Ape Man*, with Johnny Weissmuller as king of the jungle, Maureen Sullivan as Jane; *The Stranger Wore a Gun* with Randolph Scott; and *The Wild One* with our guy, Brando. Come for the eight o'clock show. Popcorn and cokes on me. We hit the road soon as you see the words, 'The End' on the screen."

Norman stared at Neal as though he was about to make a pact with the Devil himself. He had been on the coast for about six weeks and had stayed close to Zora's house and to City Lights Books. It was time to venture out, he told himself, see the Golden State and decide if it lived up to its reputation as the land of fruits and nuts.

Like Jack and like Ginzy, he had come under the spell of Neal Cassady. Dangerous, but difficult to resist. Norman rocked on the balls of his feet.

"I could join you. But I have to be at work Monday morning."

"Where's that, buddy?"

"City Lights. Funny way to make a living, selling books. But there you have it."

"I can dig it, man. I read books, too, you know."

Neal nodded his head.

"No problema. I'll drop you off before the lights come on at City Lights. "Ha, ha, ha…Safe delivery guaranteed."

Norman studied Natalie's face. When she shot him a vacant expression, he nodded his head.

"I'll be at the theater for the Brando flic."

A sly grin broke across Neal's sunburned face.

"I knew I could count on you. Bring cash for gas. I'll spring for everything else."

Norman could see that there was no point in trying to negotiate with Neal. He would twist and turn and not be pinned down.

"It's a done deal."

Norman eyed the vacant space on the sofa next to Natalie.

"May I?"

He didn't wait for an answer, but sat down, leaned his shoulder against hers, whispered in her ear, and nodded his head. Then, he gazed at Neal who cocked his ear.

"What was that? Did anybody hear somethin'?"

Ginzy rushed to the front of the room, pulled the burlap curtain aside and peered outside.

"There's a spade at the door."

Norman glanced out the window.

"It's Ezra."

"Ahh, sooo," Ginzy said.

He sounded, Norman thought, like he was trying to mimic Sidney Toler in the Charlie Chan flic, *Dangerous Money*. Ginzy took in the whole room, as though he expected applause for his impersonation of Toler, though no one clapped.

Norman hunched his shoulders.

"Don't be nasty about Ezra. He's my rock. He and his mother, Zora, and also Shig at City Lights."

Ginzy snapped a photo of Norman scowling.

"Just trying to liberate you from the shit prison you've built in your head."

"Whatever."

Norman went for the front door, opened it wide, invited Ezra inside, and, in the big room, introduced him to the gang members, who sized him up and down. Neal seemed to take an instant dislike to him. Jack looked like he wanted to borrow Ezra's jacket and his black skin. Natalie smiled, and then reached out and touched him. He returned the smile and reached out to her, as though eager to rekindle the connection they had begun at the Blackhawk and continued at Zora's.

"Would you care for a cold beverage?" She aimed to play the hostess.

Neal rushed to Ezra's side, as though he thought it wiser to make a friend than an enemy.

"How's about a little blue pill?"

Ezra shook his head.

"No thanks, sir."

"How 'bout some horse?"

Neal laughed. Ezra jerked his head back.

"Horse ain't no joking matter."

"Just pullin' your leg. I've been there, done that."

Ezra glanced at Natalie and winked.

"I'll have a glass of milk."

Natalie was the first to laugh. The others followed.

"You mean like Hopalong Cassidy."

"I mean like Jimmy Stewart in *Destry Rides Again*."

Neal laughed again, louder this time, and gazed at Jack.

"So, the spade cat wants milk."

To Natalie, he gave a command.

"Give the spade cat what he wants."

When no one except Norman was watching him, Gregory tiptoed across the room, helped himself to a couple of pages from the top of Jack's manuscript, slipped them into his pocket, and took a few steps toward the front door.

Natalie returned from the kitchen with a glass of frothy milk that looked like it had come straight from a cow.

Ezra sipped slowly and glanced from face to face.

"I didn't mean to break up the party. Just wanted to see what kinda mischief you white boys was up to."

Kerouac gathered the sheaf of typewritten papers that sat on the table, studied the top page and shook his head.

"Okay, who's the fuckin' thief?"

He glared at Corso.

"It was you, Gregory, I know it was. Hand it over. Thought you could flog my work and pick up some cash, didn't you?"

Gregory reached into his pocket and offered Jack the sheets of paper he'd purloined.

"Just testing, Jacky boy, wanted to see if you was payin' attention."

Jack thumbed through the manuscript. When he was satisfied that all the pages were accounted for and in order, he inserted them in an envelope and addressed it to "Mr. William Burroughs, El Hombre Invisible c/o Poste Restante, Tangiers, Morocco, North Africa." He added the words, "Par Avion."

Jack turned to Norman. "I know the address by heart. Me and Bill correspond. He's our mentor, a rare genius, working on a brilliant novel that will be like none other. I call it 'Naked Lunch.'"

He sealed the envelope and turned to Ginzy.

"Lay a few bucks on me."

Ginzy obliged. Jack handed a five dollar bill and the envelope to Neal and instructed him to go to the Rincon Annex Post office.

"If you leave now it'll go out in today's mail. Hightail it."

Ginzy clapped his hands.

"Wait a minute. I want a photo of everyone." He took charge and ordered his friends about. "You, spade cat, in the middle. Jacky on one side, and Neal on the other. It doesn't matter which side. Ezra's white boy next to Jacky, Natalie next to Neal, and Gregory kneeling in front."

Gregory dropped to his knees and gazed up in adoration at Ezra. Maybe it was fake adoration and maybe it was real. The camera couldn't tell the difference and neither could Norman, who said "cheese" along with everyone else.

Kerouac opened his mouth wide.

"*Les familles heureuses ne font jamais une bonne lecture.*"

Neal scratched his head.

"See what I mean. A budding Marcel Proust."

Neal placed his right hand on Ezra's shoulder.

"Come on down to the theatre with us, fella. You won't have to sit in nigger heaven."

Ezra froze for a few moments and cleared his throat.

"Thank you kindly, I'll mull it over."

If he was hurt by Neal's use of the "n" word, he didn't show it.

Jack kicked Neal in the seat of his pants.

"You're wasting time. The mail won't wait."

Neal grabbed Natalie around her slender waist and yanked her to her feet.

"Let's scram, baby doll."

When Ginzy was sure they were outside and couldn't hear anything, he rubbed shoulders with Ezra.

"Why didn't you say nothin' to Neal 'bout his foul mouth?"

Ezra wiped the milk mustache from his upper lip.

"Why didn't you say nothin'?"

"'Cause I'm not you!"

Ezra smirked.

"No, you're not, but you're a fuckin' faggot."

"Neal doesn't mean any harm."

"But he obviously thinks you're a pussy."

"So what?"

"So, don't tell me what I should or shouldn't say. That's my business. I'll pick my own battles. You pick yours."

"Touché."

Jack enjoyed the repartee.

17

In high school and in the military, Norman had heard the four-letter words that weren't supposed to be uttered in polite society. He wasn't surprised to hear them now, and he saw that the guys were showing off and trying to attract attention. He wouldn't suddenly imitate them.

Ezra studied the faces in the room.

"I don't get Neal and Natalie. What's the deal? Why the attraction?"

Norman shook his head.

"I don't either."

Ginzy rolled his eyes.

"What's not to get. He's our number one lover boy. Doctor Kinsey couldn't believe it when he interviewed him back in '47. Neal can fuck all night."

Kerouac squirmed.

"Yeah. He can fuck, but he don't know how to make love."

Gregory walked toward the door and scowled.

"Look who's talking."

Once Gregory was gone, the room quieted, the shadows lengthened, and Lester Young's invisible omnipotent sax massaged the space in Norman's head. Jack and Ginzy sat at the makeshift table opposite one another. They shared a "J," filled their lungs with smoke, enjoyed their own alternating voices, and reveled in the words that bounced back and forth like basketballs on a court. Before long, they were resurrecting memories of their favorite professors. Ginzy led off.

"Mark Van Doren was the only poet on the faculty. Nobody taught Walt Whitman. No one ever mentioned 'Song of Myself.' That was fucked up."

Jack raised his fist.

"Yeah, but your curiosity overcame their silence. You

discovered Walt on your own, which is the best way… As for me and Alfred 'Lord' Kazin, he refused to read my stuff, even when I told him that I was writing the Great American Novel."

Norman chuckled.

"You're a modest fellow."

Ginzy puffed on the joint and blew smoke in Norman's face. Norman coughed and rubbed his eyes, which turned bright red.

"What's the story with Neal? I mean, he has a wife and kids, doesn't he?"

Jack snorted.

"No story, but the other day Carolyn found a note from Natalie to Neal in the pocket of his jeans when she was doing laundry. He's in denial and so is she."

Ginzy eyes bulged.

"That's heavy."

Norman reached for the joint, inhaled, held the smoke, and slowly exhaled.

"As far as I can see, Neal's a dickhead."

Ginzy shrugged his shoulders and reached for the end of the joint, now barely a roach.

"No, he's not. He's the last cowboy; his car is his horse." He paused a moment and added, "I'm never gonna have kids."

Jack grunted.

"You better not."

Ginzy shed a tear. Then, he broke down and really cried without a sense of shame.

"My mother, Naomi, poor dear, wanted to be a good wife and raise me and my brother to be good Jewish boys, but she was clueless. No fault of her own. My father didn't understand. I was just a kid when she cut her wrists. I had to take her to the bug house. Natalie reminds me of Naomi. But growing up it wasn't all bad. Before she totally lost it, she learned me stuff they didn't teach in school."

Jack gazed at Ezra.

"The American South was my Harvard and my Yale. I heard colored folks singin' the blues."

Ezra nodded.

"The South is where I really belong, though I'll never live

there again. They'd lynch me for being colored, lynch me again for being queer, and cut off my dick and my balls to boot."

Jack shuddered.

"We don't dig the bigots and we don't pledge allegiance to the fake flag-waving shit show. Also, we don't listen to the cock-and-bull congressmen who have their heads up their asses. Call us the disloyal opposition."

Ginzy slapped Jack on the back.

"Disloyal when we need to be."

Norman listened to the conversation, and, while nothing sounded like it was spoken in confidence, he felt like he was eavesdropping.

Ginzy noticed his uneasiness.

"We have no secrets."

Jack chuckled.

"I ain't sharin' my journals with nobody."

He paused for a moment.

"Sometimes, Neal is a louse and a loser, with the worst aspects of American manhood, but you can't quote me."

Ginzy looked as though Jack had cut him to the quick.

"We love Neal. Neal is good. Neal is great."

Jack didn't buy Ginzy's plug for the king of the road and the prince of the whorehouse.

"He ought to try Zen."

"Neal is Zen. He don't have to try."

Jack folded his hands.

"Namaste....You know, he's the only real workin' man among us."

He glanced at Norman.

"Have you seen this guy's hands? He don't have a single callus."

Norman felt the softness of his own hands. He stood up and led Ezra toward the front door.

"I'll be gone for a few days with Neal and Natalie. Tell Zora not to worry and you don't worry, neither. We're going to Anaheim together, not Mississippi. Say, can you front me some gas money? I'm short on cash and can't make it to my bank."

Ezra nodded his head.

"Some of those valley towns are as bad as the South. I been there."

Norman peered into the big room where Ginzy and Jack sprawled on the floor and giggled. He turned to Ezra, who reached into the pocket of his trousers.

Norman watched him open his wallet.

"Whatcha think of Natalie's boys?"

Ezra offered Norman two bills, a five and a ten.

"You're the only one, Norman, who really loves her. The others get some kind of vicarious thrill being around her. She's their bitch."

Norman placed the bills in his wallet.

"Thanks, man… She ought to see a shrink."

Ezra exhaled.

"She told me her mother would strip search her when she came home from a date, lock her in the closet 'cause she smelled of sex, and make her eat her own puke when she threw up the shit she refused to eat."

Norman scratched the back of his head.

"When did she tell you that?"

"At the Blackhawk, after I told her I was queer. Then you joined us at the table, and she clammed up."

Ginzy put both hands on Norman's shoulders.

"I hear you, man. But you're the one who ought to see Dr. Phil Hicks at Langley Porter. Call him. I told him I liked boys. He said, 'So?' He'll open you up, buddy."

Norman frowned.

"Thanks."

He backed away from Ginzy, zipped up his jacket and walked toward the front door. Ezra followed him. On the sidewalk they craned their necks and observed the crescent moon on the horizon. A dog howled, a car sputtered, and a radio blared from the Victorian next door.

Ezra put his arms around Norman.

"Call me if and when you get in trouble. And about Natalie… Since you're incapable of cutting loose from her, try less passion and more compassion."

Norman shook his head.

"Might be too late for that, what with all we've been through and with my attachments, but thanks for the thought, brother."

He put his arms around Ezra, hugged him, detached slowly, and left him standing in the moonlight outside LaVigne's big yellow Victorian.

You have passed a rite of passage, Norman told himself. You now have brothers.

At the payphone on the corner, he called information and asked for the number for Langley Porter. He dropped a nickel into the slot and dialed the number. A woman answered.

"I'd like to make an appointment to see Dr. Hicks."

"Why?"

"My friend, Allen Ginsberg, recommended him."

"Oh, I see…Can you come in next Monday at 1 p.m. please?"

"I'll be there."

Norman braved the winds, stumbled toward the intersection, and caught a cab.

Q|Q

18

S tanding outside the box office on Market Street, Neal shouted at the top of his lungs.

"I'm Marlon Brando's older brother, Tony. I'll trade you my autograph for a ticket for me and another one for my girl, here."

How gullible can you be? Norman wondered. Neal grabbed a flyer for *The Wild One*, signed "Tony Brando" and accepted the two tickets the cashier pushed toward him. Norman paid for himself. That's the way it was going to be. My way or the highway. In the theater, where Neal wanted to gab, it was the same story.

"You know, pal, the automobile is the way of the future. Adios, railroads and busses. The driver be the man of tomorrow. Can you dig it?"

Neal insisted on picking out the seats and sitting as close to the screen as possible. He seemed to want to insert himself into the picture and become one with Brando, though he also complained about the "dumb hat that Marlon wore." He chuckled when he heard Brando's lines, especially, "Nobody tells me what to do" and "I don't make no deal with no cop." He seemed to think the dialogue had been stolen from him.

"Ticks me off."

He spoke louder than he ought to have and was instantly hammered by the bobbysoxer who sat behind him.

"Shut up grandpa and watch the flick."

Neal shushed her.

"I don't want nobody mouthing my lines."

When he saw Mary Murphy on the screen for the first time, playing the part of the police chief's rebellious daughter, he nudged Natalie.

"Looks like you, babe, and you look like her. It's uncanny."

He puckered his lips, extended his neck and leaned forward as though to kiss the screen, but couldn't reach nearly that far. Instead, he grabbed hold of Natalie and mashed her lips.

Natalie pushed Neal away and borrowed Mary Murphy's best line, "You're a fake," which she hurled at Neal who pulled her even closer to him.

"No, I'm not."

Norman trained one eye on the screen and another eye on Neal and Natalie; two shows for the price of one, he told himself.

The picture ended and the house lights came on, but Neal remained seated, his head in his hands.

"Is that all? Why couldn't there be a Hollywood ending?"

The movie seemed to devastate him. Norman took hold of one of his elbows and Natalie the other. Together, they brought him to his feet and pushed him toward the exit.

In the dimly-lit parking lot, the cool, wet air revived Neal. He cracked his knuckles, rubbed his hands together, and tried the door on the driver's side of a '53 Ford sedan which sat along the back wall, too far away for the attendant to see it clearly. Norman watched the attendant—a Black man with white hair and a bow tie—as he sat inside the booth, puffing on a cigar and listening to music on the radio.

The door to the '53 Ford would not budge. Neal worked his way down the line of cars while Natalie kept a lookout. Norman stuffed his hands in his pockets and imagined the worst. He was catastrophizing again, he knew, and didn't try to corral his unfettered imagination. They would all end up behind bars, he told himself, forced to sleep on a cement floor, shit in a stink hole overflowing with feces, and made to eat something that looked and smelled like shit.

Natalie put her fingers in her mouth and whistled. Neal leaned into the shadows. The attendant left the booth, aimed his flashlight at the cars, and moved it back and forth until he was satisfied that every vehicle was in its assigned place. Neal blew warm air on his right hand and tried his luck again.

The door to a '53 Hudson opened with only a slight squeak. Norman slid along the red brick wall that ran the length of the parking lot. Natalie bent her tall thin body and duckwalked in the shadows.

Neal slipped into the Hudson, scrunched behind the steering

wheel, closed the door on the driver's side, rolled down his window, and whispered to Natalie.

"Push, babe," and to Norman, "Lean into it, brother."

The car rolled over the sidewalk and into the one-way street that ran behind the theater and led to Market, where Neal hotwired the Hudson like a pro. No doubt about it, when it came to cars he was as talented as Lou Gehrig with a bat or Arturo Toscanini with a baton. He opened the side doors in front and back and waited for Norman to climb aboard and for Natalie to squeeze into the front seat. She slid her body so that her left hip touched Neal's right hip.

"Nice upholstery." Neal ran his right hand over the seat and across Natalie's shoulders. "I like the dashboard, too."

He pressed down gently on the accelerator, eased the car toward the sign at the corner, let up on the gas, and came to a stop, California style. Then he took a right on Market, where he joined the flow of traffic headed South. They cruised along the Bay Shore Freeway and raced down the 101, which Neal referred to as "El Camino Real." The highway seemed to inflate his sense of himself as "the Road King."

Norman peered out the rear window expecting to see cops, and, when he didn't, he closed his eyes and hummed a Charlie Parker tune. Natalie turned on the radio and moved the dial until she found a station that was broadcasting Muddy Waters singing "Hoochie Coochie Man."

The music ignited Neal.

"You know what Coochie is, Norm don't you? No, course not. You're a city boy."

He turned his head, looked away from the road and peered into the back seat, which made Norman even more nervous than he had been.

"Watch the road, please."

"Coochie is pussy, and, though man can't live by coochie alone, he can't live without coochie, 'cause, you see, he comes from coochie and must return to coochie to be recharged, reborn, revived, resurrected, and to ensure that his tool is retooled, 'cause no man can live happily if he don't retool his tool. Ain't that right, ain't that the way it is, coochie Jackson, coochie Natalie, my squeeze, my main squeeze, my one and only squeeze, my squeeze queen?"

Norman had to admit it. When Neal wanted to, he could string words together as though they were rare beads on a necklace. Maybe he was a raw genius who only needed mentoring to blossom as a writer. Natalie put her arm around Neal's neck, kissed him on his right cheek, and left a bright red mark. Neal put peddle to the metal, passed a Chevy on the right and a Ford on the left, leaned back, and allowed the Hudson to roar down the highway as though driving itself.

Bill Haley sang "Rock Around the Clock."

Norman leaned forward.

"Drive slower, please; you're making me nervous."

Neal turned around, faced Norman and chuckled.

"The boy can't take speed. He's gonna hafta learn."

Norman watched the needle of the speedometer climb to 70, 75, 80, 85, 90, 95, and hit 100.

"Oh, fuck. We're gonna be busted."

Neal explained—actually it sounded more like a boast, not an explanation—"If the cops stop us now, they'll take us directly to jail, ya understand, boy? But we're goin' so fast no cop's gonna see us, not in this black Hudson and on this dark night. We're free."

Norman soon tired of Neal's bravado and tired also of Natalie's indulgence, which made no sense to him. He was also just plain tired, and hungry, too.

"When do we stop for grub?"

Neal laughed.

"We don't, not till daybreak.'"

"Where do we sleep?"

"Close your eyes and kick back, buddy. Catch some zzz's. We'll wake you when it's time for a pit stop."

The interior of the car felt like a pressure cooker. Neal had turned up the heat and Norman's flesh felt like it fell from his bones.

He took out his notebook, and in the dim light he wrote, "One day, Hollywood will make a movie of Neal and his buddies. It will suck every ounce of real blood from all of them. Madison Avenue won't be far behind. Every kid in every city and town in America will want to wear jeans and T-shirts, talk like hipsters, and think they're cool when they're nothing more than copycats. Remind me not to mimic these guys."

He closed his notebook, removed his shoes, and curled up in a fetal position. So why do I hang with them? he asked himself. He was too tired to answer his own question. He closed his eyes, opened his eyes, closed them again, and opened them once more, until the world faded to black. When he woke after an hour or so it amused him to keep his eyes shuttered, not move an arm or a leg, and imagine that he was a mummy in an ancient tomb, coming alive after a thousand-year slumber.

He told himself, I hang with the members of the gang because they're not like the creeps I knew in school, and not like the guys in the army who kept their mouths shut and played it safe. Neal is fucked up, but he's for real. Ginzy is insane in a lovable way, and Jack is so sad I can't help but feel for him.

Norman heard a human voice. At first, he thought it was a DJ on the radio. Then he realized it belonged to Neal.

"What you got to hide, babe? What did Norman whisper in your ear back at LaVigne's?" Neal wouldn't let up. He continued his line of "cross-examining," as Norman thought of it.

"What was the big fuckin' secret, honey child?"

Norman heard the sound of someone shifting position in the front seat and knew it had to be Natalie. She had moved away from Neal and leaned against the door on the passenger side.

Neal honked the horn.

"Come on, now, 'fess up, sweetie!"

"I don't remember."

"You don't remember, or you won't remember?"

"I can't remember. There was too much going on and I smoked too much reefer. Ginzy was taking pictures, Jacky was typing, Gregory was up to no good, and you were itching for a fight with Norman's friend, Ezra."

"The spade cat?"

"I wish you wouldn't call him that."

"What should I call him?"

"Call him Ezra and leave it at that."

Natalie paused a moment and turned down the volume on the radio.

"Sometimes I think you really are fake, like the motorcycle guy in the movie."

Norman decided to emerge from his crypt. He leaned forward so his head was in the front seat while his body remained in the back seat.

"All this spade shit that comes out of your mouth gets old fast. Why don't you give it a rest?"

Neal pressed his right foot down on the accelerator.

"Ah, the Professor has spoken."

Norman leaned back in his seat.

"Forget it. You're a lost cause."

He rubbed his forehead.

"Where are we at?"

"You're in luck, buddy. Time to stop. You were gonna cover for gas."

"Was I? I don't remember."

Neal leaned on the horn again, which startled Natalie, who turned and purred at Norman.

"You did say you would spring for gas, and it's only twenty-six-cents a gallon. Don't be a cheapskate."

So, they were ganging up on him. He didn't see a way to drive a wedge between them, though that was precisely what he had in mind.

A large overhead sign painted with red letters against a white background read, "Liberty Gasoline." Neal eased up on the gas and let the Hudson roll to a stop.

"This station has my name written all over it."

He climbed out from behind the steering wheel and sniffed the air. Norman rested his body against the sleek rear fender, glanced at the red gas pumps, opened his wallet, removed a twenty-dollar-bill and handed it to Neal, who asked the attendant—a young man wearing a uniform with a matching shirt, trousers and cap—for one dollar's worth of gas. That turned out to be almost four gallons.

Neal held out his hand for the change: a ten, a five and four ones.

"I'll keep it in reserve."

Neal handed Norman a single and pocketed the rest.

"Buy yourself a Hershey."

Inside the Liberty Gas Station, Norman studied the array

of chocolate bars and selected an Almond Joy. He remembered that ever since boyhood, he loved the combination of almonds, shredded coconut and chocolate. He paid the attendant, peeled away the blue wrapper, took a bite, and chewed.

Through the dusty window, he watched Neal and Natalie arguing, or so it seemed. He polished off the last of the Almond Joy, which he had to admit didn't taste as good at the end as it had the beginning, though he licked the chocolate and the coconut from his fingertips. He tossed the wrapper in the trash, sauntered in the dappled California morning sunlight, and hopped into the back seat of the Hudson.

"What's going on with you two?"

Natalie grimaced. Neal hotwired the Hudson and revved the engine.

"That's for me to know and you to find out."

Neal laughed and couldn't stop himself.

Norman punched him, or rather gave him a noogie.

"Not that funny!"

A short distance down the road, they stopped for breakfast at Big Boys, a "greasy spoon," as Norman thought of it. The map on the wall told him they were about two-hours north of Anaheim. Natalie was restless, Norman was cranky, and Neal was jazzed.

"We be in striking distance, kiddies."

Neal picked out a booth. When the waitress arrived, he ordered coffee, eggs over easy, a side of bacon, and a side of pork sausages, along with a short stack.

"We'll share, 'kay."

When the platters arrived, he made a show of sharing, but arranged the plates in front of him and ate nearly everything in sight.

"I need the fuel, same as the Hudson."

Natalie and Norman picked at the leftovers.

At the register, Neal pulled out his wallet and flirted with the buxom waitress, who doubled as the cashier.

If nothing else, this guy has moxie, Norman told himself.

Neal placed a kiss on Natalie's forehead.

"I gotta go wee wee pee pee."

Norman eyed him as he walked bowlegged to the back of the café.

"You know, Natalie, he'll ditch you and crawl back to his wife and kids. "

Natalie stretched her legs.

"Don't 'spect me to come running back to you, Norm. You're no piece of cake."

"I'm not the New York Norman you knew."

Natalie sighed.

"I can see you're changing, but you're still ninety-nine-point-nine percent uptight rich kid from Whitestone."

Norman winced. She knew how to hit him where he felt vulnerable.

Natalie wore a grim expression he had never seen before, and hoped he would never see again.

"You kill me, Norman. You really do. I rather be a B-girl like my friend Bette, bilking guys, than have to live with you, or even with Neal, Jack or Ginzy, who could never get it up."

Norman grimaced.

"If you think we're so toxic, get out and get away. I'll help you."

"Where would I go? Back to jerk city New Jersey?"

Neal joined them in front of the café and handed them their tickets for the day.

"Don't say I never did nothing for you."

Norman read the text. "Disneyland, July 17, 1955, Press Pass." He squinted his eyes against the sun.

"What gives?"

Neal clicked his teeth with his tongue.

"Don't ask questions."

Natalie leaned against the front bumper.

"See what I mean, Mr. Uptight? You never just go with the flow."

❧❧

19

By the time they arrived in Anaheim, most of the spaces in the parking lot were already taken. Neal was pissed.

"Jesus Christ. Everybody and their cock-sucking mother is here."

He circled three times before he found a slot. It was hot under the cloudless sky, and hotter still on the long line to enter the Magic Kingdom. There was little room to stretch arms and legs in the crowds that thronged the streets, gathered to listen to the brass band, and waited in line to get into Sleeping Beauty Castle. Natalie insisted she had to visit.

"I'm waiting for Prince Charming."

She turned and looked up at the sky as though she expected a visitation from heaven.

Without his pals, Norman took the cruise on "Mark Twain's River Boat," and later reconnected with them on the carousel, which he was initially unwilling to ride. On the spur of the moment, he hopped aboard, the circus music ringing in his ears. He clutched his horse and decided, as he went around and around, that he would shed his de Haan skin and meld with the all-American crowd.

Yes, yes, he would borrow Jack's vibes, Ginzy's reverential irreverence, and Neal's speediness. Maybe he'd earn Natalie's respect, though he didn't count on it. He aimed to practice non-attachment. He would become a Zen Buddhist, meditate and let go of his monkey mind. Nirvana in California would be his, at long last. He would have to wire his friends at the Nirvana café in Manhattan and tell them.

You're not a lost cause, not anymore, he muttered.

Later as he wandered across Disneyland—took in Mickey and Minnie, and caught a glimpse of Walt Disney himself sporting a mustache and wearing a white shirt and a blue tie—he remembered he'd grown up with Bambi, Snow White and the Seven Dwarfs.

His new-found Frisco friends, he decided, were building a magical kingdom of their own: a kind of anti-Disneyland. They could be as goofy as Goofy, the human-like dog who stood on two legs, and wore a turtleneck and a vest. Nothing wrong with goofiness. All things in moderation, even Blakean excess.

His pals, he told himself, were dope-smoking Peter Pans who didn't want to grow up and turn into their parents and teachers, become the likes of Ike, Nixon, Stevenson, and General Douglas MacArthur, who wanted to drop the big one on the Chinese and watch the mushroom cloud rise as nuclear fallout settled on the planet. Who could blame the goofy hipsters for their antics? They were children of the atomic age, and they were survivors, too,

Adults sucked.

They had fucked up the planet big time.

Weren't there alternatives to American insanity? Where was the American Sartre and the American Simone de Beauvoir, the American Bertrand Russell and the American Emmeline Pankhurst? Yes, of course, there was Eleanor Roosevelt, but to Norman it seemed that genius had skipped a generation and that adults put their heads down and ploughed ahead, or worse stuck them in the sand.

"Tomorrowland" with its space age shapes struck him as the perfect place to leave the past behind. He would flap his wings and soar above the amber waves of grain and the alabaster cities.

Ginzy was right. He had built a prison in his de Haan head and was afraid to leave it because it was a known environment. Jack was right, too. America was a beautiful country with beautiful, albeit damned people.

Weren't beautiful people always damned? Hadn't it always been the same, going all the way back to the ancient Greeks and the furies who heard the complaints of the young against the aged, children against parents, and then hounded wrongdoers to death? Norman de Haan had been hounded enough. Goodbye ghosts!

Mr. Disney with his white shirt, blue tie, and mustache could certainly make audiences laugh and cry. Norman gave him credit for that. He was a genius whose myths had become the myths of America. Ginzy, Jack, Neal, Gregory, and Natalie lived a counter myth that might not survive the cold that blew across the continent. It was too early to say.

If the counter myth were to thrive, he told himself, it would need the soulfulness of Zora and Ezra, the blues of Billie, Lester, and Charlie Parker, and the grit of the Black folks in Montgomery. Too bad that his own species had become so efficient at murder and mayhem.

He spied Natalie at the entrance to Autotopia and wanted to tell her that he still loved her. Instead, he made small talk.

"It's hot isn't it?" He looked at the sky. "No one told me it would be blazing in Disneyland."

"Is that all you can tell me? You looked like you had something deep-down important to say."

Neal cozied up to them and insisted that he had to experience Autotopia. Not Natalie or Norman; they lounged in the shade, shared a cold Coca Cola, snacked on Lay's Potato Chips, and watched the Road King race around the track faster than any of the kids.

After an hour or so, Neal climbed out of his vehicle, all sweaty and red from the sun, and looked at the sign above his head.

"What's autotopia?"

Norman held back and left it to Natalie to explain that the word was, as she put it, "a combination of auto and utopia."

"You mean like autoerotica."

"Exactly, Daddio!"

Disneyland acted like an aphrodisiac on Neal. The hordes of young, beautiful California girls and women—including the Disney cancan girls, with fake feathers, net stockings and red lipstick—stroked his libido. With his tight trousers, there was no way Neal could easily hide his erection.

"I'd like to fuck 'em all." He licked his lips. "So many women and so little time."

Neal didn't mind that his voice carried, and that moms, dads, and kids heard him.

Norman excused himself and found a pay phone on a fake island with fake palm trees. He called his sister, Toni, on the number his mother included in a letter that had arrived at City Lights.

"Sis, you'll never guess where I am."

"San Quentin?"

"No, not even close."

"San Simeon?"

"Warmer."

"I dunno. Universal Studio."

"Disneyland! Everyone in California isn't a fruit or a nut. But except for me and my pals there are no hipsters here. We'll have to invade and liberate like we did in Paris in '45."

"You, at Disneyland? I don't believe it. How the mighty existentialist has fallen."

"You remember Natalie, don't you? I'm with her and a crazy cat named Neal Cassady who can only think of two things: going very fast and getting laid, not necessarily in that order."

He paused a moment.

"Have you landed a part in a movie?"

"Working as a carhop at Mel's. Tips are good. I have an audition next week for a part in a musical comedy. Wish me luck."

"How's mom?"

"Sundays, she goes to the opera and she's brushing up on her Dutch. Wants to visit family in Rotterdam, go to the zoo there, and see the windmills, of course. She'd love it if you'd go with her… Oh, and you'll never guess who showed up at mom's the other day."

"Mrs. Jackson, Natalie's mother."

"Wow! …How do you know that?"

"Just do."

"What did she want?"

"I wasn't there, so I don't know for sure. You'd have to ask mom."

"Listen, sis, come to Frisco. It's only a short ride. We'll hang out, like old times… *Vaarwel en hou van jou.*"

"Love you, too, Norman de Haan."

❦

20

Neal, Natalie, and Norman lingered at Disneyland until they were told they had leave. They dragged themselves to the sunbaked Hudson in the parking lot and headed North, with Neal driving above the speed limit and with rock 'n' roll blasting on the radio. Natalie, who wore her dark glasses, looked "fetching," Norman told himself. The three of them, each in worlds of their own making, watched the hot sun go down slowly over the vast Pacific.

Natalie removed her dark glasses.

"Did you know my mom went to see your mom?"

"No."

He liked lying to Natalie. It gave him a sense of empowerment.

"Are you telling me the truth, Norman de Haan?"

"How would I know your mom visited my mom?"

"Your sister, Toni. I would have sworn she told you."

"Why would she tell me about their visit?"

Natalie wore a look of frustration.

"We've been in touch since before you and I broke up. I've been confiding in her, like about the time my mother took me to the Jersey shore in summer and this older guy, Mickey, showed me stuff I had only read about in books like *A Stone for Danny Fisher*. I thought Mickey was cool. But when I told him I was pregnant, he ditched me."

Neal pretended to play a tiny violin.

"Boo hoo. Poor baby. I bet the experience was good for you. Didn't Jack or somebody say that what doesn't kill you makes you stronger?"

"Nietzsche!"

Norman sounded professorial.

"Who?" Neal didn't have a clue.

"The *Übermensch* guy."

"Yeah, that's what we need now, *Übermensch*."

Natalie punched Neal. He yelped.

"The abortion nearly killed me."

"But you're here now and that's what counts. You're a survivor, Nat. You always come out on top. You give as good as you get, and you don't mind being the lone chick in the company of guys who can't make up their minds whether they're queer or not, and well… that's why I think that…"

Norman tuned out, leaned back, and watched the light slowly vanish in the western sky. Darkness enveloped the car, the highway, and the hills in the distance, and made him feel lost and lonely again. Old habits died hard. Somewhere on the road between San Juan Bautista and Hollister, where he smelled the dust of the Valley, he fell asleep, and didn't wake until they reached Redwood City.

Neal leaned over the front seat and looked back.

"I'll have you at City Lights in ninety minutes."

"I'm sure you're as good as your word. You're one of a kind, sir."

He wanted to part company with Neal on good terms. To do that, he had to seal his lips and sit on his hands.

Eighty-eight hair-raising minutes later, Neal made a U-turn and pulled to the curb at 261 Columbus Avenue. Norman gathered his belongings, stood on the sidewalk and gazed in admiration at the Hudson. The supercar had survived every twist and turn on the highway, along with all the abuse that Neal had thrown at it. The brakes didn't seem to be what they'd been, and neither did the tires. The fuel gage read empty. But the car was in one piece.

Neal would abandon the Hudson on a dead end street and hot wire another vehicle. Wasn't that his way and wasn't that also the American way? Use something, throw it away, and get something to replace it.

"Gimme five."

Neal extended his right arm and turned his hand so his fingers faced upward.

Norman slapped Neal's hand hard.

"Thanks for the joy ride."

"Later, alligator."

Natalie followed those two words with "After awhile, crocodile."

She wrapped the sunglasses around her face and Norman couldn't see her eyes. She had gone back into her shell, the little girl who had been bullied and browbeaten by her big bad mother, and who had come to California to get away from her and nonwheresville New Jersey.

Norman leaned his body against the Hudson and looked Neal in the eye.

"I won't forget your kindness."

In his way, Neal had been kind, Norman decided. He had taken him on a journey that turned out to be both sacred and profane, taken him across California and into unknown territory. In the mirror of the road, he saw who he had been and who he might become, if only he could let go of his ghosts.

He looked up and down Columbus Avenue and approached the front door to City Lights, unlocked it, stepped inside, and turned on the light above the front desk. In the makeshift kitchen, he brewed a pot of coffee, opened the cash register, counted the bills and the checks, and wrote down the total amount on an index card.

Standing in front of the window, and watching the foot traffic, he sipped coffee from a mug that read "James Joyce." He glanced at the alarming and alarmist headlines on the front page of *The Chronicle*, and perused a story about an explosion at an oil refinery in Oakland. Next, he checked the stats for his favorite baseball players on the New York Giants: Dusty Rhodes, Alvin Dark, and the "Say Hey Kid," Willie Mays, who was batting over .300 and enjoying a sensational season.

He finished his coffee and washed the cup. With an Exacto knife, he opened a large cardboard box, removed the invoice and the books, logged the titles and the names of the authors in a ledger, and lodged the books on the shelves where they belonged.

Lawrence was a genius, he told himself. He was ahead of the curve that would bring the paperback revolution around the world. When Shig arrived at the store, Norman regaled him with tales of Neal's driving, Autotopia, the faux cancan girls, the crowds of excitable and excited kids, the employees dressed up as Mickey and

Minnie, and Walt Disney's brief, albeit dramatic appearance.

Shig was not impressed.

"Humph. Remind me to skip it. Ditto, I'm sure, for Lawrence. He's having a hard time at home with Kirby, just now when sales are booming. We'll be in the black this month. Things go wrong in one place and right in another. Yin and Yang, the light side and the dark side. I hope you're meditating."

"I am. I like it, though I can see all the shit I carry in my head."

Norman knelt down on the floor, carved up the cardboard box with the Exacto knife, carried the pieces to the basement, and piled them in a corner.

When he came back, he sat down behind the front desk.

"I've been thinking that I'm not Yang enough for Natalie."

Shig nodded.

"From what I've seen, the problem is that she's too Yang for you. Compensating for something."

Norman raised his eyebrows.

"Oh, really, where have you observed her?"

Shig offered a wry smile.

"At the Foster's on Montgomery. Last week before you went South, she showed up with LaVigne, ordered french fries, poured on the salt, ate every last one, and then just started to weep, seemingly about nothing."

Shig paused a moment.

"You know, I think she doesn't feel appreciated, except by LaVigne, who was schooled by Jesuits before he got to Frisco, and who's a pretty hip guy. Jack and Ginzy don't appreciate him either, 'cause he paints and doesn't write."

Norman peered out the window and watched the cars on Columbus Avenue.

"I feel like I've turned a corner. You know, Shig, my ancestors were kind of like samurai—they were nobility, embraced loyalty and didn't pay attention to pain—only they were fucked up Dutch Calvinists who settled in Surinam before they arrived in New Amsterdam."

Shig nodded again, this time more slowly.

"You're not as uptight as you were when you arrived. Maybe it's the weed you've smoked and maybe Kerouac has rubbed off on you. Or it could be those colored people in the house where you live."

Norman reached into his pocket, retrieved the ticket for Disneyland, and, with the Exacto knife, cut it in two equal parts; he inserted one in his wallet as a souvenir, and the other he used to mark the place in the book he was reading. It was a second-hand edition of Langston Hughes' *The Ways of White Folks*, which Shig recommended.

"Just what the fuck is whiteness? Have you thought about it?"

Shig cleared his throat.

"Whiteness? You're probably asking the wrong person. It's way too complicated to explain at the drop of a hat, except to say that it brings to mind the time my whole family was rounded up and locked up at the Minidoka War Relocation Center in Idaho.

"That's when I read Melville's riff on whiteness in *Moby-Dick*. You might look at the new paperback of the novel on the back wall. It's in the literature section after Mailer and before Porter, Katherine Anne."

Norman closed the Langston Hughes book and glanced at the far wall.

"Jack Kerouac is hung up on whiteness. Ginzy is hung up on queerness, Neal is hung up on his father, and Natalie's hung up on her mother."

Shig stroked his beard.

"Sounds about right."

"What's the worst thing you could confess?"

"I worked for the U.S. Military Intelligence Service in Japan."

"You worked for the Man?"

Shig nodded.

"You could say that. During the war, when push came to shove, I felt I had to be American, not Japanese. Now the pendulum is swinging back the other way. Zen helps me."

Shig walked to the back wall, retrieved a copy of *Moby-Dick*, brought it to the front counter, and handed it to Norman, who looked at the table of contents and turned to the chapter titled "The Whiteness of the Whale." He ran his eyes down the page, and from page to page, and from line to line. He stopped and read, "all deified Nature absolutely paints like the harlot, whose allurements cover nothing but the charnel-house within."

Shig took the paperback and kissed it.

"Don't you just love Melville? Your pals will never write anything as wild and wonderful as *Moby-Dick*. They're afraid of looking at the charnel house within."

Norman turned the Exacto knife around and around in the palm of his hand, careful not to cut himself.

Shig nodded his head once again, only more vigorously this time, and fixed Norman with his gaze.

"If you haven't met him yet, you might track down Peter Orlovsky, who just arrived in Frisco. Another descendant of Russian immigrants with a crazy mother. He was LaVigne's heartthrob, only now he's making it with Ginzy. When they're all together in that big room in the house on Gough, you can cut the tension with…well… an Exacto knife."

He paused for a moment and felt the sharpness of the blade.

"Ginzy just wrote a juicy love poem about Orlovsky that he memorized, and he's been reciting it in Washington Square Park, whether anyone listens to him or not. Claims it doesn't matter."

Ferlinghetti arrived at the store just as Shig was talking to Norman about Ginzy's love poem. He stood at the front desk, his head nearly scraping the ceiling, his shoulders bent as though carrying the weight of City Lights on his own back. Norman noticed.

"You remind me of Atlas."

Ferlinghetti's eyes twinkled and a boyish smile spread from ear to ear.

"I want to see that poem of Allen's about his new boyfriend. In fact, I want to see everything he writes. You know, guys, he's going to be bigger than Dylan Thomas."

Shig looked at his wristwatch and shot his eyes up toward Ferlinghetti who towered above him, even when he slouched.

"You've been keeping banker's hours, Lawrence."

"Trouble at home. Kirby doesn't understand."

Shig sat on the three-legged stool behind the front counter.

"She knows you're cheating on her?"

"She says City Lights is my mistress. We still love one another but…"

Ferlinghetti opened his bookbag, retrieved a thick sheaf of papers, and handed them to Shig.

"I've gone over the accounts; something is terribly wrong. Books are disappearing left and right. Somebody or some bodies must be walking off with them. The two of you have gotta keep an eye out and stop the stealing."

Shig ran his eyes up and down the figures and shook his head. "Sorry, Lawrence. I feel like I've fallen down on the job."

Norman glanced at the stats.

"I'll play cop."

Lawrence jerked his head back.

"A soft cop. We can't bust anyone. It wouldn't be the right thing to do, considering." He cast his eyes about the store.

On that foggy morning, Shig and Norman took turns patrolling the aisles, watching for guilty looks and furtive gestures.

While Shig was on his lunch break, Lawrence shouted from the top floor.

"Norman, your mother's on the phone."

He dashed upstairs and grabbed the receiver.

"Hello, mom…No, that's alright… yes, yes. Toni told me you're going to visit family in Holland…I wish I could…Can't leave now…Give them my best…Really?…What did Mrs. Jackson want?… I wish you hadn't done that…Yeah, yeah…Maybe I'll see you for Christmas… That would be lovely… I send kisses, mom. Love you."

The call lifted his spirits. Downstairs, he buttonholed Shig.

"Gotta go see a shrink."

Norman bounded down Columbus, hailed a cab, and arrived early at Langley Porter for his appointment with Dr. Hicks. He showed his New York State driver's license and filled out the forms the receptionist handed him on a clipboard, though he resented the questions. Why was his military service anyone's business besides his own? And why did the doctor need to know the medical history of his parents?

Dr. Hicks, dressed in white, looked like he'd just come from a tennis court. He seemed vibrant and sounded confident. Strangely enough, there were no framed diplomas on the wall and his desk was clear.

"So, you're a friend of Allen Ginsberg?"

"I recently met him. I'm new to the city. I've just been getting to know Allen and San Francisco."

"Why did you want to see me?"

"I thought you could help."

"How so?"

"I was in psychoanalysis in New York for years. It didn't do me any good."

"You're still alive and in one piece."

"True, but sometimes I have felt like I'm going to explode at any minute."

"Maybe you're having an identity crisis."

"It feels like a permanent crisis. Secrets are eating away at me."

"What secrets?"

"That's just it. I'm not prepared to say."

"Maybe another day."

"Maybe."

"You seem introverted."

"Is there something wrong with that?"

"Listen, Norman, I suggest that you stop in at the Tom Mooney School. Get out of your own head. If you're new to San Francisco, you might make friends there. A lot of guys your age who were in the war take classes at the school."

"Thanks, doc. And when I'm ready, I'll come back."

"No pressure."

Dr. Hicks shook Norman's hand, walked him through the waiting room and saw him off on the street.

When Norman saw Natalie again, he tried to persuade her to make an appointment with Hicks. It seemed to him that she needed a shrink more than ever before, and more than he did.

"The doctor is not judgmental. He won't accuse you of having some kind of complex."

"But suppose I'm really neurotic."

"You'll deal with it."

They sat on a bench in Washington Square Park where

Norman half-listened to Ginzy read his love poem to Orlovsky out loud.

"Allen has balls."

Natalie sipped cold coffee and watched the pigeons hunt for scraps.

"The only bright spot in my life right now is the Marilyn Monroe wannabe I met at work. We hang out and talk. There's no men around."

"That's great."

"We think alike and feel alike."

"Yeah, I'd like to meet her."

"She's going through a divorce and working as a B-Girl, so when you do meet her, be gentle. The cops are cracking down on the bars and she's struggling to make ends meet."

"Welcome to the club!"

In fact, Norman didn't have to worry about making ends meet. Lawrence paid him twice a month in cash. He saved and felt fat.

☙❧.

21

Acouple of days later, Ezra showed up at City Lights, stoned. He's checking up on me, Norman told himself. Wants to see if I really do have a job. Ezra wandered about the store, though he didn't seem to be looking for a particular book to buy.

"Can I help you?"

"You have a lot of books."

"Yeah, we're a bookstore."

"Do you have bestsellers?"

"We try not to, but we do carry *Messiah* by Gore Vidal. It's a retelling of the Christ story."

"What about Ralph Ellison?"

"*Invisible Man*. We have it, though it's not new. Came out a few years ago."

"I heard guys talking about it at the Blackhawk. I think it's my kind of book."

"Definitely down your alley."

Norman retrieved the book from the shelf and rang up the sale. "*Invisible Man* captures what you'd call the *zeitgeist*."

Ezra tucked the book under his arm and saluted Norman.

"Maybe I'll catch it, too."

Shortly before noon, a woman who wore a gaunt expression entered the store, and with the aid of a cane approached the front desk. Norman knew who she was before she opened her mouth and uttered a word. He put down the paperback copy of Langston Hughes's *The Ways of White Folks* and smiled in much the same way he'd seen Natalie smile at I. Magnin.

Like her daughter, the woman who stood before him was tall and thin, with high cheek bones and dark eyes, though unlike her daughter, she was no longer vivacious. She wore a dark suit and heels, a brightly colored scarf around her neck, and pearl earrings, fake or real he couldn't tell. Norman knew she meant trouble. He wished that Shig was sitting at the front counter in his place.

"My name is Irene Jackson, I've come all the way from New Jersey because I believe that my daughter, Natalie, is in grave danger. A month ago, before she stopped writing, she mentioned that San Francisco had a new bookstore. I did some sleuthing. I knew she had to mean City Lights."

She paused a moment, cleared her throat and smiled, but only a tad.

"I was hoping you could tell me Natalie's whereabouts."

Norman didn't want to tell an outright lie to Irene Jackson, but he didn't want to divulge any information about Natalie, either. It wasn't Irene's business, he told himself, where Natalie was living and what she was doing or not doing, and as far as he was concerned, Natalie's only real danger came from Irene Jackson. His own mother, Bea, hadn't left home, stormed across the country, and come looking for him in desperation.

Norman had once wanted to be a private eye like Sam Spade. San Francisco seemed like the place to become a detective, but this didn't feel like the right time, or the right case to become a gumshoe. He stared at Irene Jackson without blinking or flinching.

"A lot of folks come through our front door, far too many to keep track of."

He paused for a few seconds and gave Mrs. Jackson the once over. She was the embodiment of the American Mother Monster.

"Where are you staying and for how long?"

Irene Jackson looked at Norman suspiciously, but she opened her purse, removed a card, and handed it to him. It read, "Carleton Arms, 1239 Turk Street, Western Addition" with a local phone number.

"I'm flying back East day after tomorrow."

Norman thought that she sounded resolved.

Mrs. Jackson raised her cane in a threatening way.

"I've been all over the city, haven't had any luck, and can't find a detective I can afford. They all want money up front."

Shig came up from the basement and was now eavesdropping. He pushed forward and stood directly in front of Natalie's mother.

"What seems to be the trouble, ma'am?"

Before she spoke, Irene Jackson studied Shig's long black hair, black beard, dark eyebrows, and his black turtleneck sweater, and backed away as though alarmed by his appearance.

"I'm afraid my daughter has fallen in with the wrong crowd. She did that in Greenwich Village before she came out here. I thought she might be living with a male friend from Manhattan. I never met him, but I heard Natalie describe him. He sounded mentally unstable."

Norman kept his cool, and so did Shig.

"What's the man's name?"

Natalie's mother raised her cane again.

"I wish I knew. If I did, it would make my life easier. I know he's a jazz nut who served in the war and comes from an old New York family."

Norman loosened his collar.

"That could be any number of people. Ex-GIs love Frisco, and so does the jazz crowd."

Shig took Mrs. Jackson by the arm, marched her to the door, held it ajar, and then helped her step down and navigate the buckled sidewalk. He waited with her at the bus stop on Columbus while she steadied herself with her cane. Norman watched from behind the window.

He grabbed a copy of *Junkie* that boasted a cover of a fanatical fellow with a hammerlock around the neck of a desperate blonde in a red dress. The fanatic was ready to stick the blonde in the arm with a needle. Norman felt prankish.

He went out the door, approached Mrs. Jackson and offered her the copy of *Junkie*.

"You'll find this eye opening."

Norman looked diabolical. If books could poison, it had to be *Junkie*. Mrs. Jackson glanced at the cover and read the text that said the book was published by "Ace" and written by someone named "William Lee." She held it in her outstretched hand, squinted her eyes, spat in an unladylike manner, and tossed Mr. Lee's book into the gutter. Shig looked at *Junkie* mournfully, offered Mrs. Jackson his right hand, and helped her climb the steps to the bus.

She turned and smiled.

"You're a nice young man."

116

She snarled at Norman who had retreated to the front door; he held it ajar with the tip of his shoe. Shig retrieved the book from the gutter and stood on the sidewalk. Inside he hugged Norman and Norman hugged him.

"Thanks. Couldn't have done it without you."

"Ditto."

"I couldn't let dear William Lee, author of *Junkie*, languish in the gutter, though I'm sure that's where Natalie's mother thinks he and his book belong."

With his handkerchief, Shig wiped the debris from the cover, adjusted the tattered pages, and placed the book on the shelf behind the counter.

Norman climbed the stairs to the editorial office and avoided Lawrence, who was preoccupied at the big green file cabinet. He sat down on a corner of the large oak desk, borrowed the phone, called the number for the house on Gough, and let it ring and ring and ring. When no one answered, he hung up, stood up, and kicked the wall.

Lawrence looked displeased.

"Easy fellow."

Next, Norman called Foster's Cafeteria, asked for Natalie Jackson, drew a blank, descended the stairs, and at the front desk commanded Shig's attention.

"I'm going to hunt for my girl. Be back soon. Don't tell Lawrence I skipped out, okay? He's preoccupied and probably won't notice my absence."

"Goes without saying."

Norman glanced at the copy of *Junkie* on the shelf, then reached for it and stuffed it into his back pocket, where it fit snugly. On the street, he hailed a yellow cab and asked the driver to take him to Foster's on Sutter, and "step on it." He glanced both ways at the traffic behind and at the traffic ahead, leaned back, and whistled through his front teeth. He turned the pages of *Junkie* and was transfixed by the amazing story of addiction that was personal, cultural, national and galactic. When the cabbie arrived at the corner of Stockton and Powell, he asked him to keep the meter running and to wait for him along the curb. Inside Foster's, he scanned the room, hoping to pick out Natalie's face.

When he didn't see her, he climbed into the cab again.

"1141 Gough, a big old Victorian painted yellow. You can't miss it and step on it. I don't have all day."

22

They arrived in no time, which happened to be 11:43 a.m. Norman paid the cabby, a young woman, a brunette, who offered him her card and purred.

"Call me anytime, day or night. I'm your girl."

Norman blew her a kiss and then did a double take.

"Are you following me? Or is it coincidence?"

He reached into his wallet, withdrew the card that the cabby had given him with her name, Abbie Stein, and handed it to her. She laughed.

"I see so many passengers, I don't remember faces. Sorry, but I meant what I said. I'm your girl. Call me."

He watched her drive off, opened the gate, and walked inside the house at 1141 like he owned it. The windows were closed, and the room was warm from the rays of the sun. The drawings of penises and vaginas were gone. Sketches of Natalie were on the walls. There was a new work, too, a portrait of a young man.

Norman heard someone sobbing and found LaVigne sprawled on the floor, behind the sofa, tears streaming down his face. He wore a white T-shirt, white briefs, and white cotton socks. He looked like he'd been hit by a tsunami.

LaVigne tried to get up and greet Norman properly, but he couldn't. A poor lovesick puppy, Norman thought. LaVigne's arms and legs wouldn't work properly. His was stricken by some strange kind of paralysis. He's beside himself, Norman thought. The phrase fit Robert to a "T."

In the kitchen, Norman filled a glass with tap water and grabbed a dry dishtowel. He returned to the front room, squatted down on the wood floor, and offered LaVigne the towel, which he used to dry his eyes and wipe away his tears. Next, Norman handed him the glass of water. LaVigne sipped slowly, sobbed again, got hold of himself, and sipped again.

Norman glanced and then gaped at the portrait on the wall:

a naked young man with a beautiful face and a beautiful body. The young man sat on a divan which was covered by a soft white blanket. His uncircumcised penis was at the very center of the canvas. The youth looked directly at Norman; Norman looked directly at him and tried to see into his head.

LaVigne sighed deeply, sat up, and looked at the portrait on the wall.

"That's my Peter. Ginzy took one look at him and fell in love instantly. They made it right here, right under my own roof."

He sobbed like a child.

"Ginzy moved to an apartment on Montgomery. Peter is hiding somewhere, afraid I won't forgive him. Jack is in Marin, in Mill Valley to be precise, and is babysitting Locke McCorkle's kids, Sita and Tasha, while Locke and his wife are backpacking in the Sierras with a Berkeley student named Gary Snyder. He studies Japanese. Neal and Natalie have moved into a cheapo apartment on Franklin. It feels like musical chairs. I'm the faded flower on the wall."

Norman went on gaping at the portrait of Orlovsky.

"So the boy gang is kaput."

LaVigne stood up, took a deep breath, and sighed.

"Not yet, but it's headed that way. Ginzy will make sure that happens. It makes for a better story, you know, looking back at a Golden Age that never really was."

Norman nodded.

"Ginzy has one foot in paradise and the other in his own private inferno. Can't make up his mind where he'd rather be. Schizoid, like his mother, or so Jack says."

LaVigne blew his nose into his handkerchief and studied his own snot.

"I'd rather have Peter than the portrait of him. Now, we're both jinxed. I never should have asked him to sit for me. I can't bear to look into those sad, sad eyes, though they do make me appreciate dear, dear Oscar Wilde and his plight. I feel like we're soulmates."

LaVigne gazed at the portrait briefly and turned away quickly as though it might turn him to stone, or suddenly make him into a withered and whizened old man.

Norman winced.

"How so?"

"Life imitates art, not the other way around. One day, the portrait will haunt both of them."

Norman sat down on the sofa where he once sat next to Natalie and whispered in her ear, though he no longer remembered what he had said to her. And to think, Neal nearly had a fit. He can dish it out, but he can't take it. A jealous fellow.

Norman fluffed the pillow on the sofa and held it in his lap. "Natalie's monster mother swooped down—cane and all—at City Lights, and claimed she came to Frisco to find her daughter. She's certain Natalie is in 'deep trouble' as she put it. I told her nothing."

LaVigne coughed, cleared his throat, and murmured.

"She's right about trouble. Natalie's headed for it big time and Neal won't be around to save her."

LaVigne drew back the burlap curtains, opened the window nearest the front door, and felt the cool breeze on his cheeks, still moist from his hot tears. He turned and glanced from the painting on the wall to Norman's bright face.

"I'd better fess up and tell you that Mrs. Jackson showed up here, rang the bell, pounded on the front door, then walked to the back of the house and pounded on the rear door. She must have sensed a warm body was inside, but I didn't utter a word, just lay on the floor too embarrassed to let her see my tears. Uncanny the way mother and daughter look alike, even with the age difference."

Norman walked toward the painting and took note of the delicate brush strokes.

"How much?"

LaVigne shook his head.

"Not for sale. It's a reminder of what might have been."

"I understand."

Norman paused for a moment as though wondering how to phrase his next question.

"Do you happen to have Ginzy's address on Montgomery?"

LaVigne laughed. It was a sign, Norman told himself, that he was emerging from the trough of his own despair.

"Why in the world would I? But Natalie would know. She's at 1041 Franklin in the top floor apartment, above a sax player who rehearses all day and all night and keeps her awake."

Norman borrowed a pencil and a sheet of paper from the

desk where Kerouac typed and wrote down the Franklin Street address. He sauntered into the kitchen, helped himself to a glass of tap water, opened the door to the fridge, peered inside, broke off a hunk of Swiss cheese, chewed on it, and added another hunk to his shirt pocket.

In the big room he faced LaVigne once again.

"I wish we could chase Mrs. Jackson back to New Jersey right now, 'cause Natalie came here to get away from her."

He placed the empty glass on the table and peered up at the portrait of Peter.

"Awfully quiet in here. Too quiet. I don't like quiet, not this kind."

He exited the Victorian through the backdoor, walked to the intersection, paced back and forth on the sidewalk until the streetcar arrived, then climbed aboard and traveled back to North Beach. In the store, Norman brought Shig up to date on the latest episode in the "Natalie soap opera," as he called it.

"I don't like Mrs. Jackson hanging around. I'm going to pay her a visit at the Carleton, where she's staying, and see if I can encourage her to get out of Dodge, pronto. I don't mind telling her a white lie."

He walked much of the way to the Carleton, whistling to himself, window shopping, and stopping to say hello to pedestrians who came toward him.

"You're a new man, Nor-man, finally. You can feel it, can't you?"

Natalie's mother wasn't in her room at the Carleton. Norman tore a sheet of paper from his notebook and wrote, "I heard Natalie went to southern California. Think you're barking up the wrong tree in Frisco. A good friend." He folded it, scrawled "For Irene" and handed it to the desk clerk, who placed it in the cubbyhole labeled "Mrs. I. Jackson."

23

Norman looked at his watch, decided it was too late in the day to go back to 261 Columbus, and instead headed for his home in the Fillmore. He found the house empty, dishes piled high in the sink, and two dozen or so pies cooling on racks that sat on the kitchen counter. They smelled of peaches, nutmeg, cinnamon and vanilla.

He resisted the impulse to cut into one and taste it, but he ran his index finger along the inside of a large ceramic bowl, licked it clean, and then licked his lips clean with the tip of his tongue. He had become addicted to Zora's pies; a healthy addiction, he told himself.

Norman undressed in his bedroom upstairs, tossed his dirty clothes in the communal hamper, showered, shaved, and put on clean clothes, then lay down on his bed with his head on his pillow and took out his notebook.

With a pencil he wrote, "Summer '55, Frisco, haven't been homesick, too much going on, been around East Coasters from the get-go: Natalie, Ginzy, Kerouac, Ferlinghetti, and Gregory Corso, who did time in Dannemora. With the exception of Lawrence, they're all on the cusp of criminality, which might explain their creativity, though they're also 'angel-headed hipsters.'

"That's the phrase Ginzy uses to describe them. I call them 'fallen angels.' Kerouac says they're 'desolate angels.' I think they're the start of something new, and maybe also the beginning of the end. Kids will copy them. They'll overdose on drugs and punish themselves with sex, all the while thinking that sex is the only true thing around. Natalie will be their saint."

He opened the bottom drawer to the dresser, took out the gun he had hidden there, and where it had lived ever since he arrived at Zora's. He held it in his right hand, moved it to his left hand, and felt the heft of it. It was good to hold it. The gun reminded him of his days and nights during wartime Europe, with desperate fascists in retreat and the whole continent coming alive again after the rule of the dictators. He squinted his left eye and peered down the barrel. He spun the chamber, removed the bullets, put them back, wiped the gun clean with his handkerchief, and inserted it under his pillow.

He lay down and dozed off with his notebook in one hand and a pencil in the other. When he woke, he heard voices from downstairs that floated up to the second floor. One of them clearly belonged to Zora, the other voices, he didn't recognize.

He went downstairs to the kitchen, where he saw two thin young Black men with short black hair wearing black shoes, black trousers, and black shirts. They were in the process of packing peach pies into sturdy boxes that read in all capital letters: "ZORA'S HOME BAKED SOUTHERN STYLE PIES." The young men sealed the boxes and added them to two larger, sturdier boxes that filled up fast.

"Jerome and Henry meet Norman, our resident white spook. Norman, meet Henry and Jerome. They're very nice boys and they're backing me one hundred percent."

Norman smiled at Jerome and at Henry and helped them carry the cardboard boxes down the steps and to a van, which was double parked. It boasted the words, "Mecca Bakery," with an address and a phone number, too. Jerome climbed behind the steering wheel. Henry sat in the passenger seat, looked in the mirror behind the visor, and combed his hair. Norman watched them drive off, then returned to the kitchen, where a slice of pie was waiting for him on the counter.

Zora opened the fridge, removed a milk bottle, and poured a glass for Norman, who sat down at the table. Zora stood and watched him eat.

He sensed that she had something on her mind, something she wanted to tell him. He got to work on the slice of pie.

"What's up, Miss Zora?"

Zora sauntered across the floor, stopped in front of the refrigerator, opened the door, peered inside, and removed a bowl piled high with whipped cream. She placed it on the table and added a serving spoon.

"Help yourself to another slice and add a dollop of the cream I just whipped."

"Buttering me up?"

Norman served himself an extra-large piece of pie and piled whipped cream on top.

"By the expression on your face, you must have something mighty big to tell me."

He lifted his spoon, stared at the pie and the cream, and waited.

Zora sat down opposite Norman and looked him squarely in the eye.

"You always were good at knowin' when somethin' was comin'. I noticed that 'bout you when I first spotted you on the Greyhound and told myself 'my my, who is this poor little white boy all by his lonesome travelin' across the big U. S. of A.? I felt sorry for you. I don't no more. I see you can hold your own."

Norman put down his spoon, folded his hands across his lap and averted Zora's gaze, though she smiled at him and raised her voice an octave.

"This ain't gonna be easy, 'cause I've grown to like you bein' in the house, and I notice you and Ezra get along, but oh Lord, you're gonna have to pack up and move on, Mr. Norman, not instant like they say on the TV, but soon."

Norman felt a lump in his throat that made it hard for him to speak.

"It's because I'm white, isn't it?"

His comment sounded more like an assertion than a question. His voice dropped when he said, "isn't it?"

Zora took a deep breath and held the air in her lungs before exhaling slowly.

"Well, it is, and it isn't because of your whiteness. You see, we got family comin' from down South and they'll be needin' a place to stay until they find a home of their own and get settled."

Norman felt the muscles on his face tighten and his jaw grow suddenly heavier. He ground his teeth and nodded slowly.

"No, no, I understand completely. Family always comes first. I'll start to look for another place tomorrow. I can ask Neal and Natalie, though I know you don't feel good about them. I got to know them better on the road. They're unconventional, but they mean well... some of the time."

Zora cut herself a modest piece of pie and added a dollop of whipped cream, which she spread evenly on top. She took a small bite, chewed slowly and deliberately and swallowed carefully.

"I was wonderin' 'bout the Disney place and meanin' to ask, but the letter came from my sister in Money and I forgot."

Norman knew that Zora loved him, but that didn't mean he could stay under her roof. He calmed himself down and gathered his thoughts.

"I didn't see no Negro people in the crowds down there. I don't even know if they're allowed."

He paused a moment and licked his lips.

"Disney has Snow White and the dwarfs, Mickey and Minnie, and Donald and Daisy Duck, and there's that all-white family in the movie, *The Lady and the Tramp*, which just came out."

He added a rhetorical flourish.

"What does that tell you?"

Zora placed her fork across her plate.

"Guess, I won't be goin' to Disney anytime soon, unless my nephews and nieces beg me to take 'em and that's not likely. They'll want to see the ships in the harbor."

At the sink, Norman washed and dried his own dish.

"Thanks for the world-class pie, Zora."

He made for the hallway, but she called him back.

"There be one other thing, Norman. I've been tidyin' up your room, which I like to do so you have a clean place to lay your head, and I see you have a gun. I wouldn't want you to do somethin' crazy and hurt yourself."

Norman's face turned red. He knew that he had no business concealing a gun. The last thing Zora needed was trouble from a white boy.

"Yes, ma'am. I wouldn't want to be responsible for bringin' anything unwanted to your door."

Zora dried the large round bowl and returned it to the cupboard.

"I'd sleep better if I knew the gun wasn't loaded."

Here she was taking a motherly interest in him. That's how it felt.

"I'll remove the bullets from the gun right away."

Zora nodded.

"Whatever it is that's troubling you, it isn't going to go away by pointing a gun at it. Don't let it get the better if you."

Norman climbed the stairs, entered his room, located the gun, and removed the bullets, which he placed on the bottom shelf in the bathroom medicine cabinet. He concealed the gun in the hall linen closet.

He felt better already. On the edge of the bed with his head in his hands, he wondered where he might go after quitting Zora's. He knew he had time and ought not to panic, but he suddenly felt the return of his anxiety. Well, not his, he told himself, but something that floated freely and attached itself to things.

With Ezra's reefer, which he located in the basement, he rolled himself a "J," lit it, opened the window, and smoked. The reefer calmed his nerves and distracted him. He enjoyed the taste and the smell. He liked the sensation of being high.

Let's see, he said to himself, there's Locke's place in Marin, where Jack must be hitting the bottle hard. Ginzy's on Montgomery, where he's writing like a tiger. I don't know what rat hole Gregory inhabits, but I wouldn't want to bunk with him, nor with LaVigne, 'cause he's so down he would depress me.

That leaves Natalie and Neal on Franklin, an easy commute, but that would put me out of the frying pan and into the fire. Bad choice, but it's my only real option.

He went downstairs to look for Ezra and found him getting ready to fix a flat tire on a bicycle.

24

H ere's a moment, Norman told himself, to share Bob Kaufman's "Abomunist Manifesto." He dashed upstairs, located the poem in the big book with Blake's engravings, and floated downstairs on a cloud. Norman had read the poem so many times that he could recite it from memory, which he did now for Ezra, who nodded his head, snapped his fingers, and applauded at the end of the performance.

Ezra fired up a Mississippi-sized reefer, inhaled, exhaled, blew the smoke above his head and handed it to Norman who took time to smell the aroma.

"Heard about your relatives comin' from down South."

Ezra put the joint between his lips, puffed and puffed some more, and sucked up the smoke.

"Six of 'em in a beat up car, two adults, Aunt Mae and Uncle James, my two nephews, Hector and James, junior, and my two nieces, Hannah, who is tall and skinny, and Cadillac, who's real smart and just turned eighteen. They've been lyin' low. We been prayin' for them to make it out safe.

"Momma's idea is for Mae to bake with her in the kitchen and for James, senior, to make deliveries with Jerome and Henry. The nieces and nephews will go to school. Start all over."

He handed the remainder of the joint to Norman.

"All they ever did was chop cotton and go to church and pray and love one another. That and survive, which took some doin'. Jim Crow is awfully punishing. I do believe it's coming to an end. Hallelujah!"

Norman squeezed the fat tire that Ezra had patched and watched him turn the bicycle right side up.

"Don't panic, Norman. They got to get here from Money

---

first, which will take a week at least. They'll have to take back roads until they get out of Mississippi. You'd think all that shit was behind us."

Norman shoved his hands in his pockets. There didn't seem to be any other place for them.

Ezra lifted the bike, carried it to the street on his right shoulder, hopped on the seat and peddled madly.

Norman decided to take the rest of the day off. He figured he needed it, and Lawrence and Shig needed a break from him. City Lights from ten to nine could be claustrophobic. He called the cabby who had given him her card and asked her to pick him up at Zora's. When he was settled comfortably in the back seat, he peered into the mirror. Abbie Stein looked at his reflection.

"Where to, sugar?"

"Tom Mooney School on Golden Gate."

She chuckled.

"Hasn't been called that for ages. Nobody knew who the bleep Tom Mooney was, so they chucked him, and it became the California Labor School. Sorta sounds patriotic."

Norman chuckled.

"They teach you to labor at that school?"

He thought he was funny.

Abbie Stein laughed a belly laugh, and, since she was a big woman, the front seat shimmied.

"That school is for commies."

Norman held on to the leather strap and kept his balance.

"I'm not afraid of commies."

The cabby peered over her shoulder.

"Know what you mean, but it seems the whole country is shitting red bricks, if you'll pardon the expression."

Norman peered out the front window and watched the stores and the houses race by.

"I was scared plenty in the war, not of commies but fascists. Thought I might get blown to bits. This strange peacetime doesn't feel peaceful."

In the mirror, Norman watched the cabby's head bounce up and down.

"You're an angel, angel. I'll let you know if I run into any commies."

Norman entered the building, wandered about, read the notices on the bulletin board, and poked his nose into a classroom. Someone had written "Cooperation vs. Competition" on the blackboard with a piece of chalk. The teacher held forth about laboring women on the waterfront in the city. The students took notes.

In the main corridor, Norman gabbed with a couple of guys who were waiting for the bell to ring so they could enter their classroom and attend a lecture. They turned out to be ex-soldiers going to school on the GI bill, one married with a family, the other one a loner. A third fellow, who was red-nosed and portly, sold Norman a copy of the *People's World*, which he sat down and read cover to cover, poring over a story about a man named Vincent Hallinan. It came with a photo of Hallinan and Paul Robeson, who was identified as "A Black baritone and actor."

Norman walked up and down the hallway. A young woman who sat at a table with a stack of leaflets asked him to sign a petition.

"We're against the Loyalty Oath Act. Please add your name, comrade."

Norman shook his head.

"No thanks."

But in the school office, he signed up for a class called "The ABC's of Marxism." He examined the syllabus and the reading list, which included *The Communist Manifesto* by "K. Marx" and a quotation that read, "A specter is haunting Europe."

In the bookstore, he bought Marx's pamphlet and read the first few lines.

"Yeah, I'd say so. Europe is fuckin' haunted and so is the U.S.A."

On the first day of class, a Saturday, he sat patiently through the lecture, which was about something the instructor called "dialectical materialism." Norman decided that he was a dialectician, but probably not a materialist. After all, he reminded himself, he believed in ghosts.

At the end of sixty minutes, the students in the class on Marxism took a quiz and graded themselves using the answers the instructor provided on the blackboard. Norman earned a perfect score and decided he didn't want to take another class or another quiz. Still, he walked to the table with the leaflets, said "Hello" to the woman he'd met previously, took pen in hand, and signed the petition.

"Get rid of this loyalty act crap. I'd be suspicious of anyone who thought he had to swear loyalty to this country of ours."

25

Fog inched across the bridge and drifted into the Fillmore. Tourists swept into town, rode the cable cars, tried the famed sourdough bread, wandered across Golden Gate Park, hunted for the notorious, elusive bearded bohemians of North Beach, and escaped with their wallets lighter, their stomachs larger, and their heads filled with picture postcard images of the bridge, the bay, and the pelicans. San Francisco could be presented, Norman recognized, as an advertisement for itself.

Zora's house settled into a routine, suitable for summer, though it didn't feel like summer, and certainly not like any summer that Norman had ever known on Long Island. Especially not when he lived with his grandparents in the big house in Oyster Bay. The walls of the dining room boasted portraits of his de Haan ancestors, who gazed down at him while he stared up at them and tried to read their minds.

They would have been surprised to see their descendant thriving on pie, and selling a whole pie a week for $1 to his buddy, Jack Kerouac, who enjoyed Zora's pies so much that he had to meet her.

Bob Kaufman, who had arrived in San Francisco on July 1, heard about the pie maker from Mississippi after talking with Norman at City Lights, where they reconnoitered. Bob accompanied Jack to Zora's where he admired her drum. When she invited Kaufman to play it, he took a deep breath and nodded with an expression of reverence.

"It's amazing our ancestors brought their music all the way from Africa across the Atlantic to the plantations where the white masters bred them like animals."

Kaufman played the drum quietly. Jack enjoyed his impromptu performance, though he knew he ought not to try to beat out a rhythm of his own.

"I know the bongos, but that's about all. My musical skills mostly have to do with playing records on a turntable, and singing along with Frank Sinatra."

In the kitchen, Bob sniffed the air, cut himself a piece of pie, sat down and ate it little by little.

"Your reputation is well deserved, Zora. You could be the pie queen of Africa and America."

Jack studied Zora's sweet, sweet face.

"You remind me of someone."

Zora blushed.

"Don't jive me, mister Jack." She meant to be polite, even while she challenged him.

"No really ma'am. I was in Denver in the colored part of town and decided I wanted to move there and live there like the colored folk."

Kaufman found Jack's comment funny, as in strange rather than ha ha ha.

"If you lived side-by-side with me and traveled around with me from South to North, East to West, you'd see what racism is really like."

Zora stared at Kerouac as though she didn't know what to make of him. He was handsome and polite and sad in a bluesy kind of way. He also seemed to inhabit a fantasy world of his own making. Zora wondered about his grasp of reality.

Did Mr. Jack really want to live among the colored folk of Denver? Did he believe in miracles, as he claimed, and did he really think that there would be a resurrection for everyone, as he insisted?

Jack licked his fork clean.

"I believe in Jesus and in the Buddha. I believe they both will show us the way."

Zora rested her head in her hands and went on staring at Kerouac.

"I can tell you're not dumb, Mr. Jack, but you don't really want to live like us colored folks."

"Zora, ma'am, I beg to differ. Fact is, I'm a dumb Canuck. Proof is, I write books no one will publish and still I keep writing. What does that tell you? I'm a dumb Canuck!"

An hour or so after they first sat down to eat and talk, Bob, Jack and Zora were still at the table in the kitchen. Bob felt at home and helped himself to more pie. Jack and Zora kept trying to connect across a divide that seemed continental. Jack clenched and unclenched his right hand as though pumping himself up. He leaned toward Zora.

"Ma'am there ain't no Canuck Lester Young and no Canuck Billie Holliday. Ain't no Canuck juke joints, not anywhere from Quebec City to Lowell, Mass., where I was born and raised. Didn't know no English 'til I went to public school where I was teased and bullied, and so I got out of Lowell as fast as I could, went to the big city, but I still say ain't!"

He laughed and said something that Norman recognized as *joual*, the language of the French Canadian working classes, but he didn't understand what Jack was trying to communicate. Nor did Zora and Bob. Jack quickly switched back to English.

"Canucks think they'll get rich by praying to the Lord and workin' in a factory, makin' shoes, like my mother and they…"

He would have gone on talking but Zora interrupted him.

"Ain't nothin' wrong with workin' hard and prayin' hard and countin' your blessings. I do every day."

Jack snorted.

"Yeah, but white folks mainly go through the motions. They don't know nothing about the blues. So, I hope you forgive me, ma'am when I say I wish I was a Negro. I don't mean no disrespect."

Zora nodded her head and offered Jack another piece of pie, which he accepted ceremoniously, ate slowly and deliberately.

"Your pie is holy, and you are holy, and Norman de Haan and Bob Kaufman, the Black Rimbaud, are also holy."

Bob took the plates and the silverware to the sink, washed them and dried them and sat down facing Zora.

"He's trying, ma'am. We ought to give him credit for that."

Bob helped Jack to his feet, walked him toward the front door, stopped at the houtar and touched it with his finger tips.

"This drum be holy." He paused and added, "You be safe and sound, ma'am, and take care of my white friend, Norman de Haan."

Long after Jack and Bob left Zora's, Norman sat at the kitchen table with his notebook open and a pen in hand.

He wrote "Jack is about the only one in the gang who seems

genuinely curious about me, but he's curious about everything and everyone. Bob is also curious, but he's not exactly in the gang, at least not yet. When the guys get to know him they'll accept him. He's as bohemian as they are, and he's what Jack calls a fellaheen, a man of the Earth."

Norman stretched his neck, rolled his shoulders and went on writing: "Jack finds it amusing that he and I are both fascinated by Oswald Spengler's *The Decline of the West*, which we've adopted as our gospel, or at least part of it. Had a conversation with him the other day about how fast or how slow the decline might be and what, if anything, might replace it, other than chaos and anarchy. Meanwhile, we're living off Zora's pies and with Ezra's reefer."

Norman turned the page, shook the kinks from his hand, and went on filling the white space with his own words. "The other day, I went to a bar for a few beers with Jack. He got drunk and lost it. Bartender asked us to leave, which we did. Jack placed two empty beer bottles in his jacket. On the sidewalk he smashed both of them against a brick wall. He laughed and hugged me. Then he went into the middle of the street and gazed up at the sky. At the top of his lungs he bellowed. 'Please, Lord, protect Norman and me and Bob from the nightmare that Stalin and his henchmen have created in motherfuckin' Russia. Save old Dostoevsky from rotting in his grave, and the same for old Walt Whitman and Herman Melville, too. God bless their American souls.'

26

On a windy Friday night, Jack hosted a stud poker game at the house of his pal, Big Al Hinkle, who worked hard and drank hard and looked like he might live to a hundred, if he stayed away from booze and the law. The players around the card table were all white guys. Bob counted himself out, though he was invited.

Al's wife, Helen, made popcorn with real butter and lots of sea salt. Natalie Jackson, who wore Neal's overalls and his Southern Pacific Railroad cap, paraded around the room, looked at the cards everyone held in their hands, and smirked. She stopped in front of Neal, who wore one of Natalie's skirts, along with a bra and blouse.

They must think they're breaking some kind of boundary, Norman thought. Boys will have to do more than wear girls' clothes and girls would have to do more than wear boys' clothes to raise a ruckus in this circle of card sharks.

Norman noticed Natalie's bandaged wrist, though neither he nor anyone else said a word about it, not before or during the poker game that took place in a dimly-lit room at the back of a bungalow, on a side street with no overhead lights. Bird played on the turntable, a jug of red wine passed from hand to hand and mouth to mouth, and the smoke of twenty-five cent cigars hovered under the low ceiling. Norman lost big, won big, and lost big again. He couldn't stop himself from upping the ante.

During a pause to pee, Jack grabbed Norman's hand and held it.

"When you bite your lower lip, I know you're bluffing. It's called a tell."

"Thank you. I wasn't aware. I'll be more conscious."

Neal folded more often than not, and talked shit about reincarnation, the Church of Scientology, and L. Ron Hubbard, whom he revered as a saint. He talked the way he drove—non-stop—though Big Al Hinkle, told him, "Shut the fuck up, pal." Neal ignored him, though he shifted his subject matter from Scientology to the pool halls of his boyhood and growing up on the skids in Denver.

"We lost the West and the West lost us. White folk like us Cassadys was fucked over every time. As a boy I didn't have even a Chinaman's chance."

Jack smirked. Al sipped beer that had gone flat. Norman guzzled vodka and orange juice and gazed at Natalie, who ignored him. Neal kicked his chair back, stood up, and accidentally banged his forehead on the lamp shade.

"Ah, fuck. Count me out, fellas."

He grabbed Natalie, lifted her in the air, carried her into the bedroom, and kicked the door shut. Norman heard howling, squealing, and squawking. He gazed around the room; nobody else seemed to be listening. Maybe it was best to tune out. After all, what was there to say about Natalie and Neal fucking? Nothing. Fucking was what they did. Fucking was to Neal what writing was to Jack. It was his calling, his mission and his religion.

At the end of the evening, Jack sat down on the threadbare sofa, sipped red wine, and made himself comfortable. When Norman joined him they fell to talking among themselves. Jack looked pained.

"I took Natalie to the hospital and explained to the nurse that she accidentally cut herself slicing a tomato."

Jack glanced at his own wrists.

"I don't know if she meant to take her life or if she was crying out for help."

Norman puffed on his cigar.

"I think she's been crying out all summer."

"No one wants to see what's really happening."

"We're all in denial.'"

Days went by and nobody did anything. Norman had to fend off his own ghosts, Jack had to look after his own mother, who had moved across country and settled in Berkeley. Ginzy had to stop himself from falling in love with every kid he met in Washington Square Park.

The morning after the all-night poker game, Norman woke with a hangover, wrapped one of Ezra's army blankets around his shoulders, stumbled downstairs, and helped himself to coffee and a slice of pie. He swallowed a couple of aspirins and read the headlines in *The Defender*, dated August 6, 1955.

A breeze blew through the open window. The fridge hummed and the stairs creaked.

"Wait a minute! Didn't something happen on this day?"

He rolled up the paper and hurled it against the wall.

"I'm fucking fucked. We're all fucked. I swore I'd never forget."

He heard Zora's footsteps on the stairs and saw her standing in the doorway.

"Sorry, ma'am. I forget myself sometimes."

He lowered his shoulders, gazed at the worn floorboards, then up at Zora, and looked contrite.

"I get down thinking about Doomsday."

Zora dabbed her right eye with her handkerchief. Norman thought she had shed a tear, but she smiled and seemed happy.

"Something caught in there. Probably a cinder from the fire next door. Mrs. Cornbrake burns stuff she shouldn't burn." After a few moments, Zora removed the handkerchief from her eye and blinked a couple of times to make sure she could see properly. She sat down and gazed at Norman.

"I was wondering just now how old you are. You never did tell me, and I never did ask."

Norman wore an expression of indifference.

"It doesn't matter."

"It matters to me."

He had to think before he answered.

"Just turned thirty-three. Feeling sorry for myself and sorry for the whole world. I'm over the hill and have nothing to show, nothing to brag to my mother about. Ya know, Zora, on my last birthday, I took my mother to Peter Luger's, where she complained the whole time about the steak, the wine, her own widowhood, and *The $64,000 Question*, which she watches on TV like it's her fix."

Zora dampened a rag at the faucet and wiped the crumbs from the table.

"My mother, bless her soul, was born on a plantation..."

She paused and waited to see if and how Norman would respond.

Jonah Raskin

When he didn't, she asked, "Does that mean anything to you?"

Norman rubbed the back of his neck.

"Is it supposed to mean something?"

Zora glared at him.

"Sometimes you can be as dumb as your friends. Maybe even dumber."

Norman laughed.

"Well, that's because they're smarter than me."

Zora laughed with him, not at him.

Norman looked Zora in the eye.

"You're better off than your mother. That's what it means to me. We don't have slavery of the kind they had before the Civil War, but when I look at the South and see Jim Crow, it sometimes doesn't seem much better. But I read *The Defender* and I know young people are unwilling to live with injustice anymore. It's inspiring to a descendant of Calvinists like me."

Zora nodded her head.

"You're not so dumb after all."

She paused and announced that she was going to make dinner on Friday night for Ezra's birthday.

"You can invite one of your friends. Not all of them. Just one. I don't want the gang overrunning my house and then have Mrs. Cornbrake complaining like she did last time you were here with Miss Natalie."

"Thank you, ma'am." He paused a moment and gazed out the window at the empty lot next door where kids had built a fort and were playing cops and robbers.

"Right now, it feels like something's ticking in my head, something about to be born, something new."

"Oh dear, your poor, poor head. Maybe you should lie down and rest."

No such luck. He had big thoughts to think, big words to write, and at the front counter, paperback books to sell.

139

27

He unlocked the front door to City Lights.

"Hello, anyone here?"

No one responded to his cry, but he had the feeling that he wasn't the only sentient being inside Lawrence's niche. No, indeed. He found the cats, Emily and Phillis, asleep in the warmest and most comfortable corner of the store. Norman continued to wander about until he sensed he was getting closer to the hot spot. He stopped and peered around.

"Hello? Anyone here?"

No response.

He rounded a corner and stumbled on Jack who was sitting on the floor and meditating. He sat facing the wall, hands folded across his lap and his legs folded in front of him, with a bottle of red wine by his side. Was that Zen he wondered? Yeah, it was Kerouac Zen!

"Oops, sorry."

Jack didn't budge, didn't look up, didn't speak.

Norman backed away slowly and tiptoed to the cash register. After an hour or so, he heard footsteps. Jack stood in front of him in a red–and–black checked wool shirt, his hair neatly combed, and his eyes brighter than he had ever seen them.

"You gotta do *zazen* with me. Like me, you need a regular brain dump."

Norman rocked back and forth on the balls of his feet.

"I meditated once at a retreat in the Catskills. We weren't supposed to talk for forty-eight hours and I nearly went crazy, but yeah I'll sit with you, Jack."

After his shift at City Lights selling books, collecting money, and giving change, he called Foster's from Lawrence's office upstairs, asked to speak with Natalie Jackson, and was told "she ain't here, daddio." He called Robert LaVigne's and talked to Ginzy, who gave him Natalie's phone number.

He borrowed a pen and a scrap of paper, wrote it down, dialed, and listened while he gazed at the foot traffic on Columbus Avenue. Ghosts appeared out of the fog, only to disappear again. A ghostly tugboat sounded in the distance. The ghostly city haunted him.

Natalie answered the phone on the second ring. She must have been sitting and waiting for his call, he told himself. Chitchat wasn't Norman's thing. Off the bat, he invited her to dinner at "my landlady's house," as he put it, and offered to pay for a cab to pick her up and bring her back to her own place.

After he hung up, he called Ezra, who was at home studying, and asked him to please pick up Natalie, bring her to Zora's, and drive her home after dark. Ezra couldn't say no. He wanted to return the favor Norman had done for him on the way to hear jazz. Besides, he'd completed all the assigned reading for class and knew he'd ace the exam.

On Friday night, Norman paced back and forth in the dining room until he heard the front door open and saw Ezra in the hallway with Natalie a few steps behind him. Norman introduced her to Zora who wore an apron and a red cap on her head. Zora reminded Norman that they had already met a month or so earlier on the night they had gone to the Blackhawk to hear Lester.

"Of course, of course. That was the night I found out that Natalie was in Frisco. It seems so long ago."

Zora excused herself and went to the kitchen, while Ezra aimed for the liquor cabinet, unlocked it, and sorted through the bottles of booze until he found the bourbon he wanted. He poured three drinks on the rocks and departed.

"Gotta help with supper."

Norman heard mother and son fussing in the kitchen and heard the radio that lived in the front room, which served as a parlor for ordinary guests. Family members gathered in the back parlor, where it was quieter, more private, and the furniture nicer. He gazed about and realized that he had grown to love the house itself, which felt like his own skin.

He looked Natalie in the eye and admired the necklace he had given her when they were a couple. No, take that back. They were never actually a couple; they were dating. She looked especially attractive, he thought, in a long-sleeved green dress that covered her arms all the way down to her wrists. The dress looked like it came from I. Magnin, though Natalie couldn't have purchased it, not on her salary.

Perhaps, Norman thought, she'd stolen it. He had become increasingly suspicious about everything she did and said, but he wanted to make her feel good about herself.

"You look lovely, as always. Green becomes you."

Natalie faced the wall, so Norman couldn't see her expression.

"My life is a mess, though I thank you kindly for inviting me to dinner. I know you didn't have to do it."

"I didn't have to, but I wanted to."

Natalie swirled the ice cubes in the cocktail Ezra had mixed. "Al Hinkle wants me to see a head shrinker 'cause I did something I shouldn't have done. I wasn't in my right mind."

Norman peered into her eyes.

"What do you want to do?"

Natalie rolled up the right sleeve on her green dress and removed the gauze pad.

"It looks worse than it is."

Norman studied the jagged edge of the scar, winced and turned away.

After a few moments, he raised his glass and tried to be funny.

"Here's looking at you, kid."

Natalie laughed.

"We saw *Casablanca* together on our next-to-last date."

Ezra entered the room with a tablecloth and arranged it on the table. Norman helped with the forks, knives, and spoons. Natalie folded her arms and watched. Zora came through the swinging door with a platter of blackened catfish, then went back and came out again with a wicker basket that contained hunks of cornbread and a steaming bowl of collard greens.

She sat at the head of the table and Ezra sat at the foot. Zora served Natalie first, Norman second, Ezra third, and herself last.

Natalie stared at the food on her plate, looked up, and locked eyes with Zora.

"It's beautiful food, but I know I won't be able to finish it." Zora bowed her head and extended her hands, one to Natalie and the other to Norman.

"Things is bad, it's true, Lord, but how much worse it would be if we weren't here together sharing this food."

Zora opened her eyes and jumped up.

"'scuse me."

She dashed into the kitchen and came back with bright red linen napkins, which she distributed to her son, to Norman and to Natalie.

"Sorry. I forgot my manners." She laughed.

Norman chewed slowly. Natalie picked at the catfish on her plate and nibbled on the cornbread which she slathered with butter and honey. Ezra worked his way systematically from the outer rim to the interior of his plate, saving the catfish for last.

Norman watched Natalie play with her food and lost his own appetite. At times, he told himself, he didn't know where he ended and she began. That was bad, very bad, he told himself. Boundaries! Mind your boundaries, de Haan.

Ezra helped himself to seconds and wasn't bashful about it.

"I got into a fight on campus today. A student called me a name and I couldn't back away."

Norman stared at the greens and at the corn bread.

"There's a lot of name calling in the city. It feels like we're in a pressure cooker."

Natalie placed her knife and fork across her plate.

"Like the frog in the water on the stove that doesn't know it's in danger until it's too late."

Zora swallowed her food before she spoke.

"We're fortunate. In San Francisco, we've got an island of respect and another of dignity."

Norman liked what she had to say.

"Free zones."

Natalie opened her mouth as though to speak, and then closed it slowly, without uttering a word.

"What is it child?"

Zora asked so tenderly that Natalie smiled and tried again.

"I don't know how all of you do it. I feel like I'm under a dark cloud that's never gonna pass."

"It will if you let it. Nothing is forever, not even eternity. Let it go, child."

Natalie let it go long enough for warm peach cobbler and homemade strawberry ice cream.

"See?" Norman sounded triumphant. "It's not the end and you're not alone."

In the back parlor, Ezra poured cognac for himself, Natalie, and Norman, who offered to wash dishes.

Zora ordered him to sit, so he sat and tried to cheer up Natalie with lines from Bogart and Bacall movies, including "Just whistle," from *To Have and to Have Not*. They seemed to make her even more listless, as though all of her reserves had been depleted just trying to be civil. Norman felt as though he'd reached the end of his own tether, but he tossed out one more line.

"You're a stinker."

Natalie moved her index finger around the rim of her glass until it made a musical sound, leaned her head to the side, and listened. Ezra went into the front room, changed the dial on the radio, and opened the windows that faced the street and brought a cool breeze to Norman's face. Natalie shivered. Norman took off his jacket and wrapped it around her shoulders. Every little thing seemed to set her off.

"I was just a girl when you hit on me."

He wasn't ready for that one.

"How old were you?" He sounded like he really didn't know.

"Don't you remember?"

She looked hurt.

"I was wondering if you remembered?"

"How old do you think I am now?"

He smiled.

"I'm not sure, but you must have been seventeen when we first met."

"I was too young."

Norman leaned back and tried to relax the muscles on his face, which had tensed up. They wouldn't move.

"The way I remember it, you hit on me."

"Whatever."

She waved her right hand dismissively.

What was the real story, he wondered? Maybe they both hit on one another. He learned forward and reached for Natalie's left hand.

"What about me moving into your place on Franklin? Zora's expecting family and I have to leave."

Natalie offered a sly smile that Norman read as a come-on, but he wasn't sure.

"You wouldn't have much privacy and I know how much your privacy means to you."

"What about Neal?"

"What about him?"

"Would you ask him if he's cool with me crashing at your pad?"

"Ask him yourself, Friday at Bay Meadows. We're making a day of it and would enjoy your company. Neal likes you."

"I will. I promise."

He had two days to kill before the horses ran at Bay Meadows. The first day crawled; the second day seemed to take longer than all the other days in the whole month. Norman read and read, and wrote and wrote in his notebook. He finished *The Ginger Man*, read back issues of *The Defender* which piled up in Zora's basement, and discovered that he loved Langston Hughes' stories about a fellow named "Simple," who wasn't as simple as he seemed to be. He wished he could write like Langston and tried to, but he learned it was harder than it looked. At Foster's, he shared his hopes and his dreams with Natalie.

"I have an idea for a big book."

She shared her giant portion of salted French fries, smeared with mayonnaise.

"And I have an idea for a big performance, a kind of one woman show that's been building inside and that's ready to explode or I'll implode."

"You wanna tell me?"

"I'd rather surprise everyone, but I was wondering what you'd think if I did a striptease."

"You mean like at Zora's."

Natalie clapped her hands together.

"Yeah, only bigger and better."

28

I rene Jackson showed up again at City Lights and told Shig and Norman that she had delayed her return to New Jersey, and would go on looking for her daughter. To that end, she introduced herself to Ginzy, who was in the habit of hanging around the store and reading aloud from Walt Whitman's "Song of Myself," sometimes in front of the cash register and sometimes outside on the sidewalk, facing the traffic on Columbus.

Lawrence didn't like to discourage anyone from reading poetry, but Ginzy got on his nerves.

"Frankly, he's a bit much, but I suppose we have to let him do his thing. He's the future super star."

It helped that Ginzy didn't ask pedestrians for money. That was beneath him. He wasn't a panhandler or a beggar, and he didn't really care about money if he had a roof over his head, food to eat, friends, lovers, and poetry. He had consecrated himself to the written and the spoken word, though that meant nothing to Mrs. Irene Jackson, who buttonholed him at the front desk.

"I'm trying to find my daughter, Natalie. Do you know where she is?" She sounded more desperate now than she had sounded the first time she came to City Lights.

Norman stood behind Irene, wiggled his nose and ears, and managed to communicate to Ginzy that he wasn't to give out any information about Natalie. Ginzy shook his head.

"Sorry. No go."

He slipped away. Norman didn't see him again that day. In the store, Irene selected and bought a copy of Virginia Woolf's *A Room of One's Own*, and paid by check at the cash register.

"You haven't seen the last of me."

To Norman, her words sounded like a threat.

He and Shig watched Mrs. Jackson leave the store, saunter

downhill, and amble toward Montgomery with the help of her cane.

Lawrence climbed the steps to his office, removed his bowler, hung it from a hook on the wall, sat at his desk, and worked on a poem with the words "Coney Island" in the title. Norman brought him a container of hot coffee from Vesuvio, peered over his shoulder, and watched him cross out words and add new ones in the margins of his manuscript.

That night, after he turned out the lights and locked up the store, Norman heard Lawrence perform his own poetry on stage at the Cellar, along with a wild drummer, a sweet young saxophone player, and a tall, lanky fellow on stand-up bass who played like an angel. Kenneth Rexroth, the other headliner at the Cellar, looked like he'd slept in his clothes, but he came alive and jazzed the crowd with help from a slide guitarist.

During the intermission, Norman introduced himself to Rexroth who told him about the salon that met in his own house, where "everyone talks about everything."

Rexroth ran his index finger across his mustache.

"I heard from Lawrence that you're an expert on the culture that's exploding in North Beach."

Rexroth looked at the crowd that gathered around him and took in his every word.

"I'd be honored if you'd join me on my radio show, 'Books,' broadcast on KPFA. There's no payment, but we have tons of listeners. You'd be instantly famous. I promise you."

Norman smirked his characteristic smirk.

"I wouldn't call myself an expert, and I don't know what books I'd talk about. None of the guys have published anything big that has to do with North Beach or San Francisco, and neither has their buddy William Burroughs, who lives in Tangier. He has written an amazing book about drugs and drug addiction, titled *Junkie*, that he published under the pseudonym William Lee. Burroughs is the real thing. I promise you, he'll be famous.

"Of course, Jack has a story titled "Jazz of the Beat Generation," that's half memoir, half fiction, that will be out any day now in *New World Writing*, published under the pseudonym Jean-Louis, as a way to claim his French heritage. Jack swears that Ginzy is cooking up an epic about our whole hysterical generation, but I'll believe it when I hear it or read it. He's suffering from writer's block right now."

Rexroth chuckled.

"You sound like you're doing PR, man."

On the radio the following morning, Rexroth asked Norman to talk about himself, which made him feel uncomfortable. But he rose to the occasion. He cleared his throat and fussed with the microphone.

"You can find me most days at City Lights Bookstore which is owned by Lawrence Ferlinghetti, a publisher and a poet who studied in Paris, and who sees himself as a kind of outlaw or outlier who traces his lineage back to François Villon. He has this Franco-American thing going, which makes him appealing to Kerouac."

He paused for a few moments and adjusted his headphones.

"I can tell you from my own experience as an ex-New Yorker and as a soldier in the last war, there's something in the air here that you won't find anywhere else in the country. It's definitely new and it definitely captures the soul of our generation, whether we're street hustlers, financial district ad men, jazz aficionados at the Blackhawk, or students at the California Labor School. All of us have come of age with the bomb, and the concentration camps, and we have all turned to a kind of spirituality that's not part of any organized religion."

Rexroth leaned into the mic.

"These fellows, Ginzy and Kerouac, they're your friends?"

"Yes, but I think they come across better on the page than they do in person. They're artists and, as you probably know, artists can be overly fixated on themselves."

"Do they have a literary future?"

"If anyone in my generation does, it's Ginsberg, Kerouac, and Gregory Corso."

At the end of the hour, Norman fielded questions from listeners, but he was pooped and didn't enjoy the back and forth.

Rexroth agreed to Norman's request to play a track of Charlie Parker on alto sax. They both sat back and listened. Rexroth played the role of grand old man.

"The kids in Prague and in Warsaw listen to the same music as you kids do here in Frisco."

When the Charlie Parker tune ended, Norman spoke into the microphone.

"My pals are inspired by Negro jazz musicians. They want to be spontaneous, though they were taught to revise and revise and revise. It's a habit that's hard to kick."

Rexroth thanked Norman profusely, and gave him an autographed copy of a book of his poems that was inspired by the ancient Chinese poet, Du Fu, who lived during the Tang dynasty.

Norman was genuinely thrilled.

"Thanks. I believe in you, Kenneth and I believe in what you're doing here at the station, and with your translations from Asian languages, and with your salon, too."

At the bookstore, later that afternoon, Ginzy showed up wearing a tweed suit, a white shirt, and a tie.

"On Kenneth's show, you could have mentioned Louis-Ferdinand Celine and you could have provided the listeners with my bio and Jack's, too."

"Next time I will."

"Get Kenneth to invite me on his show."

Ginzy reached into his jacket, removed a single sheet of paper, unfolded it, and on the spur of the moment read "A Love Poem," as he called it, inspired by "the Roman poet Catullus."

He folded the paper and returned it to his pocket.

"Fact is, I like cock and I can see that you, Norman, don't judge me for that, but if I walked out on Columbus Avenue and said the same thing, I'd be crucified."

"I suggest you don't share your views about cock when you're in public."

"Then I wouldn't be true to myself."

Ginzy left the store in a huff. A few minutes later, Corso arrived wearing boots, a hat and scarf, a vest, and a long winter coat, though it was a warm August day.

"Hey guys, long time no see. I'm gonna browse. Okay?"

Norman turned to Shig, who was shelving new arrivals.

"You see the way he uses the same old tricks, wears layers of clothing so he can hide shit?"

At closing time, Norman counted the money in the cash register, placed it in an envelope, and added it to the safe. He turned off the lights, except for the bulb attached to a string that dangled above the front counter. Corso lurked in the shadows, ready to exit the front door. Shig blocked his way.

"Let's see what you got, Corso."

Norman came at Corso from behind and patted him down. He removed a copy of Nelson Algren's *The Man with the Golden Arm* and *Hiroshima* by John Hersey. Shig started at Corso's ankles and moved up to his hat, where he found a paperback copy of De Quincy's *Confessions of an English Opium-Eater*.

Shig chuckled.

"At least you have good taste."

Norman snarled.

"Next time the cops."

Corso fumed.

"You wouldn't fuckin' dare."

Norman puffed out his chest.

"Get the fuck outta here, asshole!"

Where did that come from? he asked himself. He was shaking. Corso pushed his buttons in a way that no one else did.

Shig tapped him on the shoulder.

"Let it go, man."

Norman went to Vesuvio, ordered a boilermaker, knocked back the whiskey, chugged an Anchor Steam, and went home feeling lousy.

Big deal, he told himself. Everybody steals something sometime. No reason to get uptight about it.

Norman knew that he had to examine his antipathy for Corso in the clear light of day. There was no better way to explore his feelings and sort them out than by reading Corso's poetry. After all, he didn't like Ezra Pound, he reminded himself. How could he? With his comrades, Norman had made his way up the Italian Peninsula inch by inch, trading bullets with bastards who swore alliegance to Benito Mussolini or who wore swastikas on their uniforms.

Pound, Dr. Ezra Pound as he called himself, was broadcasting his vile opinions on Italian radio, praising Hitler, lauding the white race and spewing filth about Jews. Still, Norman had to admit that he liked some of Pound's poetry, especially "In a Station of the Metro," which he knew by heart, along with parts of his cantos. That night, with a clear head, he dipped into Corso's poems, and found that he was won over by "The Vestal Lady on Brattle," which he read in a mimeographed edition and that reminded him that he didn't have to love a poet to be moved by his or her poetry. On the other hand, he knew that he would have fallen in love with Edna St. Vincent Millay, during her Greenwich Village days, though he couldn't bring himself to read very far at all in her work. Sure, she'd won the Pulitzer. BFD. Norman was sure that Jack and Ginzy never would and not Lawrence either.

That same night, he abstained from a piece of pie, climbed into bed earlier than usual, fluffed his pillows, and read Langston Hughes' column in the most recent edition of *The Defender*, which had just arrived in the mail. He heard the phone ring downstairs, heard Zora say, "Colvin residence, Zora speaking… I'll see if he's…." followed by a holler: "Norman, it's your woman friend."

Norman bounded out of bed, threw on his robe, flew down the stairs, and grabbed the phone.

"Yo, it's me." He was out of breath.

Natalie whispered.

"Neal would like you to go with us. But no pressure. Stand on the southwest corner of Army and Folsom at nine a.m. Look for a '47 Ford."

Anticipation hit him right between the eyes and moved about his whole body. He slept fitfully, with several trips to the bathroom down the hall, which felt like a distant outpost. When dawn arrived, he leapt out of bed, dressed, wrote Zora a note, and departed for yet another expedition with the mad, mad driver and the New Jersey redhead who rode shotgun.

It was rush hour, and Norman eyed the passing cars on Army. He was unprepared for the funky vehicle with a defective tailpipe that pulled to the curb.

The rear door opened, and Neal shouted.

"Get in."

The Ford made a U-turn and headed for the Freeway. The upholstery in the backseat had come undone and the carpet was threadbare.

"Nice vehicle." Norman's sarcasm was unmistakable.

"It'll get us where we need to go."

Neal honked the horn, passed a car on the right that was moving slowly, and shot ahead.

In Los Gatos, he pulled off the highway and took side streets until he reached Magnolia Court, hung a left, parked in the shade of an oak, and turned his head towards Norman.

"You're coming with me," and to Natalie, "Stay." He took the keys from the ignition and stuffed them in his back pocket.

He and Norman crossed the street, cut across a patch of recently mowed lawn, went around the side of a stucco house and entered through the rear door.

"I'm going to introduce you to the wife and you're going to keep her occupied while I attend to business."

The wife stood at the sink washing dishes. Her feet were bare, a cigarette dangled from her lower lip and she wore a rag around the hair on the top of her head. She might have been anyone of a dozen housewives in the neighborhood, Norman told himself, but she happened to be married to Mr. Neal Cassady, and no doubt her life could be entertaining, to say the least.

"Hello, baby doll."

Neal put his arms around the wife, drew her to him and kissed her on the lips.

She pushed Neal away and glared at Norman.

"Who's he?"

"Friend of mine. You have similar interests. He's a theater nut. Excuse me… while I use the boy's room."

He darted down the hall and disappeared in the darkness. The wife wiped her hands on her apron.

"You wanna cuppa?"

"Sure."

"He'll be forever in the bathroom. He's anal retentive."

She put up a kettle to boil, placed a jar of Nescafe on the table, and set out two cups, along with teaspoons and saucers.

"Help yourself to as much as you want."

So this was where the King of the Road endured domestic life!

The wife leaned against the refrigerator door and puffed on her cigarette.

"What do you think of method acting?"

The kettle whistled. The wife filled Norman's cup with boiling water and filled her own.

"Milk?"

"I'll take it straight."

He stirred the coffee with a teaspoon and watched the steam rise.

"I think method acting is great. Brando would be nowhere without it."

"But don't you think it's artificial?"

Norman peered into the dark hall.

"He's taking his time on the can, isn't he?"

He gazed at the wife and wondered what Neal saw in her that he didn't see.

"To answer your question: all acting is artificial. But Brando, Monroe and Montgomery Clift make it look natural."

Neal thundered down the hallway, hitching up his jeans.

"Thanks, doll. There's nothing like taking a shit at home. Give my love to the kids."

He kissed the wife on her forehead and looked at Norman's cup.

"Drink up. We're running late."

"Pleasure to meet you."

"I didn't catch your name."

"Norman de Haan. I'm Dutch, originally. Ancestors settled in New Amsterdam after they made a fortune in Surinam."

It was easier to blurt out the truth to a stranger than to a friend. Well, not the whole truth, but a chunk of it. He would have to sneak up on the truth and take it by surprise.

The wife looked like she was trying to digest the information Norman offered her. She placed his cup in the sink and dried her hands on her apron.

"I'm Carolyn, Neal's wife and the mother of his children."

"Bless you, ma'am."

◐◑

29

On the road, Neal reached into his pocket, retrieved what looked like a small notebook, and tossed it to Natalie. Norman peered over her shoulder and saw that it wasn't a notebook for writing, but a bank book. Natalie turned the pages that listed deposits and withdrawals. The number $20,000 leapt out at Norman.

From the glove department, Neal retrieved a letter with Carolyn's signature and handed it to Natalie.

"Copy her handwriting until it looks perfect."

Natalie put on a pair of sunglasses, wrapped a scarf around her head, and stared into the mirror behind the visor. She smiled and wrote on a blank piece of paper, "Carolyn Cassady," again and again until she reached the bottom of the page, and then shook the cramp from her hand.

Norman frowned.

"I get what you're up to, But I don't see how you're going get away with it."

Neal laughed.

"Hey man, this is Los Gatos. There's no crime here and no criminals. The cops are flat footed."

In downtown Los Gatos, after passing the library and the U.S. Post Office with its flag flapping in the breeze, Neal parked a block from a branch of the Wells Fargo Bank. He turned around and glared at Norman.

"You're coming with us. Everything I say, you agree with me. Got it?"

Norman laughed. Neal could be a comedian, albeit unintentionally.

"Yeah, I got it. Method acting." He paused a moment and added, "Don't I get a disguise?"

"You are a disguise, egghead."

Neal peered into the mirror, combed his hair, put on a white shirt, a tie, and a jacket, grabbed a satchel from the back seat, kicked his door closed, and escorted Natalie along the sidewalk.

Inside the bank, Neal was super slick, talking in an exaggerated accent. Norman couldn't place it precisely, but it sounded like it came from the wide open spaces of the American West, where cowboys wrangled, roped, and herded cattle. Natalie looked like a snazzy customer she might have waited on at I. Magnin, not the little shop girl behind the counter who lived a double life with the boys in the gang.

The three of them made a beeline for a banker named Thomas Wright, who sat behind a desk and offered Natalie a chair. Neal towered above her. Norman stood next to Neal who placed his hands behind his back.

"This is an emergency." He paused a fraction of a second, then went on as though it was a real emergency. "Oh, by the way, I'm Neal Cassady, this is my wife, Carolyn, and this fellow at my side is Dr. de Haan, a noted Palo Alto brain surgeon. My wife has to have an immediate procedure, right doctor?"

Norman nodded his head.

Neal produced the bank book.

"My wife's tumor has affected her speech, but she can still sign her name, right dear?"

Natalie nodded her head again only this time as though it hurt.

"She'd like to withdraw her savings. The hospital wants a down payment. Isn't that right, Dr. de Haan?"

Norman smiled graciously. Natalie placed Carolyn's driver's license on the banker's desk. Mr. Wright examined the photo and studied Natalie's face.

"You haven't aged a bit."

He picked up a pen and turned around and around with thumb and index finger.

"This is highly irregular."

Neal grabbed his throat.

"So is a brain tumor."

He reached into his jacket and produced a document that read "Southern Pacific Railroad."

"There! If I'm good enough for the good old Southern Pacific, I ought to be good enough for Wells Fargo, don't you think, Mr. Wright? Or is our money not good enough for you?"

The banker looked embarassed.

"No, no, you're loyal customers. We'll expedite this."

He opened the top drawer of his desk, removed a slip of paper that read, "Withdrawals," filled it out, and told Natalie to print her name and sign and date above the dotted line. Mr. Wright stood up, left his desk, dashed behind the counter, disappeared into the vault, and came back with a stack of bills.

"It's all here. In hundreds. I hope you don't mind."

Natalie stared at the bills in amazement.

Neal gathered all of them in both hands.

"No need to count. If we can't trust Wells Fargo who can we trust?"

He stuffed the cash into the satchel, and smiled at the banker.

"Thank you sir, you won't regret this."

Neal helped Natalie to her feet.

"Carolyn, honey, we've got to get you to the hospital right away if they're gonna fix your brain."

He turned to Norman who nodded.

"She'll be as good as new."

In the car, they laughed. Neal clapped Norman on the back.

"What did I tell you? It's funny money."

Then and there, Norman lost much of his respect for bankers, and admired Neal's grit. The car started and pulled away from the curb as though everything was copacetic.

Neal removed his tie.

"I have a system. I can't lose."

At Bay Meadows they went their separate ways. Norman got as close to the horses as he could and admired their beauty. Natalie sat in the shade under an umbrella, drank a beer, and then drank another one and another one after that, until she was juiced and didn't seem to know if the horses were running backward or forward.

It didn't take Norman long to see that Neal didn't have a system, despite his assertion. He bet on one horse because he liked the name, "Bandit," and on another horse because he liked the name of the jockey, "Joe Lawless."

His betting is as berserk as everything else he does, Norman told himself.

Neal bet big on nearly every race, then watched the horses go round the track and head for the finish line, neck and neck. He shook his head when his horse lost, but he kept on betting and kept on losing. By the end of the afternoon, he didn't have a dollar to his name. It was no longer funny money.

"Easy come, easy go." He sounded like it was no biggie.

Neal gathered his traveling companions and partners in crime and herded them toward the parking lot. In the back seat of the car, Natalie slumped over and fell asleep. The beers and the sun had walloped her. The lost twenty thousand dollars seemed to weigh on her heavily.

Norman rode shot gun for the first time, and braced for the ride to the city.

"What will you tell your wife?"

Neal accelerated.

"I'm not gonna say anything, and she's not gonna ask anything, either. In a marriage, some things are best left unsaid, ya understand, Dr. de Haan?"

That night in his room, Norman lay in bed with his pillow fluffed and the window open. He smoked a joint, enjoyed the high, and filled page after page in his notebook while he listened to the music that drifted up from downstairs, and surged through his veins. Charlie Parker, dear old Charlie Parker, never sounded sweeter. Norman read what he had written, surprised by his own candor and amazed that he didn't know what he was going to say until he saw the words on the page.

"In New York, I met white folks who hated jazz, probably because it, reminded them of their own sexuality. They wanted to repress it, and deny it, and lock up colored people because they have soul.

"I knew about the abolitionists who aided the Blacks with the underground railroad, but I didn't ever have faith that white folks would do the right thing when it came to the people they kidnapped in Africa and enslaved, shipped across the Atlantic like they were beasts, and then enslaved again after Reconstruction and during the rule of

Jim Crow. But things are stirring in the South. Living in Frisco, I've stretched my head and learned that the truth lives in the body and cannot be long buried! Good night, sweet prince, good night."

30

The next day, City Lights felt much like every other day, and yet it wasn't exactly the same as every other day. Lawrence wrote in his upstairs office, but he took longer breaks than usual, and went out for coffee at Trieste. Shig worked on the little magazine he called "Shigology," in which he published what he called "found poems" along with photos of North Beach faces and North Beach graffiti.

That day he worked on "Shigology" with more joy than usual. After he mimeographed his magazine, he gave away copies to steady customers and to strangers on the street. They were happy to have it.

Gregory didn't show up and neither did Ginzy or Jack, who, according to Lawrence, was helping his mother settle in a cottage in Berkeley.

Lawrence stood at the front counter and turned the pages of his address book.

"I've got to keep track of their comings and goings. Someone has to. It might as well be me, since I'll be publishing them."

Norman sat, kept an eye on the customers, and when the store wasn't busy, wrote in his notebook.

"I've noticed that Jack is devoted to his mother, whom he calls 'Mamere.' She hates Ginzy with a passion, and that makes me wonder. I'm the only real lapsed Catholic in the group, and happy to be a few thousand miles from my mother, but I wish Toni were here so I could ask her how she has steered clear of the de Haan ghosts and kept a level head. Though, come to think of it, she's way more driven than I. Won't be satisfied until she has a successful career in the movies."

No, indeed, no one in the gang arrived at the store that day, but all manner and make of men and some women, too, passed through the front door at City Lights, even though Shig pointed to a large hand-lettered sign above the entrance that read, "Abandon all hope, ye who enter here." Norman added those same words to the cover of his notebook because, he thought, they would keep him from indulging in sentimentality, which he abhorred as much as nostalgia.

Hipsters, intellectuals, bohemians, poets, and students—some from the California Labor School—filed into City Lights to buy books, escape from the wind and the fog, kill time, find a lover, or rendezvous with a friend. Sometimes these curious pilgrims came singly and sometimes they came in pairs, and wore more or less the same clothes and the same expressions. They had the same cold eyes, or warm eyes, the same pointy black shoes, or no shoes at all, though Shig barked, "No shoes, no welcome."

Norman watched the legions of men and women who had lecherous lips and celibate lips, suspicious grins or trusting grins, men who were clean shaven or bearded, women with glasses and without glasses, sometimes with attaché cases and sometimes not, sometimes buying books by the score and sometimes walking out empty handed, but seemingly better informed, as though the knowledge that lurked inside the volumes that sat on the shelves had infiltrated their heads. They looked wiser going out than coming in, or so Norman thought.

Mysterious men occasionally arrived: men with no fixed address and who disappeared for weeks and even months at a time. A codger who read Kenneth Patchen religiously and swore by him, lived in the International Hotel on Kearny Street. Lawrence had just published some of Patchen's poems and the codger was elated.

"He'll never be famous, but he'll always have followers and he'll never go out of style, not in North Beach."

The codger brought Norman and Shig to the nightclub called the "hungry i," where they heard comedian, Mort Sahl. The owner, Enrico Banducci, stopped at their table and told Norman that the lower case letter "i" stood for the word "Id," which housed the libido and the death instinct.

"It's Freudian."

Shig rubbed his beard.

"Yeah, yeah, I know. The Oedipus complex and all that shit."

Some of the mysterious men, who didn't seem to have a past or a future, troubled Norman. He stood or sat at the front counter of the store and grew more paranoid by the day. Maybe it was Neal and Natalie and the caper at the bank and the lost money at the race track. Maybe it was the stories in *The Defender*, or maybe it was the cops in the Fillmore.

It was the very nature of paranoia to float about, not unlike anxiety. He remembered that when he lived in Manhattan, his writer friend, Delmore Schwartz, had told him and Anatole Broyard, who was passing for white, "Even paranoids have enemies."

Norman thought that he had real enemies among the pilgrims who showed up at City Lights, and thought of it as a literary Mecca.

Some of them were members of cults and cliques. They grew testy when they couldn't find the manifestoes by their favorite authors, and assumed they had been deliberately excluded by a cabal of conspirators. Running a bookstore was a dangerous enterprise, Norman decided, though he recognized that it also brought joy to the tribe of readers.

City Lights seemed to make enemies by virtue of its very existence. Chief among them, at least in Norman's eyes, was a large, balding man who called himself by a variety of names, depending on the nationality of the person to whom he was speaking, but always beginning with the letter M: Senior Molino, who seemed to be a Mexican national, Monsieur Moe, who was French Canadian, and Herr Meister, from Alsace.

M appeared to be bookish and an intellectual, too, but when Norman scratched the surface, he turned out to be a boob who faked knowledge of esoteric subjects, or just stabbed in the dark hoping he might hit a verity on the head, which he did now and then.

M's near-constant companion, Casper Weinberger (known as "Cap"), served in the California State Assembly, where he represented land-hungry, water-greedy farmers and ranchers in the heart of the Central Valley. At City Lights, Cap shared war stories with Shig, though Cap had turned into a Cold Warrior, while Shig had turned into a "peacenik."

Because of his girth, M reminded Norman of Sidney Greenstreet in *The Maltese Falcon*, the film that introduced him to San Francisco and triggered his fantasies about being a detective, like Sam Spade. M would have been a worthy opponent.

A man of many names, he also wore many different kinds of headwear, including caps, berets, and Borsalinos. M spoke several languages, among them English, Spanish, Italian, Russian, French, and Japanese. Norman never knew whether he would say, "Hello," *"Bonjour,"* *"Ciao,"* *"Privet,"* or *"Kon'nichiwa,"* nor what language he would employ to launch a conversation.

On a Friday afternoon, M looked over Norman's shoulder and read the Dow Jones in *The Chronicle.*

"Stocks are too volatile for my temperament, so I've been investing in bonds, and I've steered away from companies doing business in certain countries like Iran and Guatemala. Keep that intel under your hat, sonny boy. It's not meant for general consumption."

"I'm not a gambler."

"You need a system."

"If I had some of my family's dough, I'd risk the stock market, but my grandfather left me an old book and nothing else."

"Poor boy. I feel for you."

M seemed to fancy Norman, though Norman didn't encourage him. Still, M persisted. He tried to convert Norman to his way of thinking about the decline of culture because, as he put it, "democracy lowers standards." M stood at the front desk and held forth.

"Norman, you and the whole City Lights gang here will have more people buying books than ever before. People who don't normally read anything other than Dick Tracy, and who have never learned how to think. These people who know nothing, but believe they know everything, will usher in what I call the time of the scorpion. We will go down together unless we defend ourselves against them."

"How do we know who these people are?"

"Ah, that's just it, Norman. They look like you and me."

"So how do we defend against them?"

M smiled in a Buddha-like way that made Norman uneasy.

"There are subtle ways that don't raise red flags. Never confront an opponent directly, unless absolutely necessary, and if and when you do, make sure you have all your ducks lined up in a row. Also, never be isolated, but rather isolate and neutralize your enemies."

31

On a warm evening, with the fog hovering along the coast, M arrived at City Lights at closing time, browsed, and bought Adam Smith's *The Wealth of Nations*. He begged to be allowed to stay after the lights were turned off, and then dropped a bombshell that took Norman by surprise, though where it came from, M didn't say.

"You were with Wild Bill Donovan!"

Norman's head jerked back.

"Maybe I was and maybe I wasn't."

"You must have a few medals lying around someplace."

Norman quickly regained his equilibrium.

"Someplace or no place."

Norman shrugged his shoulders, though he knew his paranoia level had shot up.

The next evening, M accepted an autographed copy of Shig's magazine.

"Mr. Muro, you were interned in Idaho, along with your mother and father, while Mr. de Haan was overseas spying on Himmler's boys in the SS."

M raised and lowered his bushy eyebrows. He seemed determine to impress Shig, as well as Norman, with information he scattered shotgun style.

"Mr. Muro, sir, if I might have your attention for a moment. I believe you joined the Military Secret Service, and after Little Boy put the Japs in their place, you served General Douglas MacArthur... as...well... I'm not sure in what capacity."

Shig sat behind the front counter stone-faced, his mouth sealed. M kept prodding and poking, trying to find a crack and open it.

"I can see why you two boys have gravitated toward one another. You're probably both still secretive and still paranoid. Old habits die hard."

At closing time, Shig cornered Norman.

"Where does he get his intel?"

Norman shrugged his shoulders.

"I don't know. Maybe he works for J. Edgar Hoover, or maybe he heard someone spouting off in Vesuvio."

Shig stroked his beard.

"So it's not true, what M said about you and Donovan?"

Norman scratched his head.

"I've erased everything about the war, or more precisely the war itself erased everything."

One uncommonly warm evening, when Ginzy and Natalie arrived at the store after a day in the Berkeley hills, gathering wildflowers, M took Natalie's right hand in his, kissed it gently, and invited her and everyone else within earshot to come to his apartment for "drinks, snacks, and polite conversation," as he put it. There was no way Norman or anyone else could turn him down. They were hungry and thirsty, and there was no cover charge to get into M's private club.

They were a party of six. Shig was too curious to remain at his post. Ferlinghetti grabbed his bowler and his umbrella, and insisted he had to join the "kids," as he called them. Ginzy called Gregory on the house phone, and Gregory showed up at the last minute.

Jack, Neal, and LaVigne didn't make it to M's, though they were invited. LaVigne had disappeared; no one knew his whereabouts. Orlovsky had returned to New York to mind his mad mother.

Right before Norman locked up the store for the night, a call came from Carolyn Cassady, who told him that the boys were riding the rails from Frisco to the Central Valley and looking for trouble. She allowed that she had to stay home and mind the children, otherwise she'd have joined them. In a nutshell, that was Mrs. Cassady's life, Norman realized. The boys went on the road, either by rail or by car, and she was parked at home, vacuuming, washing, drying, dusting, and raising the kids.

M's suite spread out on the top floor of an apartment building on Nob Hill, where Nabobs once thrived and where only their twentieth-century descendants could afford the rents.

At the entrance to M's penthouse, an Asian woman wearing

black trousers, a black shirt, and high heels collected hats, scarfs, and jackets and hung them in the hall closet.

"You get back when you leave. No worry. I remember."

In the foyer, there were bundles of old newspapers—*The Times of London, Pravda,* and *Le Monde*—tied with heavy cord and piled up against one wall. Interesting, Norman mused, if I had the bread, I'd probably subscribe to the same papers.

Next to the newspapers, there were cardboard boxes brimming with bric-a-brac, including statues that looked like they were purloined from Egyptian and Assyrian graves.

"I gathered them on my last trip to the Middle East. The Metropolitan is taking them off my hands. Of course, I get a tax write-off."

Initially, there was no proper place to sit, unless one displaced the sleeping cats, including a Burmese, a Persian, and a Siamese. Gregory, who was the last to enter the suite, screeched and drove the terrified kitties into the far corners of the room.

Gregory sniffed the air, then surveyed the newspapers and the boxes with the bric-a-brac.

"I smell a cop."

Norman was instantly curious.

"What kind of cop?"

"A cop is a cop is a cop."

"Local, state or federal?"

Gregory shot Norman a look of disdain.

"Interpol."

"So why has he invited us here?"

"Sucking up intel. He knows we're commies and faggots and can tell him what's really happening in Frisco."

M must have caught Gregory's comments—he was standing close by—though he gave no tangible indication that he had in fact heard him. He wandered around the room and Norman wandered with him.

"Are you following the campaign?" M popped the question to Natalie. "I mean, Eisenhower or Stevenson?"

Natalie shook her head.

"I'm drawing a blank."

"What about you, Shig, what do you think?"

"Doesn't matter who's in the White House."

Norman leaned on M's shoulder.

"Are you getting all this down, sir, for your report to headquarters?"

M clapped his meaty hands and, almost instantly, two slender Asian men with slicked-back black hair entered the dining room, cleared the top of the big mahogany table, and set down platters with smoked whitefish and caviar.

"From the Black Sea, courtesy of my dear friends in Odessa."

There were baked potatoes, and little pancakes that Norman recognized from his days at the Russian Tea Room as blini and now couldn't resist. He made a pig of himself and so did Gregory, who wolfed down a dozen.

The Asian woman in black and high heels pushed a cart on wheels into the center of the room. She stopped, opened a side door, removed a bucket filled with ice cubes, and placed two bottles of Stoli on the table.

"From Leningrad."

M beamed proudly and turned to Ginzy.

"As someone with Russian blood, you must have a taste for Stoli."

Ginzy shook his head.

"I don't drink alcohol. And I'm giving up smoking tobacco and eating meat."

Still, the Asian woman offered Ginzy a Stoli on the rocks.

"And you my dear." M appealed to Natalie. "You must be Anglo-Irish or something like that. Gregory is Italian, of course, and Ferlinghetti must be, like me, a mongrel. We have no fake loyalties or disgusting sentimentalities."

Norman sipped his Stoli.

"Where did you find these people?"

He glanced from the Asian woman to the Asian men. Spengler was right. The West was falling apart and the East was on the rise. Norman waited while M concocted a story for wide distribution. Norman saw the wheels turning in his oversized head.

"My little helpers are all from Hong Kong. They begged me to bring them to the Promised Land. Now, they're indentured servants."

M paused a moment and swirled the ice cubes in his glass.

"We're living in an era where everyone is free to move about the planet and sell himself or herself to the highest bidder. General Motors will rule the world. See if I'm not right, boys."

Ginzy shook his head.

"I'm afraid you're outdated, M, or whomever you are. Ever since '45, we've been in the age of the nuclear apocalypse. Only barbarians will save us."

M faced the big picture window and stared out at San Francisco Bay. The doorbell rang. Norman opened it and greeted a man he recognized from City Lights and the pages of *The Examiner* as Cap Weinberger, who arrived with a bottle of Dom Perignon and offered it to the host. He glanced at the unopened bottle of Russian vodka on the table.

"No Stoli for me. I'll take my own champagne."

M laughed.

Unlike me, Cap is an extremist."

Cap looked insulted.

"No, no, I'm a realist."

Ginzy laughed.

"Me and my friends are utopian romantics and detest Cold Warriors."

M wagged his finger.

"Play nice, boys. You may need Cap as your friend and ally in the days ahead."

He clapped his hands. The Asian woman appeared again and bowed to the assembled guests.

"Go ahead, please, Lotus Blossom."

She bowed once again, moved her arms and her legs ceremoniously and gave a demonstration of what Norman recognized as kick boxing, followed by *T'ai chi ch'üan.* She had clearly mastered the martial arts and would not be intimidated by the boys in the room.

"Norman, are you willing to try your luck against the lady?"

M poked him in the ribs.

"Count me out."

Ginzy laughed. Corso tried kicking his right leg into the air

Jonah Raskin

and landed on his face, but he got up, dusted himself off, lifted a bottle
of the Stoli and poured it down his throat. Ah, it went down so easily.

Cap approached Ginzy.

"What do you do?"

"As little as possible."

Cap wore a puzzled expression. He wasn't sure he understood
the young man.

"You don't work?"

"Not if I can help it."

Cap looked surprised. The young man seemed to be sober
and to have all his faculties about him.

"But you're civic minded."

"Absolutely, Mr. Cap, we want everyone to love everyone
else."

Corso licked his lips and glared at M.

"I love all my brothers and I love the bomb!"

Ferlinghetti struck him across his chest.

"No, you don't!"

"Yes, I do!"

Ginzy came to Corso's defense.

"He has a point, Larry."

Ginzy looked like the ghost of an old prophet.

"Hate the bomb and you make it more deadly."

Cap sipped the champagne.

"We need the bomb as a deterrent."

Norman rubbed his chin and stared at M.

"What is your position, sir?"

M raised his glass and sipped the Stoli.

"I'm sorry if you haven't followed me, my boy. I thought
it was as clear as the vodka in the bottle: I'm above politics. We
need a president for life. Then we'll have stability and no recessions,
depressions, or revolutions."

In one corner of the room, Ferlinghetti and Corso continued
to argue with one another about the bomb, the fucking bomb, the
bomb to end all bombs and all life. Corso would have thrown a punch,
but Natalie stepped between him and Lawrence.

"Save your energy. If you don't see the chaos that's coming,
you're blind."

169

Ginzy opened his arms wide, as though to embrace the world, then clapped his hands and chanted.

"Holy, holy, holy, holy."

Everyone in the room, excluding Cap and M, joined him.

Cap took a step back.

"Time for me to go." And to M, "Let's do lunch."

The boys polished off the caviar and the smoked salmon, guzzled the Stoli, linked arms, danced wildly, and sang the words to "The Internationale."

"This is the final struggle/Let's group together, and tomorrow/ The Internationale/Will be the human race."

M placed one hand over his eyes and another over his mouth. Clearly, he'd had enough of the antics. Lotus Blossom returned the hats, scarfs and coats to their rightful owners and curtseyed to each and every one.

Corso, on his way out, pushed M into a corner.

"I can take the old papers off your hands, pops."

M laughed, put his right arm around Gregory's shoulder, and hugged him.

"You're a dear boy and I appreciate the offer. But a fellow from the Hoover at Stanford is coming to take them tomorrow and pay me handsomely."

M handed Norman an envelope.

"I was hoping you would put in a good word with Mr. LaVigne."

Norman laughed nervously; the Stoli had gone to his head and he was dizzy.

"Whatever for?" He slurred his words.

M learned forward and whispered in Norman's ear.

"Mr. LaVigne's sketches of Miss Jackson will look lovely on the far wall."

He raised and lowered his double chin.

"Don't you agree?"

Norman giggled, hiccupped, and inserted the envelope in the pocket of his jacket.

"*Sayonara.*"

He went down the elevator with Ginzy, who whispered in his ear.

"I'm gonna put M in my mad, mad poem, but I'll disguise him, so he won't recognize himself and sue me for libel."

"Watch out he doesn't send Lotus Blossom after you."

"Don't worry. I know how to do this."

Norman opened the envelope from M, counted the cash and read the note: "For your troubles." The cool sea breeze acted like a tonic and roused Norman from his intoxicated state. You must remember to give LaVigne the money, he told himself. Before you lose it.

32

The bus took him across town. Holy, holy, holy, he chanted. Holy city, holy Black, holy the Fillmore, holy the fog, holy Mrs. Cornbrake, holy my gun and my Blake book. He walked the last leg of the journey. When he got within earshot he saw the bright lights in the house that had been his home for months. From the front porch he saw Ezra and Zora sitting next to one another in the kitchen.

"I've never been troubled by your love life, Ezra."

That's what Norman heard Zora say. "It's your business. If it makes you happy, I'm happy."

The table was bare. There was no peach pie, no coffee and there were no coffee cups.

Ezra snapped his fingers.

"Well, well, if it ain't the white spook himself." Norman wondered if the comment was hostile, or somehow meant to be affectionate.

"Have a seat." Ezra pulled a chair away from the table, and waited for Norman to get comfortable. "Zora and me were just talking about you and your ways."

"No, we weren't."

Ezra ignored his mother.

"The clock has run out, Norman. The folks from Money called and said they'd be here 'fore the end of the week. No rush, but pack up and be ready to split, pronto."

Norman took the stairs down to the basement, found the locker where Ezra kept his beer, helped himself to a cold one, opened it with a church key, and climbed to the second floor.

In his little room, with the door locked and the blinds drawn, he raised the bottle, sipped, and took his gun from its hiding place.

You're backtracking, he told himself. You shouldn't be doing this. But he did it anyway. The gun wore down his resistance. He added the bullets he had removed days earlier, tossed the gun on the army blanket that was stretched taut, military style. After a while, he retrieved John Steadman's *Narrative of a Five Years Expedition Against the Revolted Negroes of Surinam*, the only book he had brought with him to California.

Norman sat down on the bed and felt the stubble on his chin. He remembered that Mrs. Cornbrake had called him a white spook when he first arrived, and that he had begun to think of himself as a reverse Oreo: a white man on the outside and a Black man on the inside.

With his gun in hand, he laughed at his ridiculous conceit.

You're not Black inside or outside, he told himself. You'll never be Black no matter how hard you try.

He rose from the bed and looked at his long face in the mirror.

"Norman de Haan, you motherfucker, your ancestors traded rum for slaves."

He tore a sheet of paper from his notebook, stared at the blue lines on the white page, and filled them with hot words that poured from his head like molten lead.

"August 25th. Dear Natalie: I don't know if I'll ever be able to tell Ezra and Zora what I'm going to tell you now, that my ancestors, the de Haans, who were good Calvinists, quelled a slave revolt in Surinam, washed their bloody hands, moved to New York, became bankers and mercantilists, funded George Washington's army, branded themselves Americans, made a fortune, lost a fortune, and made another one in the fur trade. It makes me sick. Time to bury my ghosts. Your friend, Norman."

He read the letter aloud, crumpled it, tossed it against the wall, held the gun to his head, and put his finger on the trigger.

"Bang, bang, you're dead, White Spook!"

He laughed louder than he wanted to, and thought he might have alarmed Ezra and Zora, but when he went out on the landing and looked down to the first floor, he saw that they were talking quietly.

"Bless William Blake and fuck the Dutch slavers."

He fell sleep with Blake's engravings etched in his mind.

The next morning, he woke early and looked at his reflection in the bathroom mirror.

"Norman, it's dead wrong for some people to own other people."

He showered, shaved and put on a white shirt, a tie, slacks, and loafers. Downstairs, he hunted for Ezra and Zora, couldn't find them, drank cold coffee, smoked a cigarette and wrote a note: "Dear Zora and Ezra: Have gone to work, will see about living with Natalie, though I know you don't approve, but, but, but…I will move out of your house as soon as I'm able."

At City Lights, he found the front door unlocked and the front desk abandoned, but he heard voices from the second floor and knew instantly that they belonged to Shig and Lawrence, who sounded truly excited.

"Tell Ginsberg I want a copy of his manuscript immediately. Tell him I'll publish the book in the Pocket Poets series and give him a big chunk of the profits."

Norman walked upstairs, barged into Lawrence's office, borrowed the phone, called I. Magnin, and asked to be connected to cosmetics. When he reached Natalie, he invited her to meet him at Vesuvio. Shortly after twelve noon, she arrived with a woman who looked somewhat like Marilyn Monroe.

"Norman de Haan meet my dear friend, Bette Green. Bette Green meet Norman de Haan, formerly of New York; he's a gentleman."

Bette Green struck Norman as glamorous. She had full lips, high cheekbones, and a smile that melted Norman's reluctance to admire her beauty.

"I've heard good things about you, Mr. de Haan."

"And I've heard good things about you."

Natalie smirked.

"You two must belong to a mutual admiration society." She paused, then added, "Boring."

Norman chuckled. He was smitten with Bette, and he knew it.

"What do you do for kicks?"

"I dig rock 'n' roll and I get out on the dance floor every chance I get."

"Maybe the three of us can go together one night."

Natalie cleared her throat.

"Three's a crowd."

Norman went to the bar and ordered drinks: an Irish coffee for Natalie, a Chablis for Bette, and an Anchor Steam for himself. At the table, he set down the drinks.

"Speaking of threesomes, I was hoping you knew Charlie Wilson's phone number."

"Charlie Wilson?"

"Yeah, my buddy from the war, whom you dated for a while."

"I wouldn't call it dating."

"What would you call it?"

"Something else."

Norman didn't pursue the matter.

"I've been wondering about M, whom I met at the bookstore. Charlie Wilson is the only person I know who might know something about him. Charlie and I were in Berlin together in '45. He knew everyone, from the generals to the grunts."

Natalie opened her purse, withdrew a small black book, thumbed through the pages, stopped at the letter C, and on a Vesuvio coaster wrote "Lexington 5194." Norman read the number aloud and placed the coaster in his pocket.

"Thanks for sharing."

"Don't say where you got it."

"Not a word."

To Bette Green, who seemed more real than real, Norman offered a tentative smile.

"You can reach me at City Lights Books five days a week. Check me out."

Bette sipped her Chablis.

"I love to read. I go to the library all the time."

Back in Lawrence's lair, Norman called the number Natalie provided.

"Citibank."

"Charlie Wilson please."

"Just a moment, sir."

"Charlie Wilson speaking."

"Norman de Haan in California."

"I've wondered where you were hiding."

"I'll cut to the chase, Charlie. I met a guy, and you're the only person I can think of who might have intel on him. He lives on Nob Hill, speaks half a dozen languages, and has contacts on the other side of the Iron Curtain. He seems to think I was tight with Bill Donovan."

"Looks like Sidney Greenstreet?"

"You nailed him."

Norman cleared his throat.

"Calls himself Monsieur Moe, among other names."

"Yeah, I know him, or rather I did." Charlie went on a roll. "He's a sleazebag who worked for military intel in Seoul, Korea and then went rogue and sold himself to the highest bidder, who happened to be King Farouk. They had a sweet deal until the coup d'état in '52 when he had to get out of Cairo fast. I didn't know where he landed, but you say you saw him out West."

"In San Francisco. He has money and he's tight with a local politico who is eager for the White House to go head-to-head with the Kremlin."

"I'd be careful what I said around him."

"Why would he think I was in the OSS?"

"People talk. You know that as well as I."

"Can you ask around about him please?"

Charlie gave no reply to Norman's question, but asked one of this own.

"Say, Norman…have you seen or heard from Natalie?"

"Natalie Jackson?"

"The same."

"I bumped into her the other day. She seemed her old self."

He didn't want to say more about Natalie. Then Charlie surprised him.

"If I were you, I'd also watch what I said around her. She's kooky and Norman, if you're ever in Langley, Virginia look me up. I'm leaving the bank and moving there."

"How will I find you?"

"You'll find me."

Norman went downstairs and sat behind the front counter.

Shig came up from the basement and handed him an armful of Lawrence's new paperback, *Pictures of the Gone World.*

"Boss wants these displayed in the window."

"Don't worry. I'll do it." After a long pause, he asked, "Have you read Ginzy's new poem?"

"No, but I heard him read part of it aloud at Vesuvio. I couldn't make heads or tails of it, and the more I thought about it, the more I thought he was showing off. Lawrence was there, listening carefully, and then talked it up big time. He thinks it's brilliant."

Norman nodded his head. His long hair fell down and covered his right eye until he brushed it aside.

"I dig it. If it's not difficult it's not now."

33

Shig opened the cash register and counted the money, while Norman dressed the window with a dozen or so copies of Lawrence's new book. Soon after twelve noon, Ginzy arrived with a scarf wrapped around his neck, a long cigarette holder between his teeth, and a copy of W. H. Auden's *The Age of Anxiety* which he waved above his head.

"Food for thought."

He paused and glanced from Shig to Norman.

"I've gone beyond Auden, beyond Eliot, and beyond Pound. 'Howl' is so new, it's ancient."

He reached into the pocket of his jacket and brought out a dozen or so things that looked grotesque and that Norman recognized as peyote buttons. They brought a smile to his face. Ginsberg opened his palm wide and gazed at them, hungrily.

"Mailed to me from the source special delivery. I'm going to eat a bunch right now."

Norman stared at Shig.

"Is Lawrence in his office?"

With his handkerchief, Shig wiped the perspiration from his brow.

"No, not now. He slipped out with a bunch of poets from Tokyo. I was translating for them, though they'll do fine without me. They met when Lawrence was stationed in Japan."

Ginzy led the way upstairs. Norman followed him, and sat down in Lawrence's chair while Ginzy scattered the peyote buttons on the table.

"Go ahead. Take as many as you want."

Norman didn't know how many or how few to ingest.

"Never really did psychedelics before, though I tried mushrooms once. Saw all the colors of the rainbow."

Ginzy put several buttons in his mouth, chewed slowly, and swallowed.

"Go slow, go low. It won't kick in for an hour or so, but when it does, it will kick you into Nirvana."

Norman helped himself to four buttons, held them in the palm of his right hand, examined them as though they might bite, ingested them one by one, didn't like the taste, and made a face.

"I'm going to lie low for a while. Maybe I'll venture out after I see what this shit does to me."

Ginzy frowned.

"It's holy and it's a sacrament. It will do you no harm."

Norman lay down on the floor behind Lawrence's desk and went into his own head. He heard Ginzy descend the stairs and make lots of noise doing so, like an elephant in a circus. How long he lay there Norman didn't know, but after a while, he noticed that he felt sick to his stomach.

"Nausea," he told himself. He got up slowly, walked down the hallway holding his gut, opened the bathroom door, went inside, knelt down in front of the toilet, and heaved. Then he heaved again, until there was nothing more to heave.

He flushed the toilet, cleaned up the mess he'd made, washed his face and hands with hot water, dried them with a towel, climbed down the stairs one at a time, and hunted for the clock on the wall. He couldn't find it anywhere, and when he peered at the face of his own wristwatch, he didn't know what to make of it. He'd lost the ability to tell time. Weird! The peyote was more than he'd bargained for. Which was the hour hand and which was the minute hand? He couldn't remember.

When Ferlinghetti returned to the store with his visitors from Tokyo, Norman figured he was at liberty to venture into the wilds of the city.

"Later," he managed to say. He walked uphill toward Broadway, though he had the strange sensation that he was going downhill.

He crossed the street and walked toward Coit Tower, or at least in the direction of where he thought he might find Coit Tower on Telegraph Hill. Twice he came to streets with signs that read "Dead End" and had to turn around, but he kept going toward his destination. The vegetation looked lusher, fresher, and a brighter green than it had looked before, and the birds in the trees, birds of paradise on earth, sounded enchanting.

"Norman de Haan, you are alive!"

He shouted, or did he? He wasn't sure. Perhaps he simply imagined that he had spoken the words aloud. At that moment, it wasn't easy for Norman to tell the difference between inside his head and outside his head.

You have reached Nirvana, he told himself. When he saw Ginzy sitting cross-legged at the entrance to Coit Tower, he wasn't sure if he was hallucinating or not, not even when he heard, "Hey, de Haan." Only when he heard the cry a second time did he answer with a "Yes." It had to be Ginzy, or his twin.

They entered the tower and admired the murals, though the corridors were so crowded that Norman felt claustrophobic. He had an odd sensation: one of the murals seemed to wrap itself around him and then swallow him, like a whale swallowing a whole school of fish.

Before he knew it, he was standing next to a woman who read *The Daily Worker* and a man who held a copy of Karl Marx's *Das Kapital*. He thought he heard someone shout, "Strike!" For a moment he panicked, then he looked up, saw Ginzy reach for him and felt himself pulled into the space from which he had just come. Out there, not in here, though in and out made little sense to him anymore. How did that happen, he wondered? How did I find myself inside the mural and then how did I escape?

From the top of Telegraph Hill, he and Ginzy looked down at an unreal city. Norman thought he might reach out and touch the streets below. On the grass, he removed his shoes and socks, wiggled his toes, lay on his back, and gazed at the nearby-faraway blue that flickered between the leaves of a green tree. He got to his knees in time to see Ginzy, the Old Testament prophet, run his fingers through his long, wild hair.

"I had a vision of Moloch. He was stone and fire. He devoured whole armies and he belched black smoke. He was loveless and he was majestic, and he could only eat and shit."

Norman closed his eyes and heard the synapses fire in his brain. He opened his eyes, looked above, saw the sky darken, and felt the temperature drop suddenly and the wind pick up. With his eyes closed once again, he heard the sound of gunfire. The farmhouse on the horizon caught fire. Ashes fell on his head.

A woman spoke a language he didn't entirely understand, though now and then he caught a word or two, like *soldati* and *tedesche*. Those words had been on nearly everyone's lips from the moment he landed on the shore, climbed into the mountains, and heard a cry that went up from the village of stone.

He turned his eyes toward the Tower and saw a soldier in the underbrush. He reached for his rifle and felt something else; when he turned and looked, he saw a branch from a tree that would make a nifty cudgel. He heard what sounded like parrots, and when he gazed toward the blue, he saw a flock of them, perched in a eucalyptus tree. Ah, yes, the legendary parrots of Telegraph Hill.

He closed his eyes, rubbed his face with the palm of his hand, opened his eyes, looked down at the city, and saw toy cars and toy houses. In the distance, the towers of the bridge seemed to hold the fog at bay.

He hunted for Ginzy all around the tower. He circled it twice, clockwise and then counterclockwise, but didn't see him, so he slowly walked alone down the hill. In the foggiest of fogs, he boarded a bus that took him—in some kind of dream—to Franklin Street. All along the way, he read the numbers on the houses as they climbed higher and higher. He got off near City Hall and walked West, though he wasn't sure what was West and what was East. Norman de Haan was on one wild trip.

34

The streets eventually looked familiar, and so did the little houses where people lived and loved, and raised families, and dreamed big dreams in a place made for dreaming big. He saw a police car on the corner and hoofed it. When he glanced over his shoulder again, the cruiser and the cops were gone. Onward, peyote pilgrim. With his index finger, he pushed the button at the entrance to a three-story white building that sat on the corner. A buzzer sounded.

He climbed the carpeted stairs, heard the front door close behind him, and on the way up, collided with a man in a Borsalino who looked like M, had to be M. But the man ignored Norman and went on his way, without so much as a wink, a smile, or a friendly grunt. Peculiar, he heard himself say. I wonder what he's doing here. Couldn't be a coincidence, could it? The light from the sun burst through the stained-glass window and illuminated the stairs.

Natalie waited for him on the landing, wearing only a man's Oxford shirt, no panties, no bra, and no makeup.

"I, I, I…" he began and couldn't find the words he wanted to speak.

"Won't you come in?"

He reached the top floor and followed her down the long hallway to a sunlit room with bare floors and two big windows that faced Franklin Street.

"It's so quiet here. It has been terribly noisy in my head all afternoon, all over the city. But maybe that was the peyote talking."

The woman in the Oxford shirt hugged him.

"There is space for you here, Norman, if you want it."

He wasn't sure he understood. His hearing, his seeing and his sense of smell weren't working right.

"What was that?"

"I said, this can be your new home."

Norman felt loose, but not at loose ends. The peyote had awakened something in him. Maybe for the first time in his life, he was truly woke. He didn't have to do anything. It would all happen by itself, without his agency. He heard a sax that had never sounded so sweet.

He saw her pubic hair, her mons, and the insides of her white thighs. He felt blood rush to the head of his penis. Terribly excited, he told himself. You are too terribly excited.

Norman wanted to suck her, but he restrained himself. It took all his willpower. He stiffened while she seemed to relax. His whole body was erect and on fire. Whether she was dressed or undressed, he told himself, it was all the same to her, and she was the same whether she was one on one, or in a crowd of people. Natalie was eternally Natalie.

He asked himself what made her slash her wrists, which were still bandaged, but he found no ready answers. He didn't want to ask her, and so he lost himself in his own head. Maybe his New York shrink would be able to decipher Natalie. Dr. Lindenhoff had asked him, "Do you think of the sax as a sex symbol?" "Have you ever wanted to have a vagina?" and "Are you confused about whether you are male or female?"

"Fuck you," he'd said while lying on the couch in Lindenhoff's immaculate office.

"I think you're suffering from war trauma, Mr. de Haan. I think the whole thing about your family and your guilt is a smoke screen."

"Fuck you."

Natalie laughed.

"You can fuck me." She curled her tongue around the corners of her mouth and said with a smirk, "That is, if you're up to it."

She sprawled across the mattress, which took up most of the room, and with her right hand, patted a large pillow encased in a satin pillowcase, as though inviting Norman to join her.

He lay down, but not too close to her, and coughed nervously.

"You don't hold it against me that I hit on you, do you, when you were a kid?"

Natalie sat up and played with the hair at the back of Norman's neck.

"No, I let go of that one." After a pause, she added, "Other stuff won't leave me alone. I don't like me when I'm with Neal, but I can't leave."

"I know what you mean. I don't know what I'd do if I wasn't haunted. I have ghosts, therefore I am."

She removed her white Oxford shirt and draped it over the chair that sat next to the bed.

"Do you ever want to fuck your mother, Norman?"

She laughed, and so did he. She pushed his buttons, but he didn't react.

"Yeah, right. It's all about my mother."

He laughed again.

Natalie lay on her back.

"I want you inside me."

Norman peered into the corners of the room and glanced down the hallway as though he expected to see a ghost or two, ready to pounce and carry him far away to a place where he would never see Natalie again, never gaze at her breasts, her shoulder blades, and her neck.

He removed his trousers and his underpants and stared at his penis, which seemed to have grown to twice its normal size.

"I don't know if I can do it. I mean, I didn't come here thinking I would fuck you."

"Didn't you? Didn't Dr. What's-His-Name teach you anything about your libido, Norman?"

He stared at her pubic hair and her mons.

"He did and he didn't. This afternoon, I thought I was in the war again."

"You don't seem yourself, Norman."

"I ate peyote and threw up and walked to Telegraph Hill. I saw parrots and heard gunfire and bombs. And then I came here, though I didn't know I was coming here."

She stroked his penis until it grew harder and harder, inserted it in her mouth, and moved her lips and her tongue around the tip until Norman felt he would explode. He floated on air. She cushioned him. They fell, deeper and deeper down. He heard himself make strange sounds that he'd never made before.

One moment he had chills, and the next moment, hot flashes. Natalie's mouth was an opening to the void, her tongue a sweet serpent come to take him out of the past and into the present. He wanted her now and couldn't stop himself from longing for her. He felt her hands on his buttocks, pressing him down.

"Cocksucking." That was the word that popped into his head. "Fellatio," Dr. Lindenhoff called it, with an Austrian accent. It was okay. He liked it well enough, but he still had the urge to go down on her and didn't know if he could resist much longer. She must have known what he was thinking, though he wasn't sure he was thinking at all. He had reverted to his reptilian self. She lay on her back, placed a pillow under her buttocks, spread her legs, and guided Norman to her vagina.

"Go into every corner and crevice."

His penis had swollen again. His mouth opened wide and his tongue penetrated. He knew that she could come quickly and come often, without much foreplay or sex talk. That was her reputation. He also knew that she could turn fucking into a kind of ritual in which she was the priestess of pleasure. That was part of the legend of Natalie Jackson.

"Come into me, come into me. Come into me now, now, now."

He inserted his penis in her vagina, moved slowly in and out, saw her close her eyes and go into a zone of her own making, heard her come, and then he let go and ejaculated.

Later, when the sun went down in the West, as though for the first time ever, the shadows grew longer, and the streetlights came on. They passed a marijuana cigarette back and forth and got royally stoned and laughed and snacked on Ritz crackers with peanut butter. The weed loosened Norman's tongue and he talked about Coit Tower, Ginzy's poem, Lawrence's new book, and the money Neal lost on the ponies. Natalie listened and smiled.

"Ginzy's come a long way. He's a real writer now. Everyone is cool, everyone except me."

Norman admired Natalie's long, thin neck, her round face, and her lovely hair.

"Couldn't we make a fresh start?"

He was hoping against hope. She rolled her eyes.

"There is no going back, Norman. Time is running out. They will pick us off, one by one."

She is crazy, he decided, crazier than ever, and I want her more than ever. I have to get away this very moment, before it's too late, or I'll go down with her.

She kissed him on his eyelids and on his lips, and played with his penis.

"This is our last time together. We had better make it last, make it good and make it memorable."

Norman became hard again and Natalie wanted him again with the clock ticking and time running out. They fell into fucking until he felt fucked out, and she cried out, and he came. She was right. They were done and could only punctuate the end by furious fucking.

She put on her Oxford shirt and gave Norman the manuscript she had been typing for Ginzy. He read it aloud while he sat in bed, propped up by pillows, and felt the words enter his body and become a part of him.

"I've never heard anything like this, though it reminds me of Eliot and Whitman all mixed up and turned inside out. I can see why Lawrence wants to publish."

He showered, dressed, and made what sounded like an pronouncement.

"I'm going to Zora's, packing up, and bringing my stuff over here. It's not much. I have some clothes, and a gun, and a book that I want to show you, with engravings by William Blake."

Natalie handed him two keys, one for the lock to let himself into the building, and the other for the door to the apartment. She even showed him which way to turn the keys in the locks, since they had, as she put it "their own personalities."

He kissed her on her forehead in a brotherly kind of way, unlocked the door, opened it, stood on the landing, gazed down, turned around and reentered the apartment. He remembered what he meant to ask her, and what fucking made him forget.

He fixed her with his gaze.

"Was that M I saw on his way down as I was on my way up?"

She turned away and glanced at the clock on the wall.

"You must have been hallucinating, Norman. M has never been inside this apartment."

He nodded his head, though he wasn't satisfied with her answer. Maybe M hadn't been in the apartment, but he had surely been inside the building. He saw him on the stairs going down as he was coming up.

35

The bus moved laboriously from neighborhood to neighborhood, from Italian and Chinese districts to streets where colored folk made their homes. He told himself that in six months or so, he had learned volumes about the city and its ways. Like Ginzy's poem, Frisco had entered his body and become a part of him.

He took out his notebook, held it in his lap, and wrote in big looping letters. "I'm coming to the end of something. I can't go back to New York, though I also know I'll never fit in here, not with Ferlinghetti, Ginzy and Jack. They're too edgy for me.

"I know, too, I could never fit in with Zora and Ezra, though sometimes I feel like I should be more like them, not in my head so much, not scribbling in this fuckin' notebook that will never amount to anything. Maybe I could reenlist in the service and become a part of a team."

He knew he was getting close to his stop. He could feel it in his bones. He pulled the cord to alert the driver that he wanted to get off, crammed the notebook into his pocket, descended at the rear door, and aimed for Zora's house near the end of the block. Standing in the middle of the street, hands on his hips, he could see lights glowing downstairs and that the upstairs was bathed in darkness.

Norman heard a sax and cocked his ears. It came from above and lifted him toward the sky. It didn't matter whether it was real or not. Parked along the curb outside Zora's was a 1944 black Buick sedan with Mississippi plates that looked like it had clocked miles and miles. So, they had arrived at last. It was good that he was able to get out of their way, good that he had a place to go to.

Zora and Ezra sat at opposites ends of the dining room table. A man who looked like Zora, but who was clearly older than she, sat between her and Ezra, drinking coffee from a mug. He was as black as any man Norman had ever seen. A descendant of Africans and big, too, with a broad chest, large shoulders, and meaty hands that had chopped cotton. He took a close look at Norman, who poked his head into the living room. The Black man sang sweetly.

"Come in, please."

The lines on Zora's face seemed deeper, her skin darker, and her voice more musical than ever before.

"Norman, this is my brother, Benjamin. Benjamin this is my boarder, Norman. Mrs. Cornbrake next door took to calling him the white spook. He's been with us for a while and now he's movin' on."

Ezra watched the two men, as though he wasn't sure if Benjamin would be civil to Norman. Zora broke the silence that engulfed the table.

"They're lucky to get out of Money. I know for a fact, it's the big backlash. Every time we open our mouths they try to shut 'em."

She cast her eyes toward the stairway that led to the second floor.

"My sister-in-law and my nieces and nephews are sleepin' upstairs in the bedroom at the back of the hall."

Zora returned to her brother's face and waited for him to speak.

"There's a lot to tell. White folks in Money actin' crazier than ever. We knew we had to move fast. It's a long road from Mississippi to California."

Norman did not know what to say. Indeed, he knew that he was at a loss for words and that Zora's brother, Benjamin, had come from a world that he would never see, a world he couldn't look at through Benjamin's eyes. But he smiled. He was happy. Finally, he had something he wanted to express.

"I'm glad that you made it here safely. I'm glad you're with family."

Ezra leaned forward, placed his elbows on the table and turned to Norman.

"I can help you pack, then load up my car and drive you over to Natalie's. I'm happy for you. So is Zora."

Norman stood up and locked eyes with Ezra.

"I'll go up and pack." He paused a moment. "Much obliged."

He turned and gazed at Zora.

"It's good to know when to go."

He arched his back and extended his right hand to Benjamin, who returned the gesture. Norman smiled.

"Pleasure to meet you, sir. I trust you will enjoy Zora's home as much as I have."

A young Black woman descended the staircase and poked her head into the dining room. She wore pigtails and a white nightgown. Her brown feet were bare, and she looked as though she had just woken from sleep. Norman averted his eyes, but couldn't keep them averted for long. She must have been about the same age as Natalie when he first met her.

"This is my niece, Cadillac. Cadillac, this is Norman de Haan, my boarder."

He wanted to think of Cadillac as a Black princess. Maybe if he gazed at her long enough and implanted her image in his head, he might wash his brain, he told himself. Replace evil with good.

Zora cleared her throat.

"My niece just turned eighteen. She's a graduate of the Folk School in Tennessee, learned 'bout civil disobedience."

Norman knew she was beautiful, but wouldn't say anything.

Benjamin, who was still standing opposite Norman, put his big brown hands on his expansive hips.

"It's nearly the same now as in the old slavery days. We have to remember the bad with the good."

Norman coughed, cleared his throat, and exhaled. He turned away from Benjamin and toward the dark brown eyes of the young woman with pigtails.

"Pleased to meet you, Miss Cadillac. I trust we'll talk one day soon. I'd like that."

"And I as well, Mr. de Haan, Mr. White Spook." She laughed.

Upstairs, he opened and emptied the drawers, removed all his possessions and filled his talismanic duffel, which expanded to accommodate shirts, socks and trousers, all of which looked older and more threadbare than he remembered. It was time to buy new stuff. He held his gun, secured the safety, placed it in the small of his back, and made sure it fit snuggly.

The old book with the Blake prints went inside a white T-shirt, and rested at the top of the duffel.

He was happy he had downsized in Manhattan and had traveled light to San Francisco. Ezra carried Norman's duffle down from the second floor and all the way to his car, which was parked at the curb. Zora and her brother, Benjamin, watched from the front porch, seemingly impressed by the energy of the two young men.

Cadillac observed her uncle and Norman from a window on the second floor. Mrs. Cornbrake, in an apron and sturdy shoes, stood on the sidewalk and kept track of the proceedings.

"You lasted longer than I thought you would, white spook, only you're not spooky no more."

Norman thought about shaking her hand and decided to hell with it. Just go. He hated long drawn-out farewells, and the people who lingered and lingered and couldn't seem to tear themselves away from friends and family.

Zora folded her arms across her chest.

"Norman, ain't you goin' to say any last words to me?"

His right hand was on the car door. He lifted his eyes, shot them toward Zora and sauntered toward her.

"Ain't no last words for you. Of course, I owe you everything."

"Come back for pie and more."

Benjamin nodded his big head. He already seemed to have made himself at home.

On the ride across town, Ezra drove slowly and talked quickly about his uncle and his cousins, about the lives they led in Money, Mississippi, and about whites folks, too, as though Norman wasn't one of them. Then Ezra apologized.

"I'm sorry. I forgot myself." He peered into the rearview mirror, glanced at Norman and whispered, "You are the exception to the rule."

Norman shook his head.

"I wish it were so."

Shadows lengthened. A woman walked her dog. A bald jogger weaved in and out of traffic. Ezra parked, opened the trunk and retrieved Norman's duffle. Norman used the keys Natalie had given him to unlock the downstairs door, and then the upstairs door to the apartment.

With his right hand, Norman reached behind to make sure his gun had not gotten lost in the move. It was still there. He could breathe easy.

Ezra insisted on carrying the duffel to the landing on the third floor.

"You sure have pared down."

"It's the only way to live. Never know when you have to up and go at the last minute, like your folks from Money."

Norman heard voices from inside the apartment. One of them belonged to Natalie. The other one he could not identify, though when he entered the living room he recognized M immediately. He wore his fedora and held a cane in his right hand. What the fuck was he doing here? He didn't belong. He ought not to have stood so closely to Natalie. Norman eyes shot bullets.

Natalie shoved M toward the door.

"Time for you to go."

"So soon? I just arrived."

Ezra tossed Norman's duffel into the far corner of the front room.

Norman took two giant steps, turned and faced M.

"You heard the lady. Scram."

"Ah, Norman, my boy. It's good to see you. I was wondering when and where you were going to turn up again."

M squinted his eyes.

"I see you're in good hands with the darkie."

Norman's nostrils flared. Before he knew it, he had pushed M with both hands. The fat man with the double chin landed with a thud. He sat on his ass, chuckled, brushed himself off, and rose slowly.

"Not a smart move, Norman. You ought to learn to control your impulses."

Norman reached for his gun and pointed it at M.

"Get out."

Ezra helped M to his feet and escorted him to the landing. If he had heard M use the word "darkie," he didn't show it. Norman listened to M's footsteps, and heard the downstairs door open and close.

Ezra walked from room to room.

"Not too shabby." He glanced at Norman and at Natalie. "I'll leave you two to it."

Natalie smiled.

"No, stay a while."

Ezra closed his eyes, but not for long. He opened them again, blinked and stared at Natalie.

"I got family at home. Folks from Mississippi. Norman can fill you in."

Ezra shoved his hands into his pockets.

"See you."

"Thanks for driving me across town. I was in no mood to take the bus."

Ezra slipped out of the building without making a sound, a ghost of sorts in a city haunted by its past. It was the same everywhere, the same ghosts, the same joy and sadness and the same endless highway that carried families from one desolate place to another, haunted by hopes that rarely if ever arrived. But now wasn't the time to wallow in despair. It was time to rejoice.

36

Norman was in no mood to talk about Mississippi with anyone, least of all Natalie, but he was eager to make a new home for himself in a neighborhood where the pedestrians were white, the cars were newish, and the Victorian houses were painted pastel colors.

He carried his duffel into the room where he knew he was to sleep, and noticed the folded sheets and pillowcases laid out on the mattress. Someone had been thoughtful. Someone had considered his wants and needs.

He opened the duffel, removed the book with Blake's engravings, and placed it on top of the chest of drawers next to a small round mirror. He put away his clothes, then removed the gun from the small of his back and concealed it under the mattress.

Voices drifted from the front room. Ginzy and Gregory were singing the lyrics to "The International," but as a parody.

"Arise ye faggots from your slumber,/ arise ye prisoners of your own sexual repressions."

Jack entered the room and shouted.

"Don't profane the working class."

He sang full throated. "You will eat, by and by/ In that glorious land above the sky/work and play live on hay/ You'll get pie in the sky when you die."

Jack sat down on the floor, crossed his legs, and sipped from a jug of red wine. Gregory rolled a fat joint, puffed, and inhaled. He handed it to Ginzy, who also inhaled. Kerouac waved it away with his right hand and poured more red wine down his throat and into his gullet.

Norman joined them on the floor, sampled the pot, and sipped the jug wine.

"What's up guys?"

Gregory flicked the ash from the joint.

"What's up with you, comrade? Back with your friends, I see."

Ginzy took a deep breath and began a chant with just the word, "Ohm." His chanting went on and on, until Norman thought the poet would pass out from lack of oxygen.

With the sleeve of his lumberjack shirt, Jack wiped the drops of wine that ran down his chin.

"What's up is that we're cooking up a crazy poetry festival. Ginzy is gonna read his new masterpiece. He'll be joined by a couple of red hot poets from the Pacific North West, Phil Whalen and Gary Snyder, along with a genuine choir boy from Frisco called Lamantia, plus Michael McClure, who just blew into town from Kansas. We're the six horsemen of the apocalypse. Rexroth is gonna be the MC."

Natalie placed a silver tray with cups and saucers in the middle of the circle. She played mother and poured tea for the boys.

Norman lifted his cup, added two teaspoons of sugar, stirred, and caught Natalie's eye.

"Your mother showed up at the store."

She sneered.

"Shig already told me."

"You're not freaked?"

"What's she gonna do? Kidnap me and take me back to New Jersey?"

Jack put his arm around Natalie's slender waist (which seemed to grow thinner by the day), drew her toward him, and kissed her.

"Our pin-up girl has been writing stories. She and Ginzy taped me reading my 'Jazz of the Beat Generation' with a combo in the background. It's gonna be a real record and she's gonna be famous."

Ginzy held Natalie's left hand, squeezed it gently, and turned to Norman.

"I hope you can persuade her to perform with us at the Metropole. She's the queen bee. We're her drones. Maybe she'll read the poem about her own secret life. That would be a kick."

Before he went to bed, Norman read the newspaper reports from Money, watched the news on TV, listened to the radio, and learned that a Black teenager from Chicago named Emmett Till was accused of whistling at a white woman in Mississippi. Then he was hung from a tree, and lots more, all of it gruesome.

In the pages of *The Defender*, which Ezra left for him, Norman learned that white men jumped Till, dragged him to a barn where they beat him bloody. Then they lynched him, shot him in the head, tied him with barbed wire, and tossed him into the Tallahatchie River. They went on killing him over and over again, as though to make sure he would never come back to life and haunt them, never be resurrected and go to heaven.

In *The Defender*, Norman also learned that after Till's body was recovered, his mother, Mamie, brought it to Chicago where it would be visible in an open casket. Thousands of Black men and women would see Till at the Roberts Temple Church of God and Christ. Mamie Till was quoted in the paper as saying, "I want the world to see what they did to my baby."

News of the lynching hit Cadillac harder than anyone else in Zora's house. She and Till were born to the same generation and were separated by only a few years. Neither had memories of the ugly birth of Jim Crow, though they both came of age with segregation, and they both were aware of the global upheavals against empires, which inspired Norman.

Cadillac pored over every story about the South that appeared in *The Defender*. She and Norman swapped predictions and compared memories, though Norman, who was a almost generation older, had more memories than she. He was gloomier than ever, though he tried not to be. The lynching of Till would not leave him alone.

"It's all coming undone."

She wasn't as gloomy as he.

"It's come undone before."

"Only this time it's for real. It's worldwide."

Norman made sure to carry his gun to protect himself, or so he told himself.

He carried his gun when he went to City Lights, when he explored Golden Gate Park, and when he walked along the Embarcadero. He carried it when he enjoyed fish and chips with Gregory, who no longer rubbed him the wrong way. Gregory liked Norman and he liked guns.

"Guns become a part of you."

Late one night, after Natalie had gone to bed and Jack had joined Neal to work on the railroad, Ginzy wrestled Norman for the gun, lost their tug–of–war, went down on his knees, and prayed for his dear friend to break the habit of "packing heat." That went nowhere. Still, the next morning, Ginzy embraced Norman, called him "brother," and read his journal.

"You've been the fly on the wall, observing us when we didn't realize we were being observed. You could turn your prose into a poem."

Norman showed Ginzy Blake's etchings from Stedman's book about the insurrection of the Negroes in Surinam. Ginzy turned the pages and lingered over each image.

"In Harlem I heard Blake. It wasn't 'an auditory hallucination,' as my shrink called it. It was really Blake. It was his voice."

Norman put his arm around Ginzy's shoulder.

"I know what you mean. I hear a saxophone. It comes and it goes. It's really there."

A few days later, on a foggy Friday evening, Ginzy and Norman recited Blake's poetry before a small audience at City Lights. Natalie, who had become a master on the Webcor reel-to-reel, taped them. That weekend, after listening to their voices, Ginzy and Wally Hedrick (an artist and a Korean War vet) made plans for their colossal poetry festival.

They were derailed when James Dean died at the junction of California State Route 466 and California State Route 41.

Natalie and Neal made no elaborate preparations for the spur-of-the-moment journey to the last place where Dean was alive. They carried no food and only a small bottle of water. Neal insisted they could get anything they wanted on the road, going down and coming back.

Natalie found the spot where the crash had taken place on Jack's road map of California. She dressed in black like the old Italian women she saw in mourning in North Beach. Neal insisted he didn't need the map, but Natalie took it anyway. He drove at breakneck speed on the highway and only stopped at the intersection where Dean's Porsche crashed into a Ford Tudor. Natalie placed two bouquets of flowers along the side of the road and said a prayer.

Neal hurried her along.

"Maybe when he's reincarnated, Dean will work on the railroad."

He sat behind the wheel, made a U-turn and left a cloud of dust that swirled around and around. The ride north was terribly sad. Natalie wept bitter tears and turned away from Neal.

"I don't want you to see me crying."

Hours later, he dropped Natalie outside the apartment.

"Gotta go see the wifey and the kiddies."

He departed for Los Gatos. Not even a kiss. Upstairs, Natalie straddled Norman and described the journey to and from the intersection of 466 and 41. In her head, she had photographed every mile of the journey. She turned Dean into a saint and found comfort on Norman's shoulder.

"This world is headed for a great big smash-up. I can feel it."

When she thought about it, she realized that what mattered to Neal was the journey itself, not the arrival or the final destination. He didn't really care, as she did, about the holy place where Dean died or about Dean, either. No real man would allow himself to die in a car crash. That's what Neal believed. A man was always in control of his vehicle. Those thoughts made Natalie more depressed than she had been, though she found solace in Zora who loved to look at her finished pies and who also loved every step it took to make them into works of art. She located her Milltown, swallowed a few, and passed out.

The next morning, nothing Norman said or did, not the massage, nor the lunch at Fisherman's Wharf, lifted Natalie's spirits. When they went to the theater and saw *Rebel Without a Cause*, she cried from beginning to end.

"This will sound maudlin." That's what she told Jack who had joined them in the balcony. "Something inside me died with Dean."

Jack munched on popcorn and sipped on a coke.

"I hear you. I've always believed, from the time I was a boy and my brother Gerard was taken from us, that Jesus died for our sins."

Jack kissed Natalie oh so sweetly and spoke to her as though he was at confession.

"It came to me last night when I couldn't sleep. The two characters in my road novel are Dean Moriarty named after James Dean and Sal Paradise named after Sal Mineo. You, Natalie dear, have been my muse."

She reached out, held Jack's hand in hers and kissed it.

"Bless you, kind sir, bless you."

They were both far more Catholic than Norman would ever be again. Natalie and Jack seemed to understand one another's sorrow intuitively. Norman felt left out, went his own way, and turned in the only direction where he felt he could find solace: towards the Fillmore.

The house he had called home was the same. It hummed, sang, danced, and drummed. Zora and her sister-in-law had baked a dozen pies. Her brother and the two young men loaded them in the van and went off to deliver them. Ezra cracked his schoolbooks and bagged reefer to sell at the Blackhawk. Somehow, it all seemed so normal.

Back at his not-so-normal apartment, Norman spent more and more time alone in his room, reading and writing. At the top of a blank page he wrote, "You must stay high on words so the real world cannot fuck with you."

A picture postcard with an image of Lake Michigan arrived from Chicago and in Cadillac's handwriting. He tacked it to the wall in the kitchen. A few days later, Cadillac returned to San Francisco by train, bringing with her stories about Till's mother, Mamie, the crowds in the streets, and the shared sorrow.

"Nobody should ever have to die that kind of death. They didn't think he was human. But I bet nobody's going to go to jail for his murder."

Using a photo of Till lying in his coffin and another one of a smiling Till in Chicago before he traveled to Mississippi, Norman designed and produced a poster with the words, "No Lynching." With Shig's help and Lawrence's encouragement, he plastered the poster all over North Beach, at the California Labor School, in Foster's Cafeteria, and around the main branch of the public library at the Civic Center.

"I didn't make the posters to make anyone happy. Quite the opposite."

Everywhere Norman went, whether to Vesuvio, Washington Square Park, or the Blackhawk, he talked about the lynching in Money, Mississippi, and how it had taken the nation back to the darkest days of Jim Crow and the KKK.

In the bookstore on Columbus, with the front door open so pedestrians could hear it, he played Billie Holiday singing "Strange Fruit" and handed out a mimeographed sheet with the lyrics to the haunting song.

Some days he wanted to strike out, but didn't know how and couldn't persuade Jack, Ginzy, Neal or Corso to do something with him. They were in their own heads, in their own books, surrounded by their own voices. Norman realized that he had become one of those people he had warned others about.

In his notebook, he wrote, "Violence must be met with violence. I have been pushed to the edge by the force of circumstances. I feel like I've stepped into the pages of history."

Near the start of September, when it was warm one day and chilly the next, he entertained romantic thoughts about Cadillac, but he tamped them down. Some things were best left unsaid and unrecorded, and certainly not acted upon, though he knew Ginzy would insist that he go naked into the world.

37

Ezra called early one morning and asked Norman to meet him after work at the "new" New Zion, which billed itself as a "Bar and Grill." But as Norman discovered when he arrived, it didn't have a grill and wasn't much of a bar, either.

Old, poorly lit, and dirty, the bar boasted a sign at the entrance that read "Open until 4 a.m." That's when, Ezra explained, the last of the stragglers cleared out, went home, and slept for a few hours before returning to their jobs at the Southern Pacific Railroad and at the Port of San Francisco, loading and unloading freighters.

Ezra had been introduced to the "old" New Zion by his father, Zora's one and only husband, just weeks before it burned down. A new bar was built in the same location. Arson was suspected, but never proven.

Ezra and Norman sat at a back booth bathed in shadows.

"I dig this place because my father drank here and played the Dozens here. It's a wicked game."

"You're looking fit, Ezra."

"Pumping iron. You oughta join me in the gym. Whites are allowed."

Norman laughed.

"Yeah, I'm getting flabby."

Ezra laughed, too, and signaled for the new New Zion's one and only waitress, a young woman with conked hair who was smoking a cigarette and flirting with a customer probably twice her age.

When she didn't take notice, Norman gazed at Ezra and shouted over the din in the room.

"I'll order at the bar."

He made his way through the clumps of men in bib overalls. Nearly all of them held glasses with beer that had gone flat, but no one seemed to mind the absence of carbonation.

Norman could see that it wasn't the beer the men craved, but the company. The proprietor understood, too, and didn't bother to provide decent "libations." That was the word on the chalkboard. It must have been the same when Ezra's father frequented the place: the beer flat and the pretzels stale.

At the bar, Norman cocked his ear and heard bits and pieces of several conversations all at once. It took real effort to pick out one of them.

"They have us workin' overtime."

That comment came from a chubby man who talked to another chubby man.

"I get home after my kids have gone to bed and don't see 'em."

Norman shouted.

"Two cold beers please."

The bartender shouted back.

"Nothin' cold now. Folks drinkin' faster than I can keep 'em on ice."

Norman nodded and watched the bartender serve up two beers, neither one with a head.

A burly Black man wearing a Southern Pacific Railroad cap looked Norman up and down, and poked him in the ribs with his elbow.

"Listen here, ofay, the New Zion is for colored folks only, ya understand, so why don't you hightail it?"

Norman didn't feel like being bullied. For one thing, he had his gun with him. For another, he had a newly found sense of defiance.

"Excuse me."

"You heard me."

"I'm here with my pal in the booth at the back."

The burly Black man let his eyes wander toward the shadows.

"Fudge packer."

He spat on the sawdust floor.

The larger clump of men broke up into three smaller groups. Suddenly, Ezra stood between Norman and the gentleman with the railroad cap.

"You got a problem?"

Ezra stood his ground. So did the burly Black man, who studied Ezra for a moment or two and spat again on the sawdust floor.

The bartender reached for his shotgun.

"Play nice, assholes."

Ezra backed off and followed Norman, who walked slowly to the booth at the back of the New Zion. Ezra made a sour face.

"What did the jerk want?"

"Nothing."

"Nothin'?"

"Said he didn't like ofays."

"That all?"

"Pretty much."

They drank room temperature beer and munched on stale pretzels, which the waitress with the conked hair served them before she went back to the elderly customer who fancied her. A Black B-girl Norman decided. Another wave of working men washed into the bar and the room grew more crowded, hotter, smokier, and noisier, too.

"My cousin Cadillac is going back to Money."

"What? She must be crazy!"

Ezra nodded his head.

"She told her momma and her papa she want to be where there's more colored folks than around here and be part of history."

Norman sipped his beer.

"Even after the lynching in Money?"

Ezra gazed at the working men in overalls who stood at the bar.

"My cousin doesn't sound totally sane to me, and she wouldn't go right now, but she says that it has always been like that, mean-spirited white mobs lynchin' black folks."

"You staying here?"

Ezra picked up a pretzel.

"In Money, they'd cut off my dick and turn it into something like this."

He broke the pretzel in half and held the pieces in the palm of his hand.

"Been meanin' to ask you, Norman, why you packin' heat? You a gangster in some kind of movie?"

Norman's head jerked back as though pulled by an invisible

string. He turned away from Ezra and gazed at the burly man who stood at the bar and glared at him.

"What would you know 'bout me packin' heat?"

Ezra sipped his beer.

"Plenty."

He reached for another pretzel.

"Zora told me she peeped under your mattress."

"She shouldn't have done that."

"It's her home."

"I know, but it was my room and my shit."

He did not sound defensive now, but aggressive.

Ezra folded his arms across his broad chest.

"You got that gun and that book and not much else to your name. Just some rags. You ought to buy yourself new threads."

Norman shot a look across the table.

"Maybe I like old clothes."

Ezra placed the palms of his hands on the table.

"Just what is your business, pal?"

He sounded genuinely suspicious.

"I got things on my mind."

"What the fuck?" Ezra sounded confrontational. He paused a moment as though to gather his thoughts. "You have a curious family tree."

Norman felt a tightness in his chest.

"Poking around in my past?"

"Wait too long to talk about it, and it's gonna bite your ass."

Norman leaned forward, reached for the gun in the small of his back and placed it on the table.

"My equalizer."

The burly man at the bar must have noticed the light that bounced off the barrel. He ambled toward the table. Ezra reached for the gun and shoved it in his pocket, glanced up and smiled.

"Let's get the fuck outta here."

They didn't know where they were going except that they were going out. In the vacant lot next to the New Zion, Ezra gazed at the broken bricks, the twisted metal, and the empty beer bottles scattered on the ground. He reached into his pocket and returned the gun to Norman.

"Don't do somethin' stupid, buddy."

On the street, walking side-by-side with Ezra, Norman saw three white kids coming toward them. They carried no guns, but cudgels. One of them spat on the sidewalk and hurled the "n" word at them.

Another one waved his cudgel above his head.

"Fuckin' faggot."

Norman peered over his shoulder and saw three Black men from the New Zion coming toward him and Ezra.

"Oh shit. We're done for."

The Black men cut across the vacant lot, picked up empty soda bottles and cracked them open on the pavement so the necks were jagged.

Norman and Ezra leaned against a brick wall and made themselves as small as could be. The three white punks faced the three Black men.

"Get the fuck outta here." That came from a Black man in bib overalls.

"This ain't your turf."

He raised a broken soda bottle. His companions raised theirs. The white punks looked at one another, turned and fled.

Norman managed a smile.

"Much obliged."

Ezra raised a fist.

"Thanks, bros."

The man in bib overalls cracked his knuckles.

"You two stick out like sore thumbs. You betta keep your eyes peeled."

38

In the days ahead, Norman began to imagine crazy things he might do, like jump off the Golden Gate Bridge and plunge into the cold waters beneath the towers. Jumping had a certain poetic appeal. It was the ultimate act of defiance. But what if he changed his mind at the proverbial last second, and even as he was falling? What if he lived and regretted the leap? Those thoughts and more kept him from coming up with a plan of action.

Doctor Hicks told him he had "suicidal ideation."

"That sounds about right. I don't want to take my own life, but I also can't stop thinking of ways to end it all. The ideas come whether I want them or not."

Norman stopped smoking cigarettes and drinking alcohol and took long walks in Golden Gate Park. Shig reminded him of Weldon Kees, an occasional visitor to City Lights who shared his poems and who collaborated with jazz clarinetist Bob Helm. That summer, Kees stopped showing up at the bookstore. An officer with the California Highway patrol found Kees' car, a 1954 Plymouth Savoy, abandoned on the Marin side of the Golden Gate Bridge. The keys were still in the ignition. Kees was declared a missing person.

Norman found a copy of his book, *The Last Man*, on the shelf in Lawrence's office. The mystery of Kees' disappearance helped keep Norman from taking his own life. Little by little, his suicidal thoughts dissipated. Shig became his confidant.

"Jumping from the bridge is a bad idea. There are other ways to register my discontent, like writing and speaking out."

Shig nodded his head and offered a generous smile.

"Ginzy's making last minute changes to his poem, despite Jack's warnings not to alter a single word."

Climbing the stairs at City Lights became a daily occurrence for Norman, a kind of ritual that took him away from quotidian reality and into a kind of spiritual space.

"Oh, there you are." Ginzy shouted. "At last. I need you to type my manuscript on stencils for the mimeograph machine."

He handed Norman a sheaf of papers.

"Natalie fell down on the job. There's no one else I can turn to."

Norman glanced at the top page, which had words crossed out. He saw words inserted in the spaces between the lines and in the margins. The title, "Strophes," had been expunged and the word "Howl" added in its place, along with a dedication to a man named "Carl Solomon," whom Norman didn't know and had never heard of. There was a long section about a monster named "Moloch," who seemed to be a supernatural version of M and who looked down at humanity from above.

"Don't want to be sued for libel. I had to disguise our friend. Hee hee hee."

On Lawrence's typewriter, Norman made stencils, changing words here and there when the spirit moved him. He insisted on doing the work by himself, without input from anyone else.

"Get out now, Jack. Leave me alone."

Jack peered over his shoulder. Norman tried to chase him away.

"You're being obnoxious. It's not your fuckin' poem."

Jack leaned against the wall.

"Ah, but it is mine, as much as it is anyone else's, including Ginzy. I've lived with this baby for years, and watched it grow beyond anything any of us imagined. It has even taken Ginzy by surprise."

Norman's fingers flew across the keyboard.

"Well, you can write an essay or a book review and tell readers about the genesis and evolution of Howl."

Jack was already part way down the stairs to the first floor. He stopped, turned around, and shouted over his shoulder.

"I'll leave that work to the profs in the Ivy Tower."

In Norman's absence, Natalie sat at the front desk and collected money from impatient customers. She also kept an eye out for shoplifters, just barely. She was in danger of fading away.

On the Gestetner, which lived in the basement, Norman ran off a hundred copies of Ginzy's "Howl." It began with a quotation from Walt Whitman, and was broken into three sections that seemed like they were written by three different authors.

Natalie was the first person besides Norman to see the poem in its entirety, and though she read it through from beginning to end, she didn't know what to make of it.

"I like Robert Frost. I like his poem about the two roads in the woods that diverge. It speaks to me. I never know what road to take. This Ginzy poem…I don't know."

She sounded like a young schoolgirl finding her way in the world.

When Shig and Lawrence returned from lunch, Norman gave them copies of the mimeographed poem, the pages of which he had collated and stapled. Ginzy autographed them.

"Brilliant." Lawrence shrieked. But he became truly alarmed when he noticed the four-letter words, which somehow had previously evaded his gaze.

"Uh oh. I see trouble ahead." Lawrence scratched his head. "I'd better call Al Bendich at the American Civil Liberties Union."

His words seemed to be spoken more to himself than anyone else.

"Maybe we should have Allen's poem printed in England and shipped here as a kind of prophylactic against censorship."

39

Some days turned into mini holidays. On a Monday, when they felt like loafing, Norman and Shig locked up the store and placed a sign in the window that said, "Gone fishing." At Ming's Palace, they drank cold beer and ate sashimi. Shig ordered for both of them.

"Trust me."

Norman played with his chopsticks and watched how Shig did it.

"There's a new cat in town. Another poet. If we don't watch out we're gonna be the poetry capitol of America. City Lights is gonna be the unofficial embassy."

Norman added soy sauce to wasabi and mixed them together.

"I keep expecting to see a poet friend from New York, named Bob Kaufman. I swore he was coming out here."

Shig leaned back.

"Couldn't be the same Bob Kaufman! This guy is black, but not African black, small, thin, intense, calls himself an "Abomunist.""

Norman tasted the mix of soy sauce and wasabi.

"That's him. I met him in New York."

They finished their beers, started on seconds, and devoured all the sashimi. Shig rested his hands on his belly.

"I know where Kaufman hangs. I'll take you to him."

Norman recognized Bob's body from a block away. Upclose he looked older, the lines on his forehead deeper, his voice more mellow. Bob blinked his eyes, opened his mouth wide and let rip: "de Haan de Haan the folks all love you, the folks need you, de Haan de Haan, infamously famous Columbus Avenue, cash register City Lights, Lawrence right-hand man."

They walked to Bob's pad in North Beach where Norman met his wife Eileen, who brought out a pile of manuscripts, some of them on white bond paper, others on napkins, still others on shopping bags of all sizes.

"He's writing all the time, Mr. de Haan. He has enough poems for a book. Maybe you could say something to Lawrence."

Norman wrote Lawrence a note about Kaufman and left it on his desk.

Later the same day, Lawrence nodded his head.

"Tell him I'll be happy to look at his poems."

Kaufman read his poems while standing on a soapbox on the corner of Garibaldi and Columbus. He attracted crowds, and the crowds and the newspaper stories attracted Kerouac and Ginsberg. The poetry paradise on the street didn't last very long. It bloomed and faded and after an interlude bloomed again.

William Bigarani, a crazed officer with the San Francisco Police Department, ordered the crowds and the poets to disperse, "or else." When they didn't do as told, he raised his club, waded into the crowd and began to beat Bob Kaufman until he collapsed on the sidewalk, blood streaming down from his head which he held in his own hands.

A riot ensued. Norman watched Eileen lift Bob's beautiful battered body and carry him to safety. That night Bigarani was burned in effigy. Crowds cheered. After a while, Bob's wounds healed. He went on writing and reciting his own poetry at Vesuvio, where he stood on a table while crowds listened in awe. Now he was really the Black Rimbaud.

Bob's days and nights in the maritime union gave him organizing skills that came in handy in North Beach. The hipsters and the bohemians weren't agitated about wages, hours and working conditions, but rather about the right to congregate in public, wear beards and beads, long hair, recite poetry and use an obscenity now and then. Norman pondered the ongoing skirmishes in the culture war and summed up his feelings when he and Kaufman gathered at the bookstore.

"I'm a good Catholic boy and I just know that the Catholic Church is behind the cops. Bigarani didn't take it upon himself to club folks gathered peacefully in the street. A bishop must have whispered in his ear."

Kaufman persuaded Norman to sit down with him at a table inside Vesuvio and to draft what they called "The Hipster Bill of Rights," that included the right to perform poetry in public, the right to hear it without interference from cops and the right to what Kaufman called "one's own selfhood," no matter what it might be. Once the document was printed, Shig distributed it all over North Beach.

Meanwhile, letters flew back and forth and across the country from Norman to his mother and his mother to him. Then came phone calls. Mrs. de Haan booked a flight to San Francisco and Toni flew up from Southern California. Norman picked them up at the airport and delivered them to their hotel in Union Square, which was convenient for shopping.

Mrs. de Haan insisted they have dinner together and left it to Norman to make the arrangements. He was happy to do so. He knew the good places to eat, the places his mother could talk about when she played bridge with her friends in Manhattan and Oyster Bay. Mrs. de Haan and Toni arrived at the restaurant by cab; Norman walked the whole way and built up an appetite.

The tuxedoed waiter seated them in a booth at the back of the restaurant, and, once they were comfortable, handed each of them an oversized menu that read, "Tadich Grill: Since 1849."

"Bring us a bottle of Dom Perignon. And put it on ice."

"Yes sir."

Norman watched his mother open the menu and glance at the appetizers and the entrees.

"The Petrale sole here is very good." He genuinely wanted to be helpful.

"I'm quite capable of deciding for myself."

Mrs. de Haan turned to her daughter, who was seated opposite her and who looked, Norman thought, like a starlet aiming to make a big impression on a producer at Warner Brothers or MGM. She played the part, and played it well.

Mrs. de Haan beamed.

"Don't you think we should start with the Tadich platter, Toni? Your father always liked seafood platters with oysters and calamari."

Toni yawned.

"Sorry, mom. Didn't get much sleep. We were filming until late." She paused a moment. "You pick out everything. It's all good."

When the tuxedoed waiter returned, Norman asked him to open the champagne and pour for everyone.

After his first sip he looked up.

"We'll start with the Tadich Platter and then we'll figure out what's next."

"Very good, sir." He smiled obsequiously.

"Let's drink to us."

Mrs. de Haan raised her glass.

Toni watched the bubbles rise to the surface. Norman studied the menu again. He didn't want to choose the wrong entrée.

His mother sipped and smiled.

"Your father would be very proud of you both, making new careers for yourselves out here on the coast."

She placed her glass on the table.

"I'm planning to be in Oyster Bay for the summer. You both should visit. It'll be like old times."

Toni buttered a slice of bread and added it to Norman's plate.

"Yeah, just like old times." He sounded sarcastic.

Toni winced.

"Be nice."

"I am being nice. I ordered champagne."

Mrs. de Haan played with her necklace, real pearls, Norman thought.

"Maybe you don't remember, Norman, but you did have a happy childhood." She faced Toni. "You had dancing lessons, riding lessons and piano lessons."

"I'll be forever grateful."

"Your brother pretends your father didn't pull strings to get him into Yale."

"I was an all-star in high school. They recruited me."

"And I suppose the OSS beat down your door and begged you to join."

"I'm fluent in English, German, and Russian and I can speak French and Italian like a native. I've always gotten where I'm going on my own steam."

Mrs. de Haan shook her head.

"You weren't always as self-confident as you are now."

The waiter returned with pencil and pad and stood at attention. Mrs. de Haan ordered the sand dabs, Toni chose the rib eye "rare," and Norman opted for the salmon.

"Your father and I gave you two everything."

Norman picked up the buttered slice of bread and peered at Toni.

"Do you remember either mom or dad holding you and telling you, 'We love you?'"

"You're alone on this one, Norman."

Norman chewed the bread slowly, with his mouth closed.

"Read any good books lately?"

Mrs. de Haan laughed.

"Spoken like a true bibliophile."

"Well?"

"I read the new Michener."

"Which one?"

"The one about the GI who falls in love with a Japanese lady."

"*Sayonara.*" Toni murmured.

"Claptrap." Norman barked.

When their entrees arrived, they ate with a minimum of conversation, but with ample red wine for Toni and white wine for Norman and his mother, who had to have a cigarette the moment she finished her sand dabs.

Toni removed a cigarette, a Camel, from her silver cigarette holder with her initials, and waited for Norman to light it. Then he lit his mother's Parliament. The waiter cleared the table and handed them dessert menus. Mrs. de Haan ordered a bread pudding and a rice custard and insisted on sharing with her son and daughter. Norman declined the offer.

"Too full. Don't want to bust a gut."

Toni excused herself, stood up, tucked her little black purse under her arm and headed for the ladies room.

"Don't be bad while I'm gone."

Mrs. de Haan watched her disappear down the tiled hallway.

"I hope you're not going to insist on paying for all this."

"Of course I'm insisting. I work. I have a job. I make money."

"I looked up your home address. You're in the Negro part of town. Slumming again, Norman?"

"Forget about it, mom; I have a new address now."

When the check arrived, Norman paid with a $100 bill and left a $20 tip. His mother slid her arm through his.

"In December, I'm flying to Amsterdam to see the Rembrandts again. You should join me."

"Should has never worked for me."

"Stop beating yourself up. Civilization doesn't come cheap. Art is forever. Get it, Norman?"

On the sidewalk outside the restaurant, Norman kissed his mother and helped her into a cab. She rolled down her window.

"You will visit me in Oyster Bay. I know you will."

The driver pulled away from the curb.

Toni rolled down the window in her cab, puckered her lips, and blew her brother a kiss. Norman stood on the sidewalk, waved goodbye, and glanced up at the neon sign that read "Tadich."

40

Mrs. de Haan returned to her cottage in Oyster Bay on Long Island, Toni retreated to L.A., and a small role in a daytime soap opera on TV. Norman went back to City Lights, which became, more than ever before, the stomping grounds for the members of the boy gang, where they could express what sounded like first thoughts and last hurrahs. Bob Kaufman came to the store and philosophized. Natalie arrived after work at I. Magnin and wrote in a little notebook Jack had given her.

Norman kept an eye on her. She seemed to know that he watched her and didn't mind him doing so. Without saying a word, she slipped her notebook into the pocket of his jacket; Norman didn't know it was there until the end of the day. When he had a moment to himself, he read it. There wasn't much, but what there was made him sad.

"Families are sick. At least my family was."

Norman turned the pages.

"When it comes to families, I think the same goes for Gregory's, Jacky's and Ginzy's, though I know they have also loved their mothers. I can't say the same for myself. It feels like my mother tries to murder me at every turn. I have had no choice but to turn my back on her. She doesn't understand, never has, not even when I aim to explain.

"It's not just me. It's something about our generation, growing up with mothers who worked during the war and then resented going back to being housewives and having children and taking care of their husbands. I'll never let that happen to me, no matter what."

Norman returned the notebook and offered his thoughts.

"I'm not sure what to tell you except that it strikes me as true and beautiful, too, the way you express it."

Natalie opened the book and glanced down at the blank page.

"It's a kind of a foothold, though it feels tenuous."

Kaufman also read Natalie's work and shared some of his thoughts, without passing judgment.

"Keep writing."

On a warm autumn evening, Ginzy and a carload of poets—including Kaufman and Peter Orlovsky and friends like Robert LaVigne—piled into a four-door sedan Neal had hotwired and aimed like a rocket for a poetry reading. He roared all the way to the campus of San Francisco State, weaved in and out of traffic, and laughed hysterically nearly the whole way. Norman had never witnessed such inspired driving that seemed to be fueled by Little Richard on the radio. Rock had replaced bebop as the music that they all craved, even Kerouac. Little Richard seemed to make Neal more irascible than ever before.

Norman sat next to him and tried not to listen to him rant and rave and sing at the top of his lungs, along with Little Richard and Fats Domino on the radio.

Suddenly, Neal put his foot down on the brake, which he rarely did, and slowed to a crawl on the highway.

"Norman, you gotta keep an eye on Nat. She's been acting real squirrely. I can't be around much. You know… the kids, the wife, and the job."

Norman stared at the passengers in the back seat and noticed a crucifix hanging from Orlovsky's neck, which he had not noticed before. Orlovsky turned it around and around.

"I'd call this a real joyride."

He opened his mouth wide, revealed his teeth, and howled in the spirit of Ginzy's poem. They howled together, with the windows open, and the wind blowing their unkempt beards and the scraggly hair on the tops of their heads. Kaufman leaned outside the window and drummed on the side of the car.

Inside the Bret Harte Memorial Library, undergrads sipped wine from paper cups, snacked on canapés, and ogled Ginzy and the members of the boy gang.

Kaufman corralled Robert Duncan and sang a sailor's song. Natalie sat on one side of Norman and her friend Bette Green sat on the other side.

"I'm going to knock your socks off, and everyone else's too. I'm sick and tired of life in the audience, having to watch everyone else perform."

"Go for it."

Bette Green looked at her watch and then turned to Norman. "Natalie's been bottled up too long."

Someone rang a bell and the crowd filed into a small classroom that soon filled with cigarette smoke and chatter.

Short, plump Ruth Witt-Diamant, the power behind the Poetry Center, played hostess. Norman sketched her in his notebook. Wearing glasses, large earrings, and a necklace, she stood at the podium and heralded her Center; it had recently celebrated its fifth anniversary.

True enough, she was the midwife, though she had help from Robert Duncan, who bounded onto the stage and rattled off the titles of half a dozen of the rare books of poetry that lived in the library. He also performed the first scene from his play, "Faust Foutu," though he didn't undress as he had done on previous occasions. The academic setting seemed to chill the blood in his veins.

It also seemed as though Duncan meant to upstage Ginzy, who was after all a New Yorker and an interloper. Norman knew Duncan rose from the streets of Oakland and soared academically at UC Berkeley. He was a local boy who made good as a poet. Norman sensed the tension that existed between Ginzy and Duncan, who stood at the center of the stage, directly in front of the audience. Ginzy sat in the front row and glared.

"If looks could kill..." Norman said to no one in particular.

Duncan sat down. Witt-Diamant stood up, went to the podium again and introduced Kaufman, whom she called the "Black American Rimbaud." She portrayed him as a sailor who sailed the seas and was inspired to write after reading Apollinaire, Lorca and Langston Hughes.

Bob wore sunglasses, a white shirt, a pendant around his neck and a jacket with flowers that looked tropical. The first poem he read was titled, "I Am a Camera." The paper on which it had been written looked like it had burned, with the edges turning to ash. Norman liked the line about the soul riven to silence and the image of a pyramid of bones.

He's reinventing surrealism, Norman told himself. Bob fits right in and yet he doesn't. He's the odd man out. I think I knew that when I met him in Manhattan and one thing led to another.

There was a brief intermission after Kaufman read and then rejoined the audience. Witt-Diamant staked out a place on the stage and delivered a mini-lecture about Louis Ginsberg (the poet's father) and his brand of rhyming poetry. It struck Norman as unnecessary and inappropriate. Fathers? Their generation didn't have fathers, but rather brothers. Still, it struck Norman that Ginzy had become a poet by rebelling against Louis.

Witt-Diamant wrapped up her talk, and, after a pause, added, "Please welcome Mr. Allen Ginsberg, formerly of New York."

The audience applauded. Neal whistled, and Jack hooped and hollered. Kaufman folded his arms across his chest. Witt-Diamant sat down in an armchair on stage, crossed her legs, and leaned forward to see the performer. Ginzy sauntered to the front of the room and gazed at the students, who had brought with them books by Robert Frost and W. H. Auden. The tomes not nearly tattered enough.

Allen Ginsberg, formerly of New York. The phrase echoed in Norman's head. In a tweed jacket, white shirt, and tie, Ginzy might have passed for an Ivy Leaguer, or better yet, Norman thought, a "Jivy Leaguer." He'd heard the term at City Lights. Heard, too, from Shig that young cool cats, were beginning to come out of the closet at Columbia, Harvard, and even at Yale, the bastion of the New Criticism. One of Norman's New Haven friends had written to tell him that undergrads were rebelling against "Tough Shit" Eliot and his sermons about what was real poetry.

Ginzy closed his eyes and seemed to go into his own head. Silence reigned in the room. It was broken only when Ginzy began to recite from memory W. B. Yeats' "The Second Coming," and then to unpack the Irish poet's views about politics and verse.

"Out of our arguments with others we create rhetoric... and out of our arguments with ourselves we create poetry. That's pretty much Yeats, verbatim."

Ginzy sipped water from a tumbler, swallowed, and cleared his throat.

"I went to college to be a lawyer and to argue before the

U.S. Supreme Court, but I met Jack, Bill, and Lucien Carr, our blond Rimbaud, and my whole world turned upside down. I came to realize that our first thoughts are almost always our best thoughts." Norman moaned audibly. Two students seated in the front row turned around to see who had made the sound. Norman stared them down. He wanted to shout "Bullshit," but he controlled himself. In Robert LaVigne's big yellow Victorian, he had watched both Ginzy and Jack cross out words and phrases and add new ones to their respective manuscripts. He didn't want to challenge the master in front of the star struck students.

Natalie Jackson apparently did want to confront Ginzy. So Norman thought when he saw her standing at the back of the room. Indeed, she seemed hell-bent on stealing the show, stealing Ginzy's thunder, and turning the event into something distinctly female and definitely more dangerous than anything the enfant terrible on the stage had up his poetic sleeve.

Norman hardly recognized Natalie. She had turned herself inside out and become someone else: a public performer and a kind of Cassandra.

Wearing a tiara that sparkled and a diaphanous gown, Natalie chanted softly at first, and then loudly.

What did she want, Norman wondered? To seduce the audience? Shock it unto submission? Or something else? Yes, she stole Ginzy's thunder, but she also paid homage to him and his work.

"Holy the sex workers, holy the B-girls, holy all the women, holy the mother of God, holy me, holy my body."

Kaufman rocked back and forth, swayed this way and that way. Ruth Witt-Diamant placed her hands over her ears. Natalie was over the top. If anyone wanted an example of excess, this was it. Blake would have applauded. The two students in the front of the room, who had challenged Ginzy, now booed and hissed Natalie, and threw everything they had at their disposal: pens, pencils, and paper clips.

"Get off the stage," one bellowed. The other cried out, "Fucking bitch."

Natalie left the podium and approached the boys.

"Suck my holy cunt." She grabbed her crotch.

Soon others around the two male students also booed, though

there were also a great many cheers. At the podium, Ginzy didn't seem to know whether to silence the crowd or egg it on.

Kaufman didn't climb the stage, but he stood at the front of the room and brought his hands together as though in prayer. When the room grew silent he opened his mouth.

"Let the poet be the poet, let the voyager reach the end of her journey, let her lover find her lover, let her sing her siren song."

Natalie took up where she had left off.

"Holy pussy, holy clit, holy all the orifices of the holy body."

Natalie, who hovered now between Ginzy and Witt-Diamant, removed her gown, stood naked before the crowd, cupped her breasts and chanted again.

"Holy fucking, holy sucking, holy the egg, holy the birth canal, holy the placenta, holy the…"

She would have continued her performance, but two campus police officers, in blue uniforms and carrying guns, removed her from the stage, placed her inside a beige carpet which they had brought with them, rolled it up, and carried it and her outside. Norman followed them at full throttle. So did Kaufman who was only a step or two behind the cops.

Outside the Bret Harte Memorial Library, Norman spied Mrs. Irene Jackson wearing a tailored suit and in conversation with a man in a black jacket, a white shirt, and a red tie who looked distinctly like a college administrator, or perhaps, Norman thought, one of the trustees. Someone had made a phone call to summon the police.

Outside the library, the officers unrolled the carpet. Natalie spilled onto the cement sidewalk face down. Her nose began to bleed. A red puddle formed under her chin and extended across the pavement.

Mrs. Jackson elbowed her way through the crowd. When she saw Norman with his eyes bulging and his face on fire, she froze in her tracks.

"You sonofabitch! You bastard!"

Norman merely shrugged his shoulders, as though to say the names rolled off his back. There was no point tangling with Natalie's mother.

Kaufman lifted Natalie in his arms and carried her toward the black limousine idling at the curb with one rear door open. Norman helped him ease Natalie into the back seat. Then Kaufman wiped the blood from her face. A chauffeur with a paunch stood with his hands on his hips, chewed gum and watched the proceedings. M, in a black jacket and red tie, smoked a cigar and removed a gold watch fob from his vest.

Norman felt he'd lost a battle.

"What now?"

He looked from M to Kaufman, and from Mrs. Jackson to Ginzy, who seemed lost in the spectators who had witnessed far more than they had bargained for.

M leaned toward the chauffeur. Norman couldn't hear anything he said, except the word, "tower." He couldn't have meant Coit Tower. Surely, he meant his apartment building on Nob Hill. Norman cast about for Neal and found him kneeling on the ground, trying to let the air out of one of the rear tires of the limo. He did not succeed.

The chauffeur kicked Neal in the ass and gave him the finger. M leapt into the back seat, lifted Natalie's head, and let it rest in his lap. The doors closed, the headlights came on, and the limo sped off, leaving Neal behind.

Norman saw the vehicle's brake lights in the distance.

"Neal, let's go, man, go, go, go!"

They raced for the car, which was parked at the back of the library. Norman hurled himself into the passenger seat just seconds before Neal gunned the engine and made for the exit. Moments later, on the 101, a police officer pulled him to the side of the road. No doubt about it, he was speeding.

"My wife's giving birth to twins now. I'm up shit creek if I don't get to SF General pronto."

"Sorry, buddy you should have made better plans."

He handed Neal a ticket.

"Have a nice evening."

Ten minutes later, Neal was stopped again. This time he turned toward Norman and moaned.

"My buddy needs his insulin or he'll go into shock. Please, please let us go." That ticket went into the glove compartment, on top of the first one.

Norman looked over his shoulder to see if they were followed.

"You're addicted to speed, buddy. You let speed drive you." He meant to be kind.

In the next moment, had he not shrieked, "Watch Out," Neal would have collided with a flatbed truck carrying men in overalls, packed closely together and holding the railing for safety's sake. Neal swerved to the left, nicked the fender of his car, and drove on undeterred. Norman braced himself for the journey to the city.

"Don't speed."

"I'm not speeding."

Norman peered at the illuminated dashboard and saw they were going 80 in a zone for 55.

"If we're stopped now, they'll take us right to jail."

Norman reached for his gun and pressed it into Neal's right cheek.

"Slow down, motherfucker, or you'll kill the two of us and we won't do Natalie any good."

Neal turned and laughed.

"You are the craziest of them all."

Norman took the comment as a compliment.

☙❧

41

On Nob Hill, with the fog rapidly encroaching and the lights of the City flickering, Neal double parked in front of M's building and tossed the keys to the doorman.

"Keep an eye on her."

Norman ran to catch up with Neal.

The doorman confronted them.

"You can't go in unannounced."

By then, it was too late. The invaders had already crossed the lobby and were climbing the stairs. It was a long way to go. When they arrived outside M's apartment they were out of breath.

Neal banged on the door.

"Open up, buddy. We know you're in there." He paused a moment and shouted, "Natalie." The door opened.

Lotus Blossom bowed from the waist.

"*Namaste.*"

She ushered them into the living room.

Better not mess with her, Norman told himself, or she'll kick the shit out of you.

He gazed from wall to wall. On every wall he saw the sketches and the paintings that Robert LaVigne had made of Natalie. The real woman lay on the couch, her head propped up by a cushion embroidered with gold threads, her face mostly washed clean of blood, though a few red spots dotted her chin.

Other than a man's white T-shirt, she wore no clothes. Her eyes were closed, and she seemed unconscious. M sat next to her and applied a cold compress to her forehead.

He turned toward the Asian woman in black.

"Lotus Blossom, frisk the boys and take away their toys. We don't want them to injure themselves, accidentally."

Lotus Blossom removed the gun Norman kept at the base of

his spine, spun the chamber, aimed at the ceiling, and squeezed the trigger. The bullet ricocheted loudly.

M laughed.

"She has perfect aim, but at this range, no one could miss, not even a blind man."

Norman gazed at the largest of the portraits of Natalie that graced the wall opposite him. M stroked her forehead and glared at Norman and Neal.

"I'll give her what none of you are man enough to give."

Natalie opened her eyes, saw M sitting next to her and gasped.

"Get away from me."

She rose from the sofa and rubbed her eyes.

"Ouch. That hurt."

She seemed suddenly aware of her bruised and battered body. She lay down again. Neal held her feet in his hands and massaged her toes.

"Come on, baby, let's get out of here. This place stinks to high heaven."

Natalie's lips barely moved.

"Don't touch me, Neal. Nobody touch me."

Norman rummaged through the hall closet, found a gray raincoat, and draped it over Natalie's body so that it covered her from her knees to her chin.

"I'm going to touch you now, okay?"

She nodded her head. Norman reached down with both hands and helped her to her feet, then guided her to the bathroom near the front door to the apartment. Natalie went inside, closed the door, and locked it.

M knocked.

"Natalie, are you okay in there?"

Norman heard the sound of running water and the flushing of a toilet.

M circled the room.

"Nobody's going anywhere."

With his double chin, he motioned to Lotus Blossom, who raised the gun which she held in her right hand and aimed it, first at Neal and then at Norman.

M puffed out his chest and barked.

"Sit down everyone, while I cogitate."

Norman sat and so did Neal.

M smiled disingenuously.

"We'll have drinks and canapés, like before."

He clapped his hands and summoned his indentured servants who appeared with platters of fruits and cheeses, hard and soft, and cold beverages, including bottles of Coca Cola and A & W Root Beer. Norman recognized the staff, all of them decked out for a party. Natalie had not yet emerged from the bathroom, though Norman could hear what sounded like a shower.

It was nighttime again in San Francisco, on the edge of the continent where the Ohlone once danced and sang. The whole city made ready for bedtime. The busses stopped and so did the street cars. Bars closed, all except for the New Zion, which came to life, and at City Lights, Lawrence Ferlinghetti looked at the paperback books on the shelves and smiled. He was a happy man.

After one a.m., Jack arrived at M's apartment and appeared flummoxed.

"What's going on?"

M lit a cigarette and inhaled.

"Drinks are on the house."

Jack asked his question again. No one gave him an answer.

He found the liquor cabinet, selected a bottle of Kentucky bourbon, and mixed a Manhattan for himself and another for Norman, who drank it in one long gulp.

"Refill, please."

He drank the second cocktail more slowly than the first, but he soon lost his sense of balance. He could barely stand on his own two feet.

Lotus Blossom went on holding the gun. Norman tried to keep his eyes open, but that proved to be impossible.

How long Natalie occupied the bathroom, Norman wasn't sure. Maybe half an hour. He had lost his sense of time, again. When Natalie emerged, water dripped down from her nose and her chin. Her black-and-blue eyes bulged. Bruise marks punctuated her arms and legs.

Norman looked her over, every inch of her.

"You need a doctor."

No one seemed to hear him.

Natalie borrowed a cigarette from M, inhaled deeply, coughed and held her ribs. She inhaled again and spit up blood.

"We're all fucked. They're gonna get us one by one."

There was no point asking her who "they" were. Natalie wasn't in her right mind. She hadn't been in her right mind for a long time, probably beginning with the joyride to LA.

But she seemed to have one clear memory.

"Wasn't I great in the library? Didn't you just love my performance?"

Norman smiled.

"You were brilliant. You stole the show, you and Bob Kaufman. Ginzy was okay, too, for a Jivy League poet.

He stood up and walked towards Natalie. Lotus Blossom held his gun in her right hand. Norman stopped and backtracked.

"Is that your real name, Lotus Blossom? Or is that some kind of sick joke you have with M?"

She didn't laugh or crack a smile.

"I don't joke with white boys like you, Mr. de Haan."

Norman sat and faded. Neal stood up, and refused to sit when Lotus Blossom ordered him.

"I gotta go to work, lady."

He made for the door.

Lotus Blossom aimed the gun at Neal. M waved his hand.

"Let him go. He's harmless."

Norman had fallen asleep. Jack was awake, but out of commission. Blossom unlocked the door. Neal made his escape.

The door closed loudly and roused Norman, though he couldn't keep his eyes open. In a few moments, he was shrouded in darkness. Shortly before dawn, he began to regain consciousness. Light made its way over the hills, and the city came slowly back to life after a long anxious night.

Norman held his head in his hands.

"Oh, man what a fuckin' hangover." He paused. "We've all failed Natalie and at the very wrongest time."

M was asleep. Jack had passed out on the carpet, with a bottle of bourbon next to his head. Norman looked at his watch. The doorbell rang. Lotus Blossom went to answer it, but first she put Norman's gun under a pillow on the sofa.

"Who is it?"

From the other side of the door came a voice with what sounded like a southern accent.

"Police. Open up."

"Do you have a search warrant?"

Norman was startled by Lotus Blossom's near-perfect English. Her accent had vanished.

A moment later an official-looking paper emerged from the narrow space at the base of the door. Lotus Blossom bent down, lifted it with her fingers, and carried it to M, who opened his eyes wide and glanced at the signature on the bottom of the page.

"Let them in!"

The police entered, guns drawn. One was older, rounder, and whiter than the other.

The younger, thinner, darker one stared at Lotus Blossom. "Ma'am, are you Natalie Jackson?"

Lotus Blossom smiled and shook her head.

"No."

She backed away from the officers.

M stepped forward.

"This is my apartment. Natalie Jackson, who is mentally unstable, is my houseguest. I've been trying to help her, but apparently she doesn't want help."

With his eyes widening more and more, Norman searched the room for Natalie. When he didn't see her, he peered into the master bathroom and then into a smaller bedroom. At the large window in the smaller of the two rooms, he peered outside and saw Natalie on the fire escape, wearing only the T-shirt she had worn before he had covered her body with the raincoat.

"Wait, Natalie. I'll be right there."

Natalie didn't seem to hear him.

The officers followed the sound of Norman's voice down the hall and pushed him aide. Norman heard a car door slam shut, and, when he looked at the street below, he saw an officer on the sidewalk who craned his neck and stared up at the fire escape. Natalie was now perched at the edge of the edge.

Norman heard the sound of a saxophone that rose from the apartment below. He also heard voices from the roof of the apartment building opposite. When he looked, he saw a man in pajamas and a woman in a robe.

What they were saying he didn't know, though their lips were moving and their fingers pointing. The noise from the street muffled their voices. Morning rush hour traffic had begun with an unholy vengeance.

Norman stood behind the two officers.

"Natalie, Natalie, listen. Don't do something crazy, please. I need you, baby."

The older, rounder, whiter officer turned to Norman.

"Get lost!"

Norman stood his ground. He wasn't going to give up easily. One officer leapt to the fire escape and stretched out his right arm toward Natalie, who took a step back and then another step, until she was standing with nowhere else to go: beyond the edge of the edge.

Norman screamed.

"Get away from her." The older of the two cops took a step toward Natalie and then another.

"Natalie!"

The sax swelled up from the apartment below.

The younger, darker, slimmer officer reached into the air. Natalie's pink toenails slipped from the wrought iron edge of the fire escape. A split second later, Norman peered down three flights and saw her body on the pavement, blood streaming from her head, arms extended like the wings of a dove. The officer on the street placed a finger on Natalie's trachea, stood up, and shook his head.

❧❧

42

Norman backed away slowly, fled M's apartment and exited the building through the basement, which led to an alley and to the back side of Nob Hill. He wasn't thinking clearly. Indeed, he wasn't thinking at all. His reptilian brain had taken over. He made his way on foot to City Lights, which had just opened for business with Shig at his customary station.

"Natalie's gone." Norman was sobbing now. "I got to lie low. The cops were at M's apartment. They might show up here asking about me and a gun registered in my name."

"Goddamn, Norman, what the hell?"

Shig helped Norman set up a cot in the far corner of the basement where he would have a modicum of privacy. Later that morning, Lawrence brought him coffee, a buttered tartine with jam, and *The Chronicle*, which ran a story about a woman named "Jane Doe" who had "fallen to her death and who had refused to be rescued by two San Francisco police officers who arrived on the scene."

There was a sidebar about the poetry event at the college and the performances by Ginsberg, Kaufman and a young woman named Natalie Jackson.

"It was a mad, mad, mad evening," Ruth Witt-Diamant was quoted as saying. "I'll never see anything remotely like it in my lifetime."

Norman clipped the story and tacked to the basement wall above his bed.

Lawrence paid him his salary as always.

"Stay as long as you want. I've always thought this place might be a haven for outlaws and fugitives."

The newspaper made no mention of anyone named M, or Lotus Blossom either, though the reporter for *The Chronicle* noted that the police wanted to question "a certain witness who fled the scene." A gun had been found in the apartment where "Jane Doe spent her last night on earth." Anyone with information about the gun was asked to call the police, along with someone who might identify the body at the coroner's office.

Lawrence leaned against the wall and looked at the unopened boxes that had just arrived.

"You'll have more than enough to read, and Shig and I will bring you chop suey so you won't starve."

The next day a written message from Carolyn Cassady came to City Lights.

"Neal went to the morgue and identified the body of Jane Doe as Natalie Jackson. Carolyn."

After twelve noon, Shig found a note in Natalie's handwriting inside the copy of Langston Hughes' *The Ways of White Folks* that Norman had been reading. Shig turned the note over to Norman. It wasn't grammatical or logical, and there were misspelled words.

"I certain you find this after my body cold. Now feel butterfly broken wings. Too hard to fly you boys, though love you all death. No gravestone, no criminations. Wish I… Natalie J."

Later that day, Norman showed the note to Cadillac, who was visibly shaken. She and her cousin Ezra and Bob Kaufman created an altar for Natalie.

Ezra found a miniature portrait of Natalie by LaVigne which formed the centerpiece for the altar. Cadillac added a pair of Natalie's dancing shoes, her name tag from I. Magnin, a lock of her hair, and the tape recording she had made of herself reading Kerouac's "Jazz of the Beat Generation." Kaufman added pictures of Harriet Tubman, Rosa Parks and Emmett Till.

Incense burned around the clock. At the last minute, Norman added a photo of Natalie's body on the pavement, her arms extended as though she was trying to fly, or maybe, he thought, as though she had been crucified.

"It's not about us. It's about her and her memory."

Norman told himself he had to see Natalie one last time before her corpse was shipped to New Jersey.

With Lawrence's help, Norman fashioned a disguise. He dyed

his hair blond. The poet, Philip Lamantia, who attended mass daily at Saint Mary of the Ascension, provided Norman with the black robes of a priest, along with a crucifix and a rosary. Kaufman, who wore a denim jacket and jeans, accompanied Norman across town, on foot.

At the police station, Norman gave his name as Tom Jones and offered a bogus ID, provided by Gregory Corso, who was a master of fake papers that looked genuine. "The body, Natalie's body, the body of Natalie Jackson," Norman chanted, as though the words might salvage what was left of his own soul that seemed to have nowhere to go. He thought he might weep, but not a single teardrop would fall.

A few days after Neal identified Natalie's body, and Mrs. Jackson collected it, Cadillac brought Norman a freshly baked pie. He still haunted the City Lights basement. "An underground man," he told himself as though he desperately wanted to be one for real. Cadillac had her hair in corn rows, and wore a colorful print dress that made Norman think of Africa. She was bound for Alabama, a world that was slowly coming apart, a world that he now described as "racist." He had not ever used the word before, not to his recollection.

"I heard you're going South."

"You heard right."

"What in the hell for?"

"For the bus boycott that's brewin'."

"You'll be beaten and arrested."

"I'll take my chances."

"You're no innocent, are you, Cadillac?"

"Depends on what you mean by innocent."

"Innocent. You know about that."

"I do and I don't. I've grown up fast."

She kissed him and he kissed her in return.

"Now I'll have something to talk about when I get back to Mississippi."

"And I'll have you to talk about." He paused a moment. "How did you get your name?"

"I expect same way you got yours. Parents. A Cadillac is top-of-the-line."

Norman retrieved the book with the Blake engravings that he had lugged with him to San Francisco.

"I want you to have this."

"Why?"

"Because you are Black and beautiful. And just because. Isn't that good enough?"

He saw her to the bus stop, and then waved as she sat and looked through the window with a smile on her face.

Later that day at Zora's house, Norman took Kaufman to met Ralph Abernathy, the Baptist minister from Alabama, and a veteran of World War II. Abernathy had come to San Francisco to decide if Cadillac was ready for the bus boycott in Montgomery. He liked her instantly and gave her his seal of approval. Then he did what ministers do: delivered a sermon.

"We're headed in the same direction, though we take different roads getting there. That's the nature of human beings. We're all made in God's image and we will all have a hand in bringing down the walls of segregation. That goes for you in your way, Mr. de Haan, and you Mr. Kaufman, as it does for Cadillac."

A week later, Norman phoned Abbie, the cabby who had begged him to call her when he needed a ride. He arranged for her to pick him up, collect Cadillac from Zora's, and head for the bus terminal where he had first arrived in San Francisco on a foggy night.

Cadillac sat next to Norman in the back seat, her hands in her lap and her purse at her side. She wore her best clothes and new shoes.

"I was thinking about Natalie."

"What?"

"I think the cops pushed her. Maybe they're not killers, but they're culpable."

"Could be, but of course you don't like cops."

"Don't write to me, Norman."

"If that's the way you want it."

"We're going in opposite directions."

That was the truth, though it hurt to hear her say it.

"No sense holding on to a past that never was."

"Have you a place to stay in Montgomery?"

"Of course, with friends who belong to the congregation at the Dexter Avenue Baptist Church. If you had to, you could always reach me there."

Cadillac kissed Norman a goodby kiss that lasted too long. She had to dash for the bus.

Abbie Stein dried her eyes. Norman offered her his white handkerchief.

"Let's go and have a drink. Then you can take me to the corner of Columbus and Broadway."

"Skip the drink. I want you to meet a couple staying in the International Hotel."

Norman brightened.

"Okay if we pick up my friend, Bob Kaufman?"

Abbie Stein rolled her hips and her pelvis.

"If he's a friend of yours, he's a friend of mine."

The couple at the International Hotel looked like they came from opposite ends of the world. The woman was French and spoke English with a French accent. The man was from Chicago and talked like a tough guy. The French woman asked Kaufman what she and her companion should see in San Francisco.

"Coit Tower and Fisherman's Warf, the Golden Gate Bridge of course, jazz at the Blackhawk, the Diego murals, and Chinatown."

Abbie Stein was ready to take the wheel.

Norman smiled.

"I wanna go with."

"Ditto," Kaufman warbled.

During a long, lazy lunch, the French woman introduced herself as Simone de Beauvoir. The Chicago tough guy called himself Nelson Algren.

Simone's curiosity knew no bounds. She held Norman's face in her outstretched hands.

"Where do you live?"

"I have been in the colored part of town for months."

"That's unusual isn't it?

"I suppose so."

Simone turned to Kaufman.

"You seem like a citizen of the world."

His eyes twinked.

"Born New Orleans 1925, the seventh of thirteen children, my poor mother African and Caribbean, my father Jewish, married when it was illegal for whites and Blacks to be husband and wife. I was baptized in the Corpus Christi Catholic Church in the same city I was born, shipped out from Galveston, Texas at seventeen, ain't never looked back, ain't going nowhere again, except into my own head. I think my mother is smiling down at me."

The Chicago tough guy looked adoringly at the French novelist and intellectual, though she didn't return the adoration. Algren looked down at Norman de Haan, whom he regarded as a privilged kid who was slumming.

"You know, don't you, that you and your pals wouldn't get away with what you're doing in the Soviet Union. The authorities would call you mad and lock you up."

Norman wore a sly grin.

"That's exactly it, Nelson. We're mad in the eyes of authorities on both sides of the divide, East and West. There isn't a free world and a slave world. We're all slaves to something and someone. We all need liberation."

44

The five of them—Simone de Beauvoir, Nelson Algren, Bob Kaufman, Norman de Haan and Abbie—stood at Ocean Beach near the edge of Golden Gate Park. The wind bellowed and blew the blades of the windmill that had come all the way from Holland to California.

Later, at City Lights, Norman introduced the French woman and her lover to Shig and to Lawrence, who asked for and received an autographed copy of Algren's novel, *The Man with the Golden Arm.*

Simone browsed, collected books, and offered to pay for them, but Ferlinghetti refused to take her money. She handed Kaufman one of her cards and another to Norman, who read "Simone de Beauvoir, *Les Temps Modern*, Paris."

"Sartre and I would like to read whatever the two of you have to say. Lawrence told me you're both writers. Send us your work, *s'il vous plaît.*"

For days at a time, Norman rarely left his underground haunt, except at night when he and Kaufman prowled the city like the sly cats who patrolled the alleys and the narrow streets of North Beach and Chinatown.

Norman pieced together a narrative he came to think of as true which he shared with Bob. His narrative began with his arrival in San Francisco and it ended with Kaufman, Ginzy and Natalie reading their poetry. Norman sent it to *Les Temps Modern*, where it was translated and published in French as "*Les Blues des Beats.*"

At about the same time, Natalie was buried in a Catholic cemetery near the Passaic River, a tombstone placed at the head of her grave. "Natalie Jackson: Loving Daughter, 1923-1955."

When cornered by a reporter, who was writing a story about something called "the Beat Generation," Mrs. Jackson glared.

"San Francisco...that nowheresville was the death of my daughter."

She showed the reporter a copy of the newspaper story which described "the dance on the fire escape" and the attempts by the police to save Natalie's life.

"At mass every morning, I pray for the sinners in San Francisco."

Jack Kerouac wasn't sure what to call Natalie's death: a suicide, an accident, or something else. He sat down at his typewriter and began to craft a novel with Natalie as the main character, though he soon changed direction and made his Zen Buddhist backpacking pal, Gary Snyder, the hero of the book he called *The Dharma Bums*.

Ginzy wrote a commemorative poem about Natalie, in which he expressed his own guilt at not sharing more of his love for her. When his mother died, he flew to New Jersey, visited his father, Louis, and drafted an epic about Naomi Ginsberg and about her generation of immigrants to America.

He called that poem "Kaddish." Lawrence published it after he published "Howl." Kaufman began to work on a journal he called *Beatitude*, in which he intended to extol beauty and promote the "beatific" lives of the "mendicants, neo-existentialists, christs, poets, painters, musicians, and other inhabitants and observers of North Beach, San Francisco, California, United States of America."

Norman expanded his own book to include a section on Bob Kaufman, the abomunist communist, whom he had come to think of as the quintessential Black Beat and blues Beat. Indeed, Kaufman spanned cultures and continents. One day, Norman averred, he would be recognized for his genius and join the brotherhood and sisterhood of poets who flowered in San Francisco.

Norman gave his own manuscript to Lawrence, asked him to read it and tell him if it was publishable or not.

Lawrence was of two minds.

"I don't know. You got all mixed up with the misfits you've written about, but you're really not one of them. Deep down you're a man in a gray flannel suit. Kerouac couldn't hack it in the army, and they never would have taken Allen, but you... you volunteered and stuck it out, just as I did."

Norman seemed pleased with Lawrence's narrative.

"Maybe so. We're ghosts haunted by our own selves. We won't amount to much unless we accept the haunting."

Ferlinghetti wore a Cheshire cat grin.

"You'd be happy in uniform again. No more jeans and T-shirts."

"What about my book?"

"Give me time."

"Is it publishable?"

"It is, but it would have to be marketed the right way. I'm not sure City Lights is the right home for it."

Lawrence was preoccupied with Ginzy's "Howl" which was printed in England, shipped to the port of San Francisco, seized by customs officials, and placed under lock and key in a warehouse on the waterfront.

Then, as though by divine intervention, the books were released. "Howl" became an instant best seller which prompted the D.A. to launch an investigation. Two cops arrested Shig, took him to jail and released him. Charges were not filed against Shig, but against Ferlinghetti, Ginsberg's publisher, who was accused of giving birth to a pornographic monster.

Norman moved out of the basement at City Lights and back to the Fillmore. Zora took him in and gave him his old room on the second floor. Her brother and sister-in-law and their kids had found a place of their own.

Norman called Natalie's friend, Bette, and asked her out on a date. She accepted and brought him to the California School of Fine Arts, where she studied figurative painting and introduced him to the Diego Rivera mural that occupied an entire wall in the exhibition space. Bette pointed to the date the work was done, May 1931, and the artist's signature.

"I suppose it's obvious he was a Communist. The helmeted worker is bigger than life."

Norman gazed at the face of Rivera's proletarian, and then at the face of the woman with whom he had fallen in love.

"Workers of the world unite, you have nothing to lose but you chains." He paused and added, "My bohemian friends cry out, 'Mad men of the world, unite. You have nothing to lose but your mind-forged manacles.' There's something in that, too."

Bette brought Norman to the roof of the school where they

looked down at the city. She was the anti-Natalie, he told himself. She gets me, and she's nice, sweet, and grounded.

Married once, briefly, and divorced quickly in Mexico, she no longer entertained illusions about living happily ever after.

A month or so after their first date, Bette gave up the last vestiges of wanting to look like Marilyn Monroe. She became a brunette again and visited her parents in San Rafael, who welcomed her home after a long absence. Norman joined her and impressed them and himself.

"I don't want to change you, and I hope you don't want to change me."

They were driving South across the Golden Gate Bridge.

Norman turned to Bette, and kissed her on the cheek.

"Maybe we'll find paradise together."

Bette laughed.

"You're an optimist, aren't you?"

"A realist. You can dream for the two of us, if you want."

He and Bette took long walks, danced, had diner at Tadich, and after a month or so became a couple, officially. He bought her a ring, and suddenly they were engaged. The wedding, six months later, took place on Telegraph Hill, outside Coit Tower.

Norman knew one person he absolutely had to invite. He unearthed the slip of paper with Bob Kaufman's address, which he had buried in his wallet, and hoofed it to 1108 Van Ness, apartment 6G, where he found Bob in bed, listening to Charlie Parker and writing on a brown paper bag.

The man whom Norman had first met at the Nirvana Café in New York as the author of "The Abolitionist Manifesto" tossed aside the bed covers. He rose to his feet and embraced Norman, who explained that he was getting married to a former B-girl named Bette Green. Bob laughed. After all, Ivy League guys weren't supposed to marry B-girls. Bob tightened the belt for his trousers, which had slipped below his slender hips.

"I found my metier and I'm in love. I know we'll stay here for the rest of our lives, me and Eileen. In Frisco I know I can dive deep, which I couldn't do anywhere else in the world."

He rubbed his goatee.

Jonah Raskin

"I'm happy you're happy and that you're getting married. It works for some, though it probably won't work for Kerouac, Ginzy or Burroughs. They're tough old buzzards."

At the wedding, Lawrence served as best man. Zora played her drum. Shig welcomed the guests. Kaufman played the flute. Mrs. de Haan attended and so did Toni. Norman insisted on inviting Charlie Wilson, who flew to California and stayed at the Mark Hopkins on California Street. He and Norman had drinks and lunch and talked a great deal about the Russians, who were supposedly in the midst of a thaw in the Cold War.

Norman was impressed with Charlie's intel.

"I wouldn't mind a thaw here."

"Don't hold your breath."

Lunch led to an invitation for dinner with men and women in the Foreign Service. Then came a meeting in Langley, Virginia.

In a room without windows. Norman was asked, "Why do you want to work for us?"

"I served in World War Two. I'd like to serve again."

"It's a whole different ball game; hard to tell friends from enemies."

"I'm going into this, eyes wide open."

With his language skills and his prior experience with the Office of Strategic Services, Norman joined the Company. A man, whose name he never learned, told him he would work in a place called Vietnam. He knew almost nothing about the country, except that, as Charlie Wilson told him, "The French had their asses kicked at a place called Dien Bien Phu." Ferlinghetti was right when he said, "Norman you're an organization man." Kaufman was also right when he said, "You can't be pigeonholed."

Norman felt better knowing he was on a team once more and part of something bigger than myself.

Lawrence gave him a going away present: a copy of Alan Watts's *Zen*, which he autographed "to a fellow New Yorker who was reborn in San Francisco, your friend L.F."

Norman was delighted to have the book.

"Sometimes I'm disillusioned with the boy gang."

Lawrence shook his head.

"When you have illusions, you're bound to be disillusioned."

239

Norman showed Bette "French Indochina," in an old book of maps his mother gave him as a going away present.

He learned the names of the major cities and the big rivers like the Red and the Mekong. In a history book, he read about a nationalist named Ho Chi Minh who quoted from the Declaration of Independence:

"All men are created equal. They are endowed by their Creator with certain inalienable rights, among them are Life, Liberty, and the pursuit of Happiness."

Norman met with some of his old buddies from the OSS who were as proud as ever, albeit reluctant cold warriors.

Bette knit him a sweater and helped him pack his old, durable duffle.

"I'll visit you when you're furloughed."

"I'd like that."

"We'll live together on the other side of the world."

They had a farewell weekend together in Big Sur, camping out, cooking over an open fire and sleeping under the stars. Along with food, and drink, Bette brought a copy of Henry Miller's *The Air-Conditioned Nightmare*, which she read aloud to Norman while they snuggled in a sleeping bag.

"This country of ours can feel nightmarish."

Norman tossed a log on the flames.

"Yes, it can, but that hasn't stopped us from coming a long way together in a short amount of time."

Right before Norman kissed Bette goodbye and boarded the military transport that took him to Saigon, he called Kerouac.

"I'm back in service, only this time, not wearing a uniform. It's strictly hush-hush."

"Maybe you'll do some good."

"I'll give it the old college try, Jack."

"Hot dog, m' boy, hot dog!"

Sketch of Natalie Jackson by Robert LaVigne, courtesy of the estate of Robert LaVigne
by D.L. Gremmels and W. F. Bloxom.

Acknowledgements:

Six readers pored over the manuscript of this book as it went through many revisions. They are: Mona Helen Renney, Eric Foner, Jennie Orvino, David Madgalene, Jonathan Hunt and Lin Marie de Vincent. I believe that their insights and criticisms have made this a better book than it would have been without their input. I thank them all greatly. They helped me to see what it was I wanted to communicate and express. Immense thanks to my editor and publisher, Tej Hazarika. I have also read portions of this book to the members of the writers' group—Roger Weeks and Mark Heydon— to which I belong. Their encouragement encouraged me. Karen Hess was also there when I needed her with her tarot and her wisdom.

—Jonah Raskin, San Francisco, 2021

Jonah Raskin is a long time teacher, scholar and aficiondo of the Beat writers. The author of *American Scream: Allen Ginsberg's "Howl"* and *The Making of the Beat Generation*, which the <u>San Francisco Chronicle</u> named one of the best books of the year, he has also written about Jack Kerouac and jazz, William Burroughs' *Naked Lunch* and *Junky* and the only study of Natalie Jackson. Raskin taught Beat literature at the State University of New York at Stony Book and at Sonoma State University. The author of three noir novels and a performance poet, he has published six poetry chapbooks, including *Rock 'n' Roll Women*. An ex-New Yorker, he now makes his home in San Francisco, a city which he has written about in essays, articles and in the booklet "San Francisco: Gold Rush to Google." He writes for CounterPunch, the New York Journal of Books, Tablet, The Rag Blog and the North Bay Bohemian. He can be reached at jonah.raskin@sonoma.edu

Beat Blues: San Francisco, 1955

CPSIA information can be obtained
at www.ICGtesting.com
Printed in the USA
FSHW022126211021
85554FS